THIRD
GIRL
FROM
THE
LEFT

Also by

MARTHA SOUTHGATE

THIRD
GIRL
FROM
THE
LEFT

Martha
Southgate

HOUGHTON MIFFLIN COMPANY

Boston • New York • 2005

For information about permission to reproduce
selections from this book, write to Permissions,
Houghton Mifflin Company, 215 Park Avenue South,
New York, New York 10003.

Visit our Web site: www.houghtonmifflinbooks.com.

Library of Congress Cataloging-in-Publication Data
Southgate, Martha.
      Third girl from the left / Martha Southgate.
          p.   cm.
          ISBN 0-618-47023-9
          1. African American motion picture producers
      and directors—Fiction. 2. African American
      motion picture actors and actresses—Fiction.
      3. African American families—Fiction. 4. Con-
      flict of generations—Fiction. 5. African American
      women—Fiction. 6. Mothers and daughters—
      Fiction. 7. Grandparent and child—Fiction.
      8. Los Angeles (Calif.)—Fiction. 9. Tulsa (Okla.)
      —Fiction. 10. Grandmothers—Fiction. I. Title.
          PS3569.O82T47 2005
          813'.54—dc22   2005040403

Book design by Melissa Lotfy

Printed in the United States of America

QUM 10 9 8 7 6 5 4 3 2 1

For my father,
Robert Southgate,
and mother,
Joan Southgate,
who taught me the
importance of history

Author's Note

This is a work of fiction. I have freely and often manipulated time and event (yes, blaxploitation buffs, I know there's no dialogue in the fight scene in *Coffy*). I even invented one film (*Street Fighting Man* starring Fred Williamson is fictional), but I have tried to be true to the spirit of the places and times I describe. Please don't look to this novel for a strict reporting of fact. In writing the novel, I used many fine works of nonfiction (and watched a fair number of films). In understanding the Tulsa Race Riot of 1921, I was greatly helped by *Riot and Remembrance* by James S. Hirsch, *The Burning* by Tim Madigan, *Black Wall Street* by Hannibal B. Johnson, and *They Came Searching* by Eddie Faye Gates. *The Bunny Years* by Kathryn Leigh Scott is a detailed oral history of early Playboy Bunny life that is alternately amusing and disturbing but always informative. *Easy Riders, Raging Bulls* by Peter Biskind provided useful information about the film industry in the 1970s. *What It Is . . . What It Was!* by Gerald Martinez, Diana Martinez, and Andres Chavez, as well as Isaac Julien's documentary *BaadAsssss Cinema*, were crucial in my understanding of the blaxploitation genre.

Everything is
habit-forming,
so make sure
what you do is
what you want
to be doing.

WILT CHAMBERLAIN

THIRD

GIRL

FROM

THE

LEFT

MY MOTHER WAS AN ACTRESS. IN SOME WAYS, SHE doesn't look very different from the way she did back then. She still has honey-colored skin and eyelashes that make you think of fur or feathers. Her movies were all made in the early 1970s, before I was born. You know the titles of some of the big ones: *Shaft* and *Super Fly* and *Blacula*. She wasn't in those. Then there were the little ones that blew in and out of the dollar theaters in Cleveland and Detroit and Gary inside of a week, until the last brother who was willing to part with $1 had done so: *TNT Jackson* and *Abby* and *Savage Sisters*. She's in some of those. You wouldn't know her, though. She was no Pam Grier. These are her credits: Girl in Diner, Murder Victim #1, Screaming Girl, Junkie in Park. She was the third girl from the left in the fight scene in *Coffy*. When I was little, sometimes she woke me late at night and we sat down in front of the television to watch a bleached-out print of a movie with a lot of guys with big guns and bigger Afros. They ran and jumped and shot. They all wore leather and bright-colored, wide-legged pants made of unnatural fibers. They said, "That's baaaad" as percussive, synthesized music perked behind them. The movies made their nonsensical way along, and then suddenly my mother said, "See, see, there I am, behind that guy, laying on the ground. That's me." Or she said, "That's me in that booth." Then Richard Roundtree or Gloria Hendry or Fred Williamson sprayed the room with gunfire, and my mother slumped over the table, her mouth open, her eyes closed. Blood seeped slowly out from under her enormous Afro. I looked away from the television at the mother I knew. She smiled watching the gory death of her younger self. Her pleasure in her work was so pure, even though all she was doing was holding still as dyed Karo syrup drained from a Baggie under her wig onto a cheap Formica table.

My mother never said, but I knew, that I ended her acting career. I liked to think that my father was somebody like John Shaft, striding through the streets of Manhattan, a complicated man, a black private dick who was a sex machine to all the chicks. But I suspected that my father was a bit player like her. Thug #1. Or Man in Restaurant. Once I learned how dull a movie set is when you're not running the show, I imagined the two of them, in those endless, drifting hours, slowly beginning to talk to each other, my mother looking up shyly but oddly direct, the low bass rumble of my father's voice as he asked her name, then asked her out. They didn't have folding canvas chairs, their names written on them, the way the director or the stars did. They would have started talking as they stood around in extras holding, a few words at a time. I imagine my mother looked at my father's face and saw in it someone who would make everything perfect.

My mother believed in the power of movies and the people in them to change a life, change her life. I can count on my two hands the number of stories she's told me about my father. And then only when I've asked. She didn't even tell me his name until I was grown. But exactly what she wore in the fight scene in Coffy? And what Pam Grier said to her before they started shooting? I've heard that story a thousand times. In that scene, Pam Grier rips my mother's dress nearly off her body. It hangs, ragged, over her shoulders in two scarlet shards. She wears a fierce, sexy smile and a crooked, reddish wig. Her breasts are very beautiful. Here is what Pam Grier said to my mother right before filming began: "That dress looks good on you, girl. Too bad I gotta tear it." My mother held these words as a talisman against whatever else life might bring her. Pam Grier thought she looked good.

When I told my mother I wanted to go to film school, she was silent for a long minute. Then she said, "Not too many women direct movies, do they?"

"Not too many. But remember that movie *The Piano*? You never saw it, but that was a woman. And there've been others."

"Any of them black?

I hesitated. "A few. Julie Dash. Euzhan Palcy. Kasi Lemmons. You know how it is, Ma. Maybe I can help change that. Even if I can't . . . it's what I need to do."

"How you gonna pay for it?"

"I'll get a scholarship. I'll borrow money. I'll figure it out, Ma."

Ma looked at me. "Yeah, you probably will. I remember when I came out here. I was broke as hell. But it wasn't much that could have stopped me. Guess that's how I know you're my girl. Hardheaded. Just like me."

So I applied to a lot of film schools. I got into NYU. I remember holding the admissions letter, staring at it, thinking, Spike Lee and Martin Scorsese, Spike Lee and Martin Scorsese. Stupid, huh? But that's all I could think. I'd lived in Los Angeles my whole life. I knew New York from only a thousand noir pictures and *Mean Streets* and *Sweet Smell of Success*. (Here's my favorite, favorite scene: when Burt Lancaster gazes over the lights of the city, hot jazz blasting behind him, and he says, "I love this dirty town." My second favorite scene: when Burt, a key light under his chin to give him a menacing glow, says to Tony Curtis, "I'd hate to take a bite out of you. You're a cookie full of arsenic.") I went to grad school in 1999. It took me three years after college, working like a dog, to get up the nerve and to earn the money to pay for it. I knew it wouldn't be like a black-and-white movie. More like *Do the Right Thing*. But New York was still . . . so not LA. I thought it would be the home I never had, the place I should have been born.

I got in with a short I made about my mother. I did it in our kitchen. A couple of lights, my old video camera. I'd kept it working, even though I'd had it since I was twelve. Her girlfriend, Sheila, was there, like always, but I framed the shots so that only her arm and hand were in the frame. The main thing you saw was my mother's face. She was still so beautiful, her hair slicked back into a ponytail, her clothes just so, even on a Saturday afternoon. Maybe she had more lines around her eyes than she used to. I didn't notice them until I looked through my viewfinder. "So, Ma," I asked as the film rolled, "how'd you end up in Los Angeles?"

"Couldn't stand the country town I was from another minute." She laughed. It was like the camera was her home.

"What country town was that?"

"Tulsa, Oklahoma. You don't get no more country than that, sweetheart. That is the countriest I ever hope to be."

"Did you always live there?"

"'Til I was twenty." A drag on the cigarette, a look out the window.

"Why'd you leave?"

She looked back at the camera. Her eyes glowed in the late afternoon sunlight. "I was gonna be a movie star." She smiled a little. "The biggest there ever was." A slow lowering of the eyelids, another drag on the cigarette. "Didn't work out that way, though. It hardly ever does."

"What do you think it would have been like if it had?"

She smiled. "Good Lord, Tam, I don't know." She looked airily around our small apartment, then briefly at Sheila. "We'd have a house, that's for sure. Not this ratty little apartment. Maybe a pool. You'd have liked that when you were little, huh, Tam? I never really have been much of a swimmer. But that would have been nice. A house in the hills. Maybe a garden. And a big-ass car!" She yelled this last, then gave Sheila a high-five. "We'd be rollin'. No more piece-of-crap used cars. That's for damn sure." She paused, picked up her cigarette again. Took a drag. As the smoke entered her lungs, she seemed to return to where she really was, who she was now. A forty-eight-year-old who was a receptionist for a plastic surgeon and rented DVDs and videos and looked for herself in the backgrounds of old movies. Her eyes narrowed. "But that's not happening, is it?" Then she fell silent.

Later, when I looked at the footage, I was amazed. I'd never seen my mother look like this, so serious and direct. Always, whenever she was talking to me, her attention was elsewhere. But now, as I held the camera, she was there, fully present, every inch of her focused. Her eyes were shiny and hard. You couldn't look away. I couldn't figure out why her directors had never noticed that quality. You couldn't see it when she wasn't being filmed. But when she was? Good God. I couldn't look away. I must have run the tape for an hour, over and over, looking for the words that would explain my mother's life. House. Car. Damn. Rollin'. A star. Gonna be a star.

Part I

ANGELA

1

I T WAS 1972. THERE WERE AT LEAST FIFTY BEAUTIFUL
girls in the room. Everywhere you looked there was another
young woman, each face a different brown, here the color of a
puppy's eyes, there the color of a fallen acorn, all so heartbreak-
ing. And for once, not afraid. There was something about these
women, these new young women, that made you think that
something must be changing, that the time had come to start giving to pretty black women, not taking from them. Angela sat on a
folding chair. The room smelled of Afro Sheen.

She leaned over her clipboard intently, as though filling it
out correctly would get her the part. Name: Angela Edwards.
Age: twenty. She had really just turned twenty-two, but nobody
told the truth about that out here. It didn't take but a minute to
figure that out once you started trying to get work. The younger
the better. *Other parts.* Hmm. Her parts had been temping, working as a Playboy Bunny, and auditioning. Who would know if she
said something that wasn't quite true? She gave herself small parts
in *The Liberation of L. B. Jones* and in *Shaft.* Carefully, she attached her headshot to the form and gave it to the bored blonde
seated at a flimsy card table in front of the room. She went back
to her cracked plastic seat, a dirty orange instead of dirty yellow
this time, and dug in her bag for a copy of *Jet.* She pulled it out

to read, her left hand rapidly twisting the hair at the back of her head, the part her mother always called "the kitchen."

She waited a long time, watching other young women come and go, some looking defeated, some with an air of grinning confidence. She concentrated on taking deep, slow breaths and reading the "Weddings" page in *Jet*. The articles, as always, were tiny, hardly enough words to fill a thimble. But she couldn't concentrate on them at all. She jumped when she heard her name.

A pale white guy with lank black hair took her into the audition room. His satiny pink shirt had a couple of dingy red spots down the front. Whether they were blood or ketchup was hard to say. In the room, three more white men were seated around another card table. It was always white men around the table. The top of the table was ripped, foam sticking up from the gash. The middle one (was he the producer or the director?) had white hair combed straight back from his forehead. He held his cigarette like Humphrey Bogart in those old movies. He squinted at Angela through a haze of bluish smoke.

A softly fat man with squinty light blue eyes sat next to him. He nodded slightly when she came in. Then there was a weasely, anxious-looking third man. Angela figured him for the usual mystery man. At every audition she'd been on there was always somebody's friend or somebody's brother there strictly to check out the merchandise. She stood, fighting the impulse to twist the back of her hair again, and waited for one of the men to speak.

"So, Miss Edwards, I'm Jon Solomon, the director. You want to read for the part of Tasha?" That came from the fat, squinty-looking guy.

"Yes, sir, I do." Damn. She sounded so country.

"Well, why don't you read with Rafe here. Show us what you got." Solomon smiled. His teeth were small and yellow. They gave her some script pages and gestured to a brown-eyed handsome man she hadn't noticed before standing in the corner. He looked like one of the boys she knew from back home in front of the five and dime—like he'd lick you as soon as talk to you. He walked over, a slow smile on his face. Angela's heart squirmed in her chest like a live animal. They began reading the scene.

"I can't let no white motherfucker treat my woman like that," he said, staring at her chest.

"Yeah, well, I'm a woman who can take care of myself. I've got the gams and I've got the guns. You don't need to worry about me," said Angela. Her voice shook. What did "gams" mean anyway?

"Baby, you need a man to take care of your business. I don't want you out there getting hurt."

"Nobody hurts me. They better jump back, in fact. They're going to rue the day they messed with me."

"That's enough, thank you," said the white-haired man. Solomon looked startled but said nothing. "You can go. But please come here for a second? I need to ask you something." She walked over and he pushed his business card across the table. "I think you have real potential, young lady. Please give me a call, would you?" he said. If Angela hadn't been staring at the card in front of her, she would have seen the other two men at the table give each other sardonic looks. But she just picked up the card and slid it into her tight jeans pocket, real slow. Then she looked at the producer levelly. "Sure, Mr. Kaufman. You'll hear from me tonight."

When she was fifteen and she and her friend Louann took turns reading *The Best of Everything* and this kind of thing came up, the white girls in the book were always terrified, shocked, unwilling. She was scared, but not unwilling. She hadn't slept with a white man, but let's face it, they ran things, especially out here. She might as well get it over with. It might even be interesting. She had a brief vision of her mother's face. But she pushed it away. She knew what she had to do.

• • •

She pulled up to Kaufman's door about ten minutes late. His building was in West Hollywood, a mini–shopping strip that contained a dry cleaner, a convenience store, and a small suite of dingy offices. Angela checked her lipstick in the mirror. She ran her sweaty hands over her pant legs, and rang the bell, practicing her smile.

The lobby of the office had greenish carpet and smelled slightly of cat pee. There was a coffee table with some magazines on it and a receptionist's desk with a typewriter in the corner, but no one else was there. Kaufman greeted her, standing in the doorway of an inner office, smiling at her. "Ah, Miss Edwards, so glad you could come." He stuck out his hand. Angela took it, careful to hold it a little longer than necessary, and said, "You can call me Angela."

"You may call me Howard," he said. "And may I say that you're looking very lovely this evening?" Angela smiled again. It was kind of funny to have someone staring at her breasts without even pretending to look at her face. But it excited her too. He ushered her into his office, his hand on the small of her back.

Laid out on a table in front of a grayish, formerly cream-colored leather couch was a plate with Ritz crackers and light orange cheese on them and next to that, a straw-covered bottle of wine, two wine glasses, and a joint. Angela had never smoked pot before. She hadn't expected to have to do that too. She swallowed quickly and turned to look at him.

"Do you smoke?"

"I haven't, but I been wanting to try." *Where'd that come from?* she wondered. She had not been wanting to try. He looked pleased. "Good," he said. He led her to the sofa, picked up the joint, and lit it, smiling in a slightly threatening way as he handed it to her. "You know, it's a cliché, but you're really very talented," he said, his voice constricted as he tried not to exhale. "Here, you've got to hold it in your lungs or it won't work. Don't let it out. Yeah. That's it."

Angela felt as if someone had lit a fire in her chest. She'd had cigarettes before but never anything like this. She held the smoke for a second, then, coughing madly, gestured for a drink. Kaufman got it for her, laughing. "Everybody has a little trouble the first time. Here, don't give up. This is really good stuff."

She took the joint again, holding it the way he did, between his fingers, and inhaled. Easier this time. She passed it back and took a sip of her wine. She could taste each grape in it. Howard hit the joint again and then said, "So, where are you from, Angela?"

"Oklahoma. Tulsa. Hope I don't never go back there again." Oh my God. She'd said "don't never" in front of a Hollywood producer. She busied herself taking another hit, then noticed that he wasn't shocked at all. In fact, he was looking at her gently, a small smile on his face. She bit her lip.

"Tulsa, Oklahoma," he said consideringly. "Tell me, Angela. What did you do there in Tulsa?"

"Be bored mostly. I went to a lot of movies."

"Ah, yes. The movies." He was sitting very close to her now, tracing small circles on her thigh with his finger. She could hardly sit still. She licked her lips. They were very dry. "Well. You'll go far in the movies, Angela. I can see that already." He was slowly unbuttoning her blouse. "And I'll be proud"—now he was reaching around her back, undoing her bra—"to be the one who gave you your start." He lowered his head to her breasts and she moaned. He smelled like the wine they'd been drinking and something else, something a little bitter. He paused for a minute, lifted his head, his lips wet, his gaze unfocused. "I can see that you'll do what needs to be done. An actress's most important job." He slid her onto her knees in front of him, then took her hands and guided them to his pants, still smiling. She unzipped them and reached up to touch him. His penis was a kind of rosy pink. The color startled her. She moved her hand slightly, but then he pushed his hips forward a little and said, "In your mouth."

"What?"

"In your mouth. Haven't you ever done that?"

She gulped. He was a white man and a movie producer. It was what he wanted. "No." Her voice was small. She hoped it sounded sexy, not scared.

His voice was soft and insinuating. "You'll like it. It's OK. Go ahead."

She opened her mouth, just a little at first, then wider. Would it fit? It did. It didn't feel good, but it wasn't so bad. It was OK. She had the part.

Afterward, there were Ritz cracker crumbs on her knees. Some had made their way onto the floor. She reached down to brush them off, laughing a little, trying to act like she did this all the time. She was still stoned, so it was easier not to feel strange. Nothing mattered anyway. Kaufman helped her. Now that they were done, she felt how rough his hands were. If she hadn't been so high, she might have noticed that he didn't look at her. She ran her tongue around her teeth; not knowing what else to do, she swallowed when he came and now she was a little nauseated. They dressed in silence until she spoke.

"I enjoyed that, Mr. . . . I mean, Howard." She paused. "I hope you don't think I do this kind of thing all the time. In fact . . . I've never done that before. I mean . . . that was really good." She looked up, from under her eyelashes; a look she'd long practiced in the mirror at home. She didn't feel as if she were lying. She was just saying what the man wanted to hear. He smiled at her wolfishly and said, "Well, I'm glad. You handled yourself like an old pro." He reached out, hand under her chin. Squeezed just a little too hard. "You'll hear from me tomorrow. I'm sure we can find something for you." Angela could hear her heart pounding in her ears. Though she didn't really want to, she turned her head slightly to kiss Kaufman's hand. Then finished dressing and left without another word, making sure to switch a little from side to side so he'd think about her butt as she left. It was like Sheila said: it wasn't that hard to do what you needed to do to get what you wanted. You just had to close your eyes. She didn't think about anything but the road ahead as she drove home. It was already very late.

Midmorning the next day, the script for *Street Fighting Man* arrived at her apartment with a note attached and some sections underlined—not Tasha, the big part, the part she wanted. But a secondary girl who was in the movie for about ten minutes. On the front was a note. "I had a lovely time, Angela. We've decided to go a different way for Tasha, but I'm pleased to offer you the part of Sandy. It will require some nudity. Remember, there are no small parts. Only small actors."

Well. She ran her hands over the script, thinking about Mr. Kaufman's wet tongue moving over her breasts, the way she felt as he slid into her mouth. She took another sip of her coffee. Cold now. It wasn't the worst place to start, she supposed. The next part would be bigger. Sheila came into the kitchen, rubbing sleep out of her eyes. Like Angela, she worked at the Playboy Club and rarely got to bed before 4:00 A.M. They often had the same shift, but Angela had traded with someone to make her date with Kaufman. "Mornin'. What's that?" she said, gesturing toward the script.

"A part," Angela said, just beginning to smile.

"Are you kidding?" Sheila's voice went up in a squeak.

"Nope. Says so right here."

"You mean you're going to be the lead?"

Angela's face got hot. "Naw. I got a smaller part. But the producer says it's a good one. And hey"—here she lifted her chin a little—"there are no small parts. Only small actors." Sheila raised her eyebrows, then opened the small refrigerator for a pitcher of orange juice. "Did he say that to you?"

"Yeah."

"Mmm. Figures," said Sheila. "It's a part, though." She walked over to the table where Angela sat, put the pitcher down, and placed her hands on Angela's shoulders, rubbing slowly. "So when do you start shooting?"

Angela stretched her neck, rolled her head a little as Sheila's hands moved over her shoulders and down her back. She looked at the cover letter. "Day after tomorrow. Holy cow, they don't waste no time out here, do they?"

Sheila, who had lived in Los Angeles for five years to Angela's one and a half, stilled her hands but didn't remove them. She looked over Angela's head at the yellowish wall in front of her. "No, they don't. The sooner you learn that, the better off you'll be."

"You know, Sheil, I think I'm getting the hang of it." She thought of the look on Mr. Kaufman's face as he unbuttoned her blouse. "I think I'm getting the hang of it."

Angela's scene was set at night but was being shot during the day in an old gin mill in West Hollywood to save money. It smelled like hundreds of years of piss and beer and smoke. Every single surface in the place was chipped. The paint flaking off the walls, the neon sign flickering behind the bar, about to sputter out, the edge of the bar rubbed smooth by years of tired, drunk elbows. The crew was knocking even more paint off of every surface, trying to get each shot as fast as possible. The windows were covered with garbage bags to block out the light.

Angela had been prepped, her breasts and belly powdered down by a make-up woman who smelled of vodka and perfume and blew smoke in a steady stream as she smoothed on the powder. Now Angela stood in a corner, uncertain what to do. This morning she had learned that her part had been further reduced, to just this wordless dance on the bar. She'd had to swallow hard to keep from crying after the script supervisor told her. The script supervisor, who had long ago stopped asking herself why they always believed the producers after they fucked them, looked tactfully past Angela to a spot on the ceiling. So now Angela stood wearing a thin robe, just beginning to feel cold. No one had told her where to go or what to do. No one rushing by even noticed her. It was, it seemed, unremarkable to have a half-naked girl standing around the set. Her fingers inched to the back of her hair. Suddenly she heard a deep voice saying, "Where are those goddamn girls? We need them on the set now!" And then an announcement through a bullhorn, not so angry: "All ladies for the bar scene. All ladies to the bar, please." She saw another girl in a purple robe rushing toward the bar and she joined her, stepping carefully over the cables that snaked everywhere. She was freezing and sweating. Her nipples hardened under her robe.

There was a stool in front of the bar and a series of Xs made with masking tape all along it. The girl who'd been hustling along in front of Angela hopped up onto the bar in two quick moves, taking her robe off at the same time. No one even looked. Angela climbed up behind her, a little more awkwardly, her butt sticking out as she hoisted herself. She stood there for a minute, still holding her robe closed. The other girl stood on her tape mark X, wearing nothing but a G-string, looking intently at her long, red nails. Angela let her robe drop, felt the cold air on her body. All around her voices called. There was the sound of a hammer and then somebody saying "Goddamnit," then another bullhorn announcement. "We're ready to shoot. Mr. Williamson on the set, please."

When he came out, he leaned on the bar right in front of her. He was wearing a buttery-soft tan leather coat and his skin looked polished, though his eyes were a little bit red. A white actor whom Angela didn't recognize came and stood with him, made a joke and they both laughed. They never looked at the girls standing behind them. "All right, we're rolling. Silence, please." The men took their places and the first assistant director pointed at Angela, moving his finger in a slow circle. She started swiveling her hips and sticking her butt out. The refrain of that Delfonics song, "La-La Means I Love You," kept going through her head. The other girl danced too, a bored look on her face. But Angela wasn't bored. Cold and a little bit scared. But not bored.

The girls danced without music for about twenty minutes as the actors went through the scene twice—one time the white guy messed up a line so they had to do it over—then the director said, "Cut and print." And the first assistant director said, "That's a wrap. Next scene in fifteen." Angela hopped off the bar and so did the other girl. They were done. They still hadn't said anything to each other. Mr. Kaufman, Howard, was on the set, standing just a little behind the director's chair. He looked at Angela once with blank indifference. She tied her robe around her waist.

Angela walked back to the corner of the room that had been marked off for the girls with makeshift sliding walls and a sheet on the floor. There were a couple of rickety steel stools in there and a clothes rack made of piping pounded sloppily together. A thick-painted, greenish radiator hissed in the corner. The other girl peeled off her G-string and picked up her underwear, which wasn't much more generously cut, without a word. Angela finally got up the nerve to speak. "This right here is my first movie," she said.

"That's nice," the other girl said in a flat tone.

"How about you?"

"Oh, I don't know. I've done a lot of them." Now she was wiggling into her jeans. They were very tight. "It doesn't get much better than this. But it's a living, I guess."

Angela looked around. Not much better than this? "I'm going to have it better," Angela said.

The other girl laughed and rolled her eyes skyward. "Where have I heard that before?" She snapped her fingers. "Oh, yeah.

That's what every girl in this town thinks." She sucked in her breath and buttoned her pants. "You go right on believing, kitten. See where it gets you." She picked up her fake fur bag, took a final look at herself in the mirror, and shoved the cheap curtain aside, exposing Angela's half-naked body to anyone passing by. "See ya 'round the cattle calls, baby." And then she was gone.

2

TULSA, OKLAHOMA, IN THE EARLY 1960S WAS NOT a place that a smart black girl would want to linger. What the future held for such a girl was as circumscribed and prim as the dust and doilies on every surface. Greenwood, the section of town where most black families lived, felt as if it was about to go out of business. Life proceeded, but the pace was slow and uncertain. Angela Edwards of the Greenwood section was a smart black girl, though her mother never said that to her. What her mother said to her was this:

Girl, ain't you got sense to come in from out in the rain?

I ain't raisin' no heathens.

You bet' come on in here and get that hair combed. You can't be runnin' around lookin' like who-shot-john-what-for-and-don't-do-it-again.

My mama didn't raise a fool. You better have finished washin' every dish by the time I come in there.

You best be careful around those boys.

There was always this need to do things right, to be seen to be right, never to be too mussed or too loud or too worked up or too anything. When she was in kindergarten, Angela brought home a drawing she'd made. It was furious with red and pink and orange crayon. Smiling faces and suns. A green star in the corner. Mildred took one look at it and said, "Girl, what's all them colors about? Can't make head or tail of it." And Angela brought home no more pictures. She didn't know that her mother found that picture later and smoothed it out and kept it. Angela missed the bright fury of the colors, the pure concentration of making the work. She could never get that moment back, but sometimes that feeling was there, just around the corner. Sometimes she paused on the stair landing, feeling her hair ribbon coming untied and tickling her neck (again), holding a pile of neatly folded laundry, and she would hear this hum in the back of her neck, just below the threshold of audibility. It seemed to her that it was the hum of everything, of understanding. If she stood there long enough, stood still and quiet long enough, she might begin to understand what it was she was supposed to do, where exactly she had failed. Why her mother was so nervous about things being right. She could never be quiet long enough. But she stopped on the landing often, trying to hear that hum.

She was pretty sure she was loved. She knew she was taken care of. Her mother's rough hands pulling through her hair, lingering just a second longer than necessary to fix a bow. The softening in her eyes when she looked at Angela sometimes. Everybody knew the kids in town who never got that look, never got the hair bows or the smoothing hands. They were the ones with the dusty faces and ashy legs. They were the ones who always smelled of pee and soda and would ask you right out for a quarter if they saw you at the ice cream parlor. They hit one another a lot. Angela and her brothers and sisters had good home training. Their legs shone with Jergens, their faces gleamed with Vaseline. If they hit one another, they did it out of sight of their mother. Or their father. They didn't hit much. They knew they had to act right. But Angela always wondered why. What would happen if she just stopped?

She was seven, she was ten, she was fourteen going on fifteen.

Her best friend was Louann Parsons from next door. Angela had long, honey brown legs with slightly knobby knees, small breasts that she spent a lot of time standing in front of the mirror examining, and a neck that, even as young as she was, made a man think about the hollow at the base of it. She and Louann loved to go down to deep Greenwood on a Saturday after their chores were done with nickels begged from their fathers and get ice cream. The best part, though Angela never said this aloud to anyone, was walking past the barbershop where the old men and the young bloods hung out, spitting into a brass pot put there for the purpose and talking what Angela's mother called a lot of nonsense. Their rich voices wove together like a sweet bluesy tune, rising and cresting as the girls approached and then dropping to a croon as they went by. The older ones tipped their hats, the younger ones simply looked on steadily, their eyes heavy with appraisal, their teeth parted behind their lips with possibility. As Angela walked away she bit her own lip, her heart rattling at the thought of the eyes that watched her retreating form, the legs that shifted together, then apart as she left. She touched the back of her hair, lifting her arm so her breasts would be outlined under her dress. Louann looked at her as if she were crazy. "What you doing, Angie? You know they all looking at us."

"I know. I had an itch."

"Well, it makes your dress hitch up when you do that."

"Can I help it if I had an itch? Don't be such a worrywart."

Louann sucked her teeth elaborately. "All right then, Miss Fast Thing. What kind of ice cream you want?"

"I don't know. Vanilla. What you gettin'?"

"What I always get. Chocolate."

Old Mr. Evans who ran the ice cream shop had a picture up behind the counter of his former ice cream shop, which had stood in the very same spot (and had nicer stools to hear him tell it). The old shop, which had been his father's before him, had been burned to the ground in the attack in 1921 and he never tired of telling any child who would listen—or anybody at all—of how he stood in the bell tower of the First Baptist Church, firing his gun until it was empty and then using his brother's when his was depleted. "Them white folks went crazier'n mad dogs that day. Burned my daddy's shop right to ashes. But I stood my ground. I wasn't much older than you then. You girls are steppin' tall. But you don't know. You don't never know when they gonna just turn on you."

The two girls listened politely, their hands waiting for their cones, their eyes solemn. They received their ice cream at the end of the story, said "Thank you, Mr. Evans" in chorus, and walked out into the brilliant sunshine. Louann's tongue worked around the edge of her cone. "Don't you get sick of him talkin' about that riot all the time?" said Angela, her tongue darting in and out.

"Yeah, but what are you gonna do? Grownups always talk about that old-timey stuff. 'Sides"—Louann's tongue darted out again—"my daddy says he's right. He was a little boy then. He says it was the worst day ever come to Tulsa. White folks is crazy."

Angela was quiet, considering. Her parents never talked about that day. But her daddy walked on the same side of the street as a white person only when he absolutely had to. And one time, when her mama asked her to clean out the hall closet, Angela found a brownish old picture of a beautiful woman. She had steady eyes and an oval face, an almost too full mouth. She wore a high-collar dress and a dreamy expression. Angela stared at the photograph for a long time, then took it to her mother, who was hanging the wash outside. "Mama, who's this?"

Her mother looked down, distracted, a clothespin in her mouth. "What, Angie?"

"I said, who is this in this picture?"

Mildred pulled the clothespin from her mouth, her distant

look vanishing. She reached out and snatched the photograph from her daughter's hand. "That ain't nobody you need to concern yourself with. Just an old picture. She been gone since the burning in twenty-one. Now get back up there and finish cleaning that closet like I asked you to." Her eyes brightened with sadness. She was looking at Angela when she first took the photograph from her but now stared down. Her hands shook. Angela knew better than to ask why she was so upset.

"Yes, ma'am."

She went back upstairs, back to her task. But she couldn't stop thinking about the woman whose picture made her mother cry. She folded heavy sheets, put away hot, itchy blankets, swatted summer moths away from her face. But she could feel the beveled edge of the photo frame in her hand, its light weight against her fingers. A picture of someone who had the dreamy eyes of a girl who would stand on the landing and listen for the hum of the universe. Who was she?

Her fifteenth birthday came and went. When she was nearly sixteen, she started keeping company with Bobby Ware. Her parents approved. He was the son of Dr. Ware and a football player for the colored high school. He was tall and chocolate-skinned and polite to grownups. He had legs that ran through the dreams of half the girls in town and a mouth that you found yourself watching when he talked. Lips so pretty it didn't matter much what he said. Whenever he talked to Angela, his voice a slow caress, she found her feet doing an independent, twisting dance of their own, her heart slamming into her ribs. And she became the chosen one. In all the good seats at the games. Walking home with him after church. Wearing his letter sweater slung casually over her shoulders. Sitting with his hand on her leg at the movies. She knew she ought to make him move it, but it felt so good there, warm and gentle, the feeling between her legs so delicious. It was dark in the theater, the only light that which beamed from Sidney Poitier's face as he showed a group of unworldly nuns the meaning of life in *Lilies of the Field*. No one could see them. She allowed him this liberty. She lay in bed after he brought her home, always well before her curfew, and rested her hand on her leg in the same spot he had rested his.

The way it happened was like standing in water up to her waist and suddenly finding it was over her mouth. First she let him keep his hand on her leg, then when they went to see *The Birds*, her belly, then when they saw *A Hard Day's Night*, she let him touch her breasts, outside the bra. She knew her mother would kill her if she knew, but she also could not believe how good it felt. How desperate she was to keep going.

So finally she did. She was with Bobby under the football bleachers after a game. He still smelled of the shampoo he'd just used. The air was sweet and cold, about to turn fall. When he reached under her bra and moved his fingers over her nipples, her eyes opened wide in shock. She must have looked like a cartoon. She had no idea she was capable of feeling such pleasure. What could be bad about it? She shifted her legs underneath him, wanted to reach down and rub herself the way she did before she fell asleep some nights. Only this was better. It was nice to hear his hoarse breathing, feel where the soft flesh met his springy hair on the back of his neck. She liked that intent look on his face —like she was the last thought he was ever going to have. She took his hand and slid it between her legs, a move that surprised him so much that he was still for a moment. But soon his hand began to creep, at first hesitantly, then when he met with no resistance, a little more quickly, into her underwear, moving gently over the soft places underneath. She moved her hips to encourage him, surprising both of them with her small, unselfconscious moans and gasps. After a minute, his hand went still again and he finally spoke: "Can I? Girl, what you want me to do?"

She thought her heart would break if he stopped. "Go ahead," she whispered. "I want everything." They looked at each other a stern moment, legs shifting against the rough plaid wool blanket. He slid a finger in, experimenting. She cried out, pleased, and he grinned a little. "OK, then." He unhooked her bra and got to work. Her last clear thought was: *Boy, I'm really going to have to leave town as soon as I'm old enough. Folks are going to hear about this.*

Girls who felt the way she did about Bobby Ware under the bleachers didn't last long in the Greenwood section of Tulsa. Not long at all before everybody was calling them "fast" and looking the other way when they came down the street.

After they finished, Bobby lay stroking her face, not speaking. She didn't say anything either. She felt the whole world had opened up between her thighs. Sam Cooke's voice was in her head, like silk. She knew it wasn't right, but she couldn't stop beaming.

"What you smiling at, girl?" Bobby said after a few minutes.

"You," she replied. He liked that. He smiled and kissed her. But she didn't really mean it. She liked the way he made her feel. She liked that her mind was free of words, that there were so many sweet green moments of being completely out of control. That's what made her smile. But she didn't know how to say that. He seemed satisfied with her answer. She sat up, pulled up her panties, brushed at her skirt, kissed him with an open mouth, and said, "We probably ought to be getting back. My mama's gonna be worried."

That night at dinner, her stomach kept swooping downward unexpectedly. She had trouble eating. She kept remembering some moment—Bobby's mouth on her nipples or the way he ran his tongue, just once, around the edge of her earlobe—and she had to close her eyes, a gasp almost escaping her. Her father didn't notice anything, going on about Miz McNulty coming in to get "something for her monthlies," and not wanting to talk to him about it, so he had to spend twenty minutes looking around for a woman she could talk to until he finally had to haul Tilly Ransom off the street and Miz McNulty whispered in her ear and then Tilly Ransom whispered in his ear and he soberly reached down the bottle of "remedy" (which was about ninety proof) and wrapped it in paper and handed it to her. "And all I could think," he concluded in a too loud voice, "was as old as she is, that monthly visitor's been hanging around a good sight longer than most. I think she just likes the medicine. If you know what I mean." He laughed and shook his head, shoveling in a forkful of mashed potato. He had grown much franker in his dinner-table talk since Angela's older brother and sister had married and moved out.

"Now, Johnny Lee, that ain't no way to talk in front of Angie," said Mildred.

"What? She's a girl, ain't she? And it ain't nothin' this old druggist ain't seen. She might as well know what goes on in this town. Why shouldn't I talk in front of her?"

"It just ain't seemly, that's all."

"Hmm." Johnny Lee retreated to sullen silence. Angela shifted in her chair, flushed. What he was talking about made Angela especially uneasy this time. Mildred's eyes bored right through her. *What if she was pregnant?* They'd have to be careful next time. No way was she having any babies. No way.

Every Saturday after chores, Angela and her mother went downtown to the movies. Mildred was an old-fashioned moviegoer. She was willing to see everything. It used to be fine to do that. Everybody saw everything. Johnny Lee never cared much for the pictures, but she never thought twice about bringing the children. There wasn't anything at the movies they couldn't see back then. Times were changing. But Mildred and Angela weren't. Not about this. The previous Dreamland, a place of magic with a glittering chandelier and acres of plush Oriental carpet, had burned to the ground in the riot and was rebuilt brick by painful brick in the years later. No one had told Angela that. And the chandelier was gone by the time she was old enough to have noticed it. But she loved the theater. She thought it had always stood there in its fading but still palpable glory. In 1964, the fading was far more apparent than the glory. The neon out front flickered and the lobby smelled of rancid oil and there were always a couple of letters missing from the awning. Today's film was Y AIR LADY. But they didn't care about the popcorn hulls underfoot, their feet sticking to the floor, the faint smell of old, squeezed-out sweat. Everything important was on the screen.

Mildred generally smelled of lavender sachet and wore her hair pulled back in a smooth chignon. To Angela, she only seemed truly relaxed in two situations: one was singing in church, which she did fervently to every hymn, even though she was never in the choir, her eyes closed, her round tones like butter in the air. The other was at the movies every Saturday. Inevitably at emotional moments or in musicals, as the lead actress—Audrey, Judy, Debbie, Dorothy, Deborah, whoever it might be—burst into song, Mildred sat, mouthing the lyrics gently, tears rolling down her face. The first time this happened, when they went to see *The King and I* when Angela was six, she happened to look over during "Hello, Young Lovers" and was terrified.

"Mama, why you crying?"

Mildred wiped hastily at her face and gazed down at her daughter with a look she never forgot. Even though it was dark in the theater, her mother's face was sufficiently lit by the sudden arc of light from a daytime scene, the brightness reflected from the screen. It was the same look Angela saw later in the woman in the photograph she found, the same look she sometimes saw in her own eyes later in life, when she looked at herself in the mirror until she was dizzy, falling into the brown pool that was her face.

It was a look of longing, of rivers unheard and songs unsung and dances never danced and paintings never painted. She seemed not to recognize her daughter. "I'm not crying, baby," she said. Then she said, "I mean I am. But I'm not sad." Angela didn't believe her, then or ever. But she knew better than to ask any more questions. She just got used to her mother's tears during movies. Now, with sixteen looming just ahead of her, she was beginning to feel the same way, sometimes. Like there was something there that if she could just reach it . . . But it was always hiding behind the music. She felt her mother's tears in her own throat sometimes.

Like today, when Audrey Hepburn came down the stairs in that column of white, her hair piled upon her head like that of a princess. Angela's breath disappeared. What could she say? What could she say about something like that? She looked at her mother. But neither of them said anything. Just kept reaching into the shared bag of popcorn, eating quietly and methodically.

It was these Saturdays that made Angela decide she wanted to be an actress, although she didn't say so. She started using her allowance to buy every movie magazine she could. The funny thing was, her mama didn't stop her. She usually didn't hold much truck with what she called foolishness, but she dusted around the ever growing piles of *Photoplay* and didn't say anything about the pictures of Sidney Poitier and Warren Beatty and Natalie Wood and Diahann Carroll up on the wall. And they kept going to the movies together. It was the only fun they had with each other.

Today, after Rex had reclined in his chair, feet up, to inquire in his velvet-cream voice, "Eliza, where the devil are my slippers?" mother and daughter walked out together in contented silence. They never talked much after a movie. They relished the remembered pictures in the quiet between them, the early-evening crickets just beginning to be audible, even in town. After a while, though, Mildred spoke. She touched her own hair quickly, making sure it was in place, and said, "Angie, you're not doing anything with that Bobby Ware that you shouldn't be, are you?"

"What, Mama?"

"You heard me."

"I did, ma'am. No, ma'am. I'm not doing anything I shouldn't." She surprised herself with the bold calmness of her lie. It didn't even feel like a lie, really—what they were doing didn't feel like a shouldn't. "We're just keepin' company, that's all."

"Well, I know what these young boys out here are like," said Mildred firmly, settling her hat on her head. "You got to watch your step. A young girl like you can easy end up goin' the wrong way."

"Yes, ma'am."

"Don't let him take no liberties."

"No, ma'am."

There was a school dance that night. Angela and Bobby danced all the fast dances and held each other through all the slow ones. Bobby sang the words to the songs into her ear. It was a warm spring night. They went out by the bleachers again, the sky vaulted above them, a deep blue blanket studded with stars. The moon cut a silvery path down the field for them. They fell on each other right away, hands sliding into clothes, buttons unbuttoning, mouths open, burying themselves in each other. Bobby fumbled around until he found his condom; as a measure of his devotion, he'd gone two towns over to get them. He couldn't very well buy them from Angie's father. This time, together, they figured out that if they rubbed spit on it, he could slide in much more easily. Angela didn't mind the rubber. It was just as good with a condom. It was the best feeling she'd ever had. Her mother just didn't know.

3

THE WORST THING ABOUT THE COSTUME WAS THE tail. Large and puffy white, it made sitting down impossible, going to the toilet a feat of Olympian proportions (you try wriggling out of that skintight bustier, sitting down, and keeping that thing out of the bowl). Aside from dealing with the costume and the toilet (which there was barely time to use anyway), there was so much to learn. Truth be told, not being able to sit down wasn't really a problem because you weren't allowed to sit down anyway. You could only lean, legs aligned seductively, in "the Bunny perch," against the back of a chair, the edge of a sofa or a railing. Always ready. Always willing. You had to call in your drinks in a sequence that never ever varied and then arrange them with military precision on your tray. You always had to remember to stand in "the Bunny stance" when you weren't moving, your pelvis tucked forward like an offering, your legs together, back arched (but don't lose your balance in those three-inch heels). When you were serving, no matter how bad your feet hurt, you had to do that "Bunny dip" so your titties weren't right up in somebody's face. You'd lean back, again with the pelvis forward, arch the back, then bend the knees. Make them think about resting their hands on the small of your back, or between your legs. But if they ever tried to touch . . . uh, uh, uh. A laugh

31

and a gentle pivot away. No drunken businessman was going to get it for free. He wasn't supposed to get it at all. The Bunny Mothers watched the girls with smiling firmness to make sure that this rule was never violated within the club. But you could always slip someone your phone number. Or meet him later.

Angela didn't do that stuff, at first. She took the rules very seriously and couldn't imagine going out with any of the key holders anyway. They were all white, all fat, all bald, it seemed. They called everyone honey, and thought their unfunny jokes were hilarious ("I love hot chocolate," they were always saying to her), and drank Scotch straight up until their words were a liquor-edged blur. They were always plucking at her tail and trying to get her to lean forward over the table so they could get a good look at her tits.

The money, however, was unbelievable. She often took home $200 or $300 a night in cash. The first time a guy slipped her a $100 tip, she almost gave it back; she'd never seen a $100 bill before. She wasn't sure it was real, and then, when she saw how much it was, she couldn't believe he'd meant to give it to her. She perched next to Sheila for a second during one of their infrequent lulls. "Sheil, this guy just gave me one hundred dollars. Do you think he meant to do that?"

"Girl, you look like a million dollars in that outfit." Sheila poked her in one of the rigid stays that made her tiny waist appear even tinier. "You bet he meant to give it to you. You keep it and keep working that shit. There's plenty more where that came from."

And so there was. Angela had a drawer full of cash until Sheila told her she really ought to open a bank account. She could buy any pretty clothes she wanted, but a lot of the money just sat there. She was so tired all the time. She still wanted to be an actress, but she wasn't at all sure how to make that happen. The days slipped quietly by. As soon as she and Sheila got some rest, it was time to go back to work. The only thing that kept her going was Dexatrim. She couldn't afford to gain a pound, and the pills gave her a buzzy feeling that she liked, especially before work. They rarely got home before 4:00 or 5:00 A.M. (if neither of them had a date). The days were spent sleeping until noon or so and then massaging each other's sore feet and running to the drugstore to buy more Dexatrim. In their refrigerator was a cloudy glass of water, three cans of Tab, two lemons, an old bag of carrots, and a moldy Chinese takeout carton. Angela loved it. She loved walking out of their tiny apartment and standing on the corner, inhaling the mingled scents of car exhaust and gardenia, and standing on the edge of everything good.

Not long after she and Sheila had become roommates, Sheila took her to Venice Beach. Angela, though she'd lived in LA for a few months by then, had yet to see the ocean. She hadn't known how to get there and she had no one to go with. Sheila laughed and took her hand. "Girl, you are so country!" she said. Angela felt sheepish but curiously thrilled at Sheila's warm hand wrapped around hers. They were silent as they drove to the beach.

To get to the water, they had to make their way through a dizzy hubbub of stoned white people. A blond girl with eyes that had long ago left this earth smiled sleepily at Angela and Sheila as they picked their way past. She sat next to an enormous, full-to-bursting backpack and a draggle-haired, dirty white guy. They both wore fringed leather vests. Sheila took a quick look at Angela and said, "Don't worry. These hippies don't bite. Too high." Then, "Look, Angie, there it is."

All the air rushed out of Angela's chest. Her hand flew to her heart, just like in a movie. The ocean glittered blue and green, sun-touched, just like in a movie. But with the salt on her face and the sky above and her body warmed by the air all around her.

She had come to where she was meant to be. Sheila stood next to her, grinning. "Nice, huh?"

"Oh, Sheila, I can't even tell you."

"I know. I thought you'd feel that way." Without speaking they moved a step closer to each other. They stood looking at the water for a long time, the sound of the waves in their ears, the noise of the city behind them forgotten. They might have been alone in the world.

When Angela met Sheila, she was close to giving up. Her work as a Katharine Gibbs girl was disappearing. She was a fast typist, but when she met Sheila she'd worked only three days out of the previous ten. She had no idea how she was going to pay the rent at her pay-by-the-week hotel, and she couldn't bear taking the bus one more second. She had to get a car. She was sitting behind the desk at Goldstein and Associates, a casting agency she'd been sent to that morning. She had her headset on and was staring at the wall in front of her, trying to stay awake. She'd gotten only five hours of sleep the night before. Her neighbors, two extremely large transvestites, were screaming at each other at glass-shattering levels most of the night. Her eyes were grainy and her neck felt loose; she kept drifting off. She woke up when Sheila came in. It was as if a lioness had entered the room. She had skin the color of a buckeye and about the same satiny smoothness. She had the walk of a runway model, one foot swinging way in front of the other, her fake-fur-trimmed ankle-length orange maxicoat swinging open with every step to reveal a tiny white mini and black go-go boots. Her hair was wrapped in yards of blue silk that matched the shirt that clung to her. She walked up to Angela: "I'm here to see Mr. Goldstein," she said. Her deep voice was cool water in the desert.

"Yes, ma'am."

The woman laughed, giggled really. Her sophistication fell

away for a moment and Angela realized that they were about the same age. " 'Yes, ma'am?' Where you all from?" she said in an exaggerated fake southern accent.

"Tulsa, ma'am. I been here about nine months."

"Nine months, huh?" The beautiful woman looked speculative. "You been working here the whole time?"

Angela blushed and looked down. "Not really. I want to be an actress. I've been working wherever I can. This is just a temp job." She sighed, uncertain why she was telling the truth. "This ends tomorrow. Then I don't know what I'm going to do." The phone rang and she busied herself with it for a moment. The woman watched her sympathetically. She considered something, then decided. "Listen, my name is Sheila Jenkins. I'm an actress too, and I need a roommate. Here's my phone number. Why don't you call me after work and we can talk. I think I might know a place where you could work too." She smiled. "I know how it is when you first get here. You're gonna get famous right away. And then when you don't . . ." They smiled at each other. Angela slipped Sheila's note into her pocket, feeling as though she might cry. "Mr. Goldstein will see you now," she said. But what she wanted to say was "Thank you. You're saving my life."

She moved in with Sheila a week after that conversation. Sheila came over to help her move her two boxes and one suitcase. She looked around the hotel room, her mouth in a little pout of disgust. "How long you been living here, Angela?"

"The whole time I been in LA."

Sheila hoisted a box under her arm. "Hmm. I stayed in a place like this too. Cried myself to sleep every night." She looked at Angela. Angela was suddenly very aware of the chocolate-cream texture of Sheila's skin, the large depths of her eyes. "I don't cry anymore, though. You'll stop too, you knock on enough doors. Come on." They left without checking for things under the bed or in the drawers. Nothing left behind was worth keeping.

The apartment wasn't far from the hotel. Sheila drove like the first woman allowed into the Daytona 500. Angela clutched the door handle and didn't speak. She kept looking at Sheila, who pushed the pedal to the metal as soon as the light changed and threw her cigarettes out the window like *she* was on fire. She talked the whole drive, offering to get Angela an interview at the Playboy Club where she worked. "The money's good and there's lots of movie types there. I been there two and a half years. It's good."

"I'll have to wear that little costume, though, huh?"

Sheila looked at her quickly. "You sure as hell will. You'll look good in it, though." She glanced up at herself in the rearview mirror. "I do."

Angela's final interview took place at the large Mission-style house that Hugh Hefner rented to use when he was in LA; the mansion was still a few years away. She'd made it through the big cattle-call audition in town and Mr. Hefner's brother, who ran the auditions, said, "Don't worry. You've got what we need." He patted her butt briefly and shoved a wrinkled slip of paper with a phone number and address on it into her hand. On the assigned day, Angela smoothed her very short red skirt over her hips and pushed the doorbell. It played the first few notes of "Take Five" by Dave Brubeck. A butler Bunny answered the door. She was heavily made-up and pushed-up, wearing the full Bunny costume augmented by a small white collar and a black bow tie. She led Angela from the brilliant white marble hall with the zebra-print rug to an anteroom with blood red walls and a black bear-skin rug. She was kept waiting there for the better part of a half hour. The rug still had a head. Angela stared into its glass eyes. It had many yellow teeth. Finally, she was summoned in to see Mr. Hefner—or Hef, as his brother had told her he liked everyone to call him. Sheila had told her that he took great pride in briefly meeting as many of the Bunnies as he could before they were officially hired. She walked into the room and a tiny gasp escaped her. Her future boss sat before her in an enormous tub full of constantly bubbling water—she found out later that it was called a Jacuzzi and was the latest thing. With him were two naked, blank-looking blondes. He looked at her levelly. He had a very raspy voice. "So, Angela . . . that's your name, right, Angela? You want to be a Bunny?"

"Yes, sir, I do." She tried not to look at Hef's penis, only somewhat obscured by the bubbles. One of the blondes idly ran a hand over her left breast, stopping to finger a large pink nipple.

"Well, what makes you think you can do it?"

"I've got a lot of energy, sir. And I like people." She was trying to sound as she would on any other job interview. That seemed the safest thing to do.

"Hmm." His hand traced small circles around the shoulder of the right-hand blonde. "That's good." He paused. "Take your clothes off, would you?"

"Sir?"

He smiled, and repeated his words as calmly as though she had misheard a request to hand him a glass of water. Angela's stomach slid down to her toes, which curled involuntarily. Was she going to have to get in the tub with three naked white people? How could Sheila not have told her about this? OK. OK. So take the skirt and top off. That's Hollywood. Tears stung her eyes sharply. She swallowed twice. Hard. Reached around to undo the zipper of the skirt, pulled the shirt off, wiggle, twist, out. She reached around to take off her bra and stepped forward, but Hef held up his hand magisterially. She dropped her arms and stood in her clean white bra and panties, her arms loose at her sides. The blondes didn't look at her.

"You have a nice rack," Hef finally said.

Angela sucked her breath in quickly and straightened up. She'd come so far. She didn't fold. "Glad you think so, sir."

He laughed and slid his arm around the blonde on his left.

"Turn around, would you?" Angela did what he asked, turning slowly. "Nice ass, too. You'll do well at the club. Lot of my customers want a little hot chocolate. Good to bring you girls in."

"Thank you, sir."

"See Mr. Jensen on your way out. He'll get you all signed up and outfitted. You'll have orientation next week, I think. And listen to your Bunny Mother. She won't steer you wrong." He stretched one leg out in front of him. "Welcome to our little family, Angela. I think you'll enjoy working with us."

"I'm sure I will, sir." But she wasn't sure he heard her. He was sloppily kissing the blonde on the right, whose hands moved rapidly beneath the bubbles. Angela didn't look too closely at what she was doing. They didn't watch her put on her clothes. When she got into the car, which she had borrowed from Sheila, she sat for a long time, the heels of her hands pressed into her eyes. But when she started driving, she felt OK. She'd done what she had to do.

When she got home and reported that she'd had to take her clothes off for the interview, Sheila pulled an "oops, I forgot" face and said, "Dag. Sorry. I should have told you about that. Sometimes he asks to see some of the girls before he hires them. I had to do it." She looked at Angela intently. "You did it, though, right?"

"Yeah. Sure. I woulda liked to known what to expect, though."

Sheila laughed and punched her in the arm like an affectionate big sister. "Girl, you don't *ever* know what to expect in this town. I thought you knew that already."

When Angela first left Tulsa, she didn't call her parents for a week. They were frantic. The first time they spoke after she left home, her mother cried wordlessly into the phone for five whole minutes. Her father asked all the questions: "Angie, Angie, we were so worried. What on earth were you doing, leaving us like that with just a note? Where are you?"

She told them that she was in Los Angeles (which caused a sudden change from sobbing to shrieking) but that she had found a job and a nice place to live (an outright lie). She told them no, they shouldn't come visit her but that she'd call as often as her busy schedule would permit. She told them that she was all right. They said they would pray for her. She thanked them. Then she hung up the pay phone in the filthy, savagely battered phone booth and watched a roach scurry up the grayish green wall. The hall smelled of urine. She sighed and blinked back tears. It was difficult to believe that Sidney Poitier or Jane Fonda or any of them had ever lived this way. She went back to her moldy, damp bedroom and cried until she fell asleep.

Once Sheila took her in and she went to work at the club, it was immeasurably better. She was able to send money and little presents home sometimes. Her parents thought this was all being funded by her work in a dentist's office as she tried to make it as an actress. But even though things were better, even though she liked the Playboy Club, it wasn't getting her into any movies. Sheila had the same problem. They both auditioned some — not enough — and were passed over plenty. There just weren't that many parts for girls like them yet. And they didn't know how to get the ones that were there. They could smell the change all around them, but they didn't know how to touch it. They lamented their situation often, but nothing happened until late one hot morning when they were watching TV together, not talking. Sheila was rubbing Angela's feet, which felt so good she was almost asleep. Suddenly Sheila's voice cut through her stupor. "I can't believe we didn't think of this before!"

"What?"

"This!" She picked up a copy of *Ebony* lying on the floor next to the sofa on top of a pile of dirty clothes. On it was a picture of Cicely Tyson, her hair in a neat Afro. "We need to change our hair."

"Change it into what?" said Angela, genuinely puzzled.

Sheila shook the magazine. "This. We need to look today. Hot. Happening. We need naturals!"

Angela's hands flew to her head. "You mean let our hair go back?"

Sheila rolled her eyes. "Yeeees. It is almost 1972, after all. And we look just like every other girl who goes on an audition in this godforsaken town. We all look like Diahann Carroll in *Julia*. Nice. Sweet. Enough of that. It's time for power to the people. Let's do it. OK?"

Angela fingered the hair at the back of her neck. It was starting to go back already. What would it feel like to have that softness all over her head? "Well. OK. If you don't think they'll give us a hard time at work."

"No. We can just tell them it's the next big thing. You know they'll listen to us 'cause we're black chicks. We're always ahead of everybody else. It'll look good. Look at her, Angela. She's beautiful."

Angela looked. Cicely was smiling, confident. Beautiful. She was beautiful. Angela's hair had not been left to its natural texture since she was five years old. Her mother was not raising any nappy-headed little ragamuffins. In Tulsa, a girl would no sooner have run around with unstraightened hair than she would have run around naked. It would have been worse than running around naked, letting everyone see your naps. Angela touched the photo, a little self-conscious. OK. She came here to become someone new. It was time to look different too.

They both had the night off so they started right away. Despite Sheila's bold proclamation, it had been so long since either of them had had more than the slightest contact with their God-given tresses that they weren't sure how to proceed. Finally, Angela proposed that they wash their hair so it would go back and then go to a barbershop to get it cut. "Just to start with," she said. They washed each other's hair in the sink. The oil used to press it slid down the drain in thickened swirls. Angela felt Sheila's hair rise up beneath her fingers like bread dough, thick and pliable. She rubbed Sheila's scalp, finding it curiously comforting. She remembered when her mother used to wash her hair over the sink. Every Saturday, the hot comb sizzling in wait on the stovetop, her mother humming to herself, usually an old hymn. Angela dreaded the comb—her mother liked a hard press and usually burned her at least twice—but she enjoyed those soft moments before, the quiet of the kitchen, the sound of her breath in her lungs. There was no smell of burnt hair and oil yet, no infinity of sitting still. Just a quiet hymn and her mother's hands moving on her, getting her ready. It was odd to find herself in the opposite position with Sheila, her hands moving through her friend's hair. "OK, I think I'm about done now. You can sit up."

Sheila sat up, her eyes slightly glazed, and wrapped a towel around her head. "Your turn," she said. When Angela was done, they regarded each other, towel-headed. "You really want to go to the barbershop looking like this?" said Sheila. "You know how those guys in there are gonna be, all checking us out and talking about us. And we'll have to wait with our hair looking all crazy."

"Well, what do you want to do?"

"I used to cut my brother's hair all the time and I still have my old clippers. I wasn't thinking at first. I can do yours and then if we prop up the mirror I can tell you how to cut mine."

"I don't know, Sheil."

"Oh, you'll be fine. Here. Off with your towel." Sheila snatched the towel off Angela's head. Her hair stood up all over, frizzy and wild. "Come on, Sheena, Queen of the Jungle, let's get to work." They both laughed and Sheila went to find her clippers. Angela watched her friend's retreating back and rubbed her fingers together, remembering the spirals of hair under her hands.

Sheila emerged from the bedroom, holding clippers and a pair of barber scissors. "I can't believe I forgot all this stuff. Come on, Sheena, sit down."

Angela sat obediently. "We need a little music for this operation," Sheila said. She put the Supremes on the stereo, loud, and started combing out Angela's hair and dancing around. Then she got out the clippers, plugged them in and started cutting. Angela jumped as the first large clump of hair fell into her lap. "Don't worry, Angie. I know what I'm doing. And don't jump—that'll get you messed up for sure." From then on, Angela sat like a child chastised by her mother. Her hair fell around her. Finally she had to close her eyes. She remembered her mother's screams on the phone when they talked after she moved out here. What would she say now? After about half an hour, working first with the clippers and then, quick and sure, with small barber shears, Sheila said, "There. I do believe you're an African queen." She held up a mirror. Angela's eyes widened. She barely recognized herself. She had never looked more . . . well, OK . . . she had never looked more astonishing. Her eyes were large and luminous, the midlength hair soft and inviting. It made her neck look longer still. She did indeed look regal. "We gotta go over to Melrose and get your ears pierced and get you some earrings, girl. You gonna be knockin' 'em dead in no time."

"Oh, Sheil, I can't believe it."

"Believe it. Diahann Carroll is dead."

Angela was very nervous cutting her friend's hair, but Sheila was a patient instructor. She too looked gorgeous when they were done, her darker skin a contrast to Angela's honey coloring. "We have *got* to go to the store," they shrieked, almost in unison as they looked at themselves in the mirror. They did a fast, sloppy job of sweeping up their old hair, tossed it in the trash and headed over to Melrose. Two African queens out for an afternoon's shopping. Who would stand in their way?

· · ·

They came back just moments before dark, exhausted and laden with bags of new clothing they could not possibly afford. "So much for next month's rent." Angela laughed, shoving her hip into the door. Her earlobes ached a little from her new gold posts. Sheila was wearing new black-and-white-striped hoop earrings. They dropped their bags inside the door and collapsed on the ugly gold sofa. They both started laughing for no discernible reason, their legs entangled, their heads at opposite ends of the sofa. "You look good, Sheil," said Angela.

"So do you, girl."

Silence fell between them. A police car's siren wailed in the distance. They stared at each other for a long moment. Angela was the first to speak. "You really do look beautiful."

Sheila shifted her feet a little, rubbing them against Angela's thighs. Angela didn't move away. Sheila crawled around awkwardly and brought her legs in line with Angela's so that they were head to head. Their faces were very close. Sheila touched an earring experimentally. "Do those hurt?"

"No. Not if you don't mess with them." Angela's breath was coming a little faster, and she was utterly confused. She knew only that she didn't want to stop, just like back under the bleachers with Bobby, whatever this was. Sheila's hand slid to the side of Angela's face and she shifted around, straddling her now. Angela moved her hips a little and spread her legs. Sheila smiled. "So this is all right?"

"Yeah." Angela paused. "Well . . . what? Is what all right?"

Sheila smiled easily. "This." She leaned in. They kissed, mouths open. Angela's mind jumped from sensation to sensation. She opened her mouth a little wider, concentrating on the feel of Sheila's tongue, her hands moving lightly across her breasts. She had a sudden odd flash of those blondes in the tub, but then she opened her eyes and it was Sheila, only her Sheila. It was all right. Sheila had saved her after all. And now here she was, saving her again. Once they got each other's clothes off, they both laughed for a minute. Angela was uncertain exactly how to proceed. But it didn't take long to figure it out.

They lay together on the slightly lumpy orange carpet afterward, staring at each other. The strangest thing was not feeling strange. Angela had never even heard of two women together like that. She was sure it wasn't allowed back home. But something that had been knotted in her all her life, just below her breastbone, had been untied. And now it was done. She was loose. A loose woman, what her mother always used to fear so. She took a deep breath. Sheila spoke first. "You OK?"

Angela stretched, slid her hand across to touch Sheila's cheek. "Yeah, I'm fine." She pushed up on one elbow. "I've never done anything like that before, though."

Sheila laughed. "You're awfully good at it."

"Well--I had a good teacher." Angela paused, drew a small circle on Sheila's stomach with her finger. "Have you done that . . . done what we did with other girls?"

"Once or twice. I'm not no dyke, though. I just do it for kicks . . . if I really like someone."

Angela frowned. "What's a dyke?"

Sheila stretched. "A dyke is a big, mannish woman who hates men and only sleeps with other big mannish women. Not like us. We just do it for fun." She looked at Angela intently. "Wanna do it again?"

Angela laughed. "Sure. Let's go to your bed this time, though." She crawled over and kissed Sheila deeply. She had never felt less self-conscious in her life. "Let's go," she said again, standing up and extending her hand. They went into the bedroom with their arms around each other, like girlfriends on the playground.

The next morning, Angela woke up in Sheila's bed. She felt wide open. Her eyes. Her heart. Her ears. Everything was wide open. She could hear every sound in Los Angeles.

She had an audition that afternoon before work. Sheila helped her get made-up, picked out her outfit—a Kelly green mini and high black boots—and gave her a big kiss as she sashayed out the door. "Go get famous."

Angela smiled. "You know it."

She walked into that audition room like the queen she was. Everyone turned to look at her. She laid her headshot down on the desk and took her seat with the others. After a long while, they called her name. She entered a small room where three white men sat at a table across from her. She said her name, read a few lines from the script they gave her. "Do you mind nudity?" they asked. "No, I like it," she replied, laughing. They looked startled but then laughed too. "We'll get back to you, Miss Edwards," they said. She left. That night at work, she made more in tips than she'd ever made, didn't bump into one single person with her tail. Everybody was talking about her and Sheila's hair, how terrific they looked. The next day, there was a call on her service. She had a callback for a part in *Big Doll House*, to be directed by Jack Hill. It was her first callback. She felt so good that day she didn't even care later that she didn't get the part. Things were changing. The work had begun. When she told Sheila about the callback, she said triumphantly, "The queens will not be denied!" Sheila laughed and took Angela's hand, throwing it up in the air like a prizefighter's. "No they won't. They certainly will not."

4

WHEN ANGELA BROKE UP WITH BOBBY WARE, not long before she left for Los Angeles, people thought she'd gone right out of her mind. They'd been keeping company for nearly five years, and making love for about four and a half of them (though folks didn't know that). Neither of them knew much about the other's body when they started, but they were open and eager. Angela felt as if a great secret had been kept from her. All her mother's talk about being a lady. If ladies didn't get to know what this was like, then she plain didn't want to be one. On nights she wasn't with Bobby, she slid her own hands between her legs, thinking about all kinds of things, different people, figuring out different ways to conjure that feeling, sighing and moaning into her pillow. She could see why people didn't talk about it too much: the power of it seemed dangerous. It didn't feel *wrong* exactly—just risky. But she didn't want to stop.

Louann was the only person Angela told. That was how it began to end. She brought it up one day as they walked home from secretarial school. Louann was going on and on about her boyfriend, Mitchell: ". . . he said he just wanted to slide one hand up under my bra for one minute, and I said, Oh no, mister, that's as far as we're gonna go and—"

"Lou, don't you want to?" Angela spoke without thinking.

"Don't I want to what?"

"Let him. Do it. You know."

"I do not." Louann hugged her books closer to her chest as though someone was going for her breasts right then and there.

"Never?" said Angela.

Louann smiled a little bit and lowered her books. "Well, sometimes." She rolled her eyes. "Sometimes it's nice. But you know . . . you just can't. He ain't never gonna buy the cow if he gets the milk for free."

"Louann, sometimes you worse than my mama." Angela skipped a few feet ahead and turned toward her friend, overtaken by a wild impishness. "I've done it. Been doing it. I like it too."

Louann stopped dead. "You what?"

"You heard me."

Louann clutched her books back to her chest. Her eyes widened. "Angie. Wow. I knew you was always kind of fast, but—"

"But what? Now we ain't friends?"

"No. That ain't it. But now you gonna have to marry him. Or something. How you gonna do the nasty with him like that and then just go on? What all would folks say?"

And in that moment, Angela saw. She'd lived in Greenwood all her life, but she'd let herself be blind. She remembered the firm, possessive way Bobby took her elbow when they went out, the confident way he looked at her when she came over to have dinner with his folks, the way he opened doors for her with a flourish. All things that had seemed nice when they'd just been having their own little secret. But now she had to think about what folks would say. He cared about that too. He would never let her go now that they'd been lovers for so long. And she knew. Knew like she knew her own name, that she could no more marry him than fly to the moon, no matter what he'd been thinking. She would have to stop. There was no way to do what he would want of her now. She felt a deep and sudden twisting in her stomach. And one word and one word only in her head: no. She and her friend stared at each other, shocked by what they knew.

She saw Bobby the next night. They had just made love, having grown adept at avoiding the bumpy parts of the car and finding the right parts of each other. They were snuggled together in the back seat under a stadium blanket, the windows cracked to let out the steam, the air snapping in bright and cold. Angela could hear her breath in her lungs and Bobby's heart beneath hers. The opening riff of "You Keep Me Hangin' On" buzzed in her head as she looked out the window at the stars. She was having trouble breathing.

"Bobby," she finally said. "What do you wanna be doing in ten years?"

"What?"

"What do you wanna be doing in ten years?" Even though she'd asked him this before, she was hoping he'd surprise her.

He shifted up on one elbow, looking bemused. "You know. Living 'round here. My daddy's probably gonna retire soon and I'm going off to Howard for college and med school, but then I'm coming right back here. Be married too, I think." Here he stopped and looked at her, but she didn't say anything. "I'd like to live right around from my parents so I can help out."

Angie's head pounded. She liked Bobby a lot. He always made her laugh. And she loved the feel of his hands on her; that was always good. But now he'd told her. Now she knew. He wanted a life that would kill her. She couldn't do it. Why hadn't she seen it sooner? Bobby was looking at her, only love in his eyes. How could she break that good heart? "I can't, Bobby. I'm not even going to stay here. I'm gonna be an actress. In the movies."

"What?"

"I'm not staying here. I . . . I'd better go." She finished straightening her clothes and reached for the door. The truth. She owed him that. Even though she hadn't been totally sure what the truth was until the words came out of her mouth. She never did forget the look on his face as she climbed out of the car. Like something had hit him from behind. Or what it was like not to take his calls, to avoid him in the street. She carried those memories with her on the bus all the way to Los Angeles, a heavy weight. But they didn't stop her. She knew she couldn't stay.

Things that mattered to her were always like that. It was the same when she found herself with Sheila. She had been aware of the way Sheila's hips moved, the way she used her hands when she was talking, the elegance of her mouth before they were ever lovers, but until they kissed she didn't know she could want a woman this way. She didn't know she could feel this kind of satisfied with a woman. But now it was true. There was no hiding from it. She still liked men, she could still look appreciatively at a man or take pleasure in a man's touch. She thought she still might even be able to love a man. But Sheila was the fact of her. She couldn't deny it.

Two years had passed since Angela had come to LA. She never went home to visit; she didn't call often. Every week at first, halting, filled with pauses, then every month. There were no friends to talk to back there. Louann, married and pregnant already, would not even begin to understand. And her brother and sister remained the strangers they had always been. She did talk to her parents, lying with almost every word she spoke. She told them that she auditioned as much as she could on her lunch hour from the fictional dentist's office. That she lived with two other girls in a nice part of town. That she was dating nice young men and not letting any of them go too far. That she'd heard about this new marijuana, but, no, she didn't know anyone who'd tried it.

Her parents never suggested visiting and eventually they stopped pressing her to come home. Sometimes this made Angela feel a little sad, but other times she thought they could hear that she was a different person now and they didn't want to know about it. She didn't tell them about the movie she was in, the slow hip swivel on the bar.

One cool fall night, when she answered the phone, she didn't recognize the voice. It sounded like a woman's, but it was hard to tell. "Naked. Naked up there" was all the voice said.

"Who is this?" Angela said. She almost hung up, but her hand tightened around the receiver at the same moment.

"You know who this is," the voice went on. "It's your mother. Though God help me, I never raised you to do anything like that."

Angela's hand went from tight to boneless. She nearly dropped the phone.

"Angela, you know you are to answer me when I'm speaking to you. I could not believe what I was seeing."

"Mama?"

She went on. "I *wouldn't* have believed it except I saw it with my own two eyes. Everyone in town is talking. That's why I went. And there you were, right up on that bar. Naked. Naked!"

"Mama, I—"

"What in the name of all that is holy are you going to say to me? What are you going to say to me about that?"

Angela felt her mouth working, tried to think of what she could say. But nothing would come. "You've got nothing to say, have you, miss?" More silence. "Well, I don't want to speak to you until you do. Until you can somehow explain this to me. And I don't see how that day is ever going to come." Then came the slam of the phone in Angela's ear. Angela sat there, her beautiful face a fist. She could feel all her muscles under her skin, the skin that her mother had seen when she was a baby, the skin that horrified her now. Her hands rested on her smooth brown thighs, the thighs that frightened her mother. Her breath came hard in her throat. She thought she might vomit.

Sheila was out shopping. Angela choked on the silence in the apartment. Her hand worked furiously twisting her hair in back. After a while—she couldn't have said how long—she got up, took off her robe, and walked into the bathroom. She looked down and surveyed her body. Her skin was the color of pennies underwater, stippled here and there with moles in unexpected but oddly inviting places, like one side of her left knee. Her stomach was a little bit rounded, her breasts medium-sized perfect globes. She cupped her hands underneath them, touched the nipples experimentally. This is what her mother hated and feared—the amount of pleasure her body could give someone, even herself. Her mother would never understand the power of being wanted. The way she felt when she was just a little high and making love, like she was in charge of everything. She slid her hands over her stomach again, felt the insides calm down a little. The outside still looked good.

Angela was sitting in the dark when Sheila came home. She had not risen from the sofa for an hour. Her head hurt. She jumped at the sound of the key in the lock. "Sheila?" Her voice shook.

"Yeah, it's me. What's going on? Why you sitting here in the dark?"

"I just . . . My mama called. She saw one of the movies." Her voice was tiny as though her throat were stuffed with cotton.

Sheila sat down next to her. "Not too happy, huh?"

"You could say that." They sat in silence, legs touching, for a while. Finally Sheila spoke. "I've got some good dope," she said.

"That would be good," said Angela, wiping at her wet eyes.

"Come on, then. Let me just put my stuff down." Sheila put her packages into her room, and came out clutching a little Baggie. "A cure for what ails you." She waved it cheerfully. Angela smiled a little.

Sheila always made a big deal out of putting a joint together. First the picking out of the seeds, then the spreading out the leaves, and, finally, with a noisy, small rattling, shaking out the paper to roll the joint. Angela felt like slugging her. She didn't want to wait for the smooth absence to take her over. She just wanted to be there.

She didn't have any difficulty holding the smoke in her lungs anymore. In fact, she could no longer clearly remember the fear she'd felt when she was faced with that first joint, how nervous she'd been. Now it was all pleasure. She smoked until she couldn't remember her mother's call at all. Well, she did, but it didn't mean anything. What else was her mother going to say? She was her mother, after all.

Once they were high, they rested on the sofa, their legs entangled for a while, their feet lazily rubbing up and down each other's calves.

After a long silence, Sheila spoke. "I got invited to a party in the Hills. All kinds a people gonna be there. Let's go. I don't want"—she sighed deeply, rubbing her hands through the back of her hair—"I don't want to just sit here all night . . . let's get with somebody. Somebody who can do us some good."

Angela nodded, her eyes still closed. "Yeah," she murmured. "Let's go."

So they moved to the bathroom, together, as though underwater. The air was lined with fur. Felt good against their skin, slow, like they could eat it, like chocolate. Sweet.

They chose their outfits together, tight and shiny and beautiful. They leaned toward the mirror together, smoothing on gleaming reddish brown lipstick. They both put on big hoop earrings, earrings that twinkled, small spots of cheap light against their brown skin. They put in eye drops to get rid of the red and picked their hair out to its fullest glory. They put on false eye-lashes. They were so stoned that it took a long time. One of Angela's lashes got stuck to her cheek as they laughed helplessly, trying to remove it, then making crooked attempts to glue it onto her eyelid. Finally, they were ready. They fired up another joint that they shared in the car, then had to stop for doughnuts on the way, and then they were winding down the road, out to Bel Air, up to the top of a mountain, Sheila's little orange Bug putting the road away underneath them, gasping a bit at the difficult turns. They laughed a lot at nothing, that kind of obsessive laughing that takes your breath away and makes your eyes water. They didn't want to because it made their mascara run, but they couldn't help it. Everything was just so funny. Sheila drove with her hand on Angela's thigh.

Finally, they pulled up at an enormous house, ablaze with floodlights. Cars dotted every inch of gravel around it. What you could see of the roof was flat and angular, punching the night sky at odd angles. Angela wiped at her eyes and finally said, "Whose house is this? It's fucking huge."

"It's fucking Wilt Chamberlain's, that's whose," said Sheila.

"Fuck. No!" Angela screamed. "You got us an invite to Wilt's house! Oh my God! And I was just sitting there all crying and shit when you walked in the house. Why didn't you just tell me?"

"Well," Sheila said, checking her eyes in the mirror. "I didn't want to make you all nervous, you know. And you were so upset when I came home . . . I don't know. I thought it would be a nice surprise."

"Hell, yes," said Angela. She fussed with her hair, reached out and took the lipstick Sheila extended toward her. "Everybody's gonna be here."

"Damn straight," said Sheila. "Let's go."

They jumped out of the car, their four platformed feet hitting the ground at the same instant. Tossed their keys to the valet, who caught them on the beat. Colors pulsed from inside the house, orange and red and bright pink. They turned their heads toward each other, grinned. Walked in the door.

According to an article Angela had read in *Ebony*, the soft gray fur of the enormous conversation pit, had been gleaned, along with the fur for Wilt's gigantic bedspread, from the nose fur of seventeen thousand Arctic wolves. The grayness was covered by brown bodies dressed in every silky shade of the rainbow, and over to the left, on a bed set into the middle of the floor, bodies half-undressed, entangled, flashes of breast and hair, a hand moving. The air was sulfurous with the mixed tang of pot and cigarette smoke. "Freddie's Dead" pounded out of the stereo speakers, making their flared pant legs vibrate. Hundreds of people talked, embraced, screamed, pulled slowly on joints, and hoovered coke off a low glass table and off the belly of a blond woman who lay on the floor, spread-eagled, her eyes closed, her shirt off, slowly rubbing her nipples as if she were alone in her bedroom. Angela took it all in with the diffidence of the truly high. Then she felt a hand on her neck as she made her way toward the scene. "What's up, lovely ladies?" Some man she'd never seen before, good-looking but still . . . She needed to find out who he was before she did anything. Her heart hummed in her chest.

"I'm doing all right. This is my friend . . . ," she trailed off. Sheila was gone. "Well, she was right here."

"Yeah, I saw her go. You're the one I wanted to talk to anyway." The smile. The look. The joint offered. The dance begun. He had a name. What was it? Sam or Tony or Reggie or John. This one was named Rafe. They always stood too close. They always looked at her face for one minute and her breasts for five. They always offered her joints and she always took them, inhaling deeply, feeling her head waft away from her body. Her mother wouldn't have believed she could be so fast, going on the pill so she could fuck whomever she pleased, whenever she pleased, without worrying. Sizing it up. Looking for kicks. Filling her lungs with that sweet smoke and then dancing with him. He smelled good, like some kind of flower. She was so high that it was getting hard to stay awake, but she didn't want to sleep, she didn't want to miss this, so when he held the little mirror out to her, the powder heaped in a line, she took the rolled bill gratefully. As soon as she snorted it, she felt the top of her head explode, all light stars inside. In a minute or so she thought she might never need to sleep again. All she needed to do was keep dancing, keep talking, keep feeling Rafe's lean hips against hers. She felt like every good idea ever conceived. She could see Sheila across the room in the conversation pit and she laughed and waved. Sheila laughed back. She had caught the night's real prize; her leg was thrown casually across Wilt's long, long leg as if Sheila found herself hugged up to the world's most famous basketball player every day. He was rubbing her neck. They weren't in a hurry. They both knew how this scene would end. Sheila smiled up at him, then back at Angela. "That your friend?" said Rafe.

"Yeah. Looks like Wilt's gonna get lucky tonight," said Angela.

"Wilt? How would you know he's getting lucky with your friend?"

Angela smiled mysteriously. "A girl can just tell." She ground her hips into his a little. "If you play your cards right, you might get lucky too." She could see he was trying to figure out the deal between her and Sheila. She could tell it turned him on too, which just got her more excited. The song had changed to "Ben." Angela saw Wilt get up, extend his hand to Sheila. They left the room, he lowering his hand to cup her ass briefly. Rafe looked at them speculatively. "Guess you're right about Wilt." He paused. "You know, the playroom—where they're going—is just down that hall. Wanna go with?" Angela had been running her tongue around and around her teeth. She felt the separation of each one with particular intensity. "Sure. Let's see what they're doing." She looked at him, her eyes challenging.

They went down the hall, which was dimly lit every few feet with sconces that gave off a warm purple light. Rafe backed Angela up underneath one of them and started kissing her before they even got to the playroom. She couldn't open her mouth wide enough underneath his. Couldn't pull him close enough to her. He stopped after a minute and pulled her the rest of the way down the hall.

The playroom. What to say about the playroom? There wasn't a pinball machine. The room had five sides, three of them mirrored, and a vast pink circular sofa surrounding a huge open surface that undulated gently from the weight of the bodies already moving on it: the biggest waterbed Angela had ever seen. When she and Rafe entered the room, Sheila and Wilt were already there, had already begun. They stood in the doorway a frozen moment, quiet. Angela's high fell away just for a second; she remembered what it was like to crouch in her mama's backyard with her sister, watching a box they had propped up on a stick and waiting for a bird to blunder underneath. They always thought that someday they'd catch a bird that way. But they never did. Where'd that come from? That memory somehow propelled her into the room in front of Rafe, propelled her onto the bed next to her friend. Sheila opened her eyes and looked at Angela steadily. She was so lovely; Angela wanted to kiss her. Wilt was still working away on Sheila's breasts, but Angela knew in that moment that Sheila was thinking of her. Wilt never looked up. Angela swallowed and sank onto the bed, and Rafe came up behind her on his knees, his hands on her breasts before she could even exhale. She could feel his breath hot on the back of her neck. "You done this before?" she murmured.

"Done what?"

"You know—more than one person," she said.

"No." He turned her to face him, started unbuttoning her silky blouse. "But I'm always willing to try new things. I think a person ought to be willing." He had her shirt off now. "To try new things," he said.

"Right."

His mouth closed on her breast. She stopped thinking. Her favorite part was when her mind went off altogether. The bed moved beneath them. She was unbearably excited by Sheila's moans, by the bed waving and swirling beneath them, by the knowledge that this man was a stranger to her, by the mouth on her breasts, by how far away it was from Tulsa, from anything anybody ever thought of in Tulsa, by knowing that her mother would never understand this in a thousand years. She pulled him—what was his name? oh yeah, Rafe—inside her. She cried out, just after Sheila. Everything seemed very clear. And then it was over.

The next thing she knew, she was home in her own bed. She had no idea how she'd gotten there, where Sheila was, what had transpired after the events in Wilt's playroom. Her mind turned gray at just that point, covering a harder-edged truth. She looked at her yellowing shade, could feel that her hair was totally flattened, her mascara smeared all over her eyes, lipstick a pathetic reddish memory. She was still wearing her jeans. She skinned her hand into her pocket, drew out a small piece of paper. "In case you want to get to know me better . . . 555-8976. You something else, girl. Rafe." Rafe. Hmm. They usually didn't give her a number. It might be worth calling.

While she was considering this, Sheila came to the door and leaned in the doorway. Her hair was matted on one side and bushed out on the other. Her eyes were reddened and her mouth looked bruised. Angela looked at her, smiled slightly, and said, "Girl, you look a mess."

"Well, you ain't exactly ready for your close-up either, girl."

She pulled absently on the flattened side of her hair, then came and lay down next to Angela. "Some night last night, huh?"

"Who you telling?"

They were silent. "Think Wilt's gonna call you?"

"Nah." She went quiet again, looking at the ceiling. "He was something, though. I never been with somebody so tall. Hadda keep scooting up and down. Felt like a damn fireman on a pole." Angela laughed and took her hand. The sun suggested itself, warm and inviting, outside her window. Living in a way nobody in Tulsa could ever even have dreamed of, she felt not the least bit dirty. Not this morning. She didn't even mind that Sheila had been with someone else. They were just two girls doing what a girl's got to do. They'd always have each other. She ran her tongue around the inside of her mouth. It tasted as though a desert resided there, hot grit and sand and the rot of dead things. She sat up, told Sheila she was going for a shower, walked to the bathroom. Once she got there, she looked at herself for a long, long while, her face out of focus from time and sex and cigarette smoke. She had a sudden moment, just a moment, where everything fell away, where she knew that her mother was right, this was never going to work out. But she pushed that thought away, drew a deep breath, turned on the shower. Another day begun. Another day begun.

5

HERE WAS THE THING ABOUT LOS ANGELES THAT year: it was hot. Not just hot: the Santa Anas blowing 100 degrees so that you could barely breathe half the time. Not just hot: the air like sandpaper on the skin, the sun like a weapon. Not just hot: you had to spread newspaper on the seat of the fanciest car in order to have any hope of sitting there. But it wasn't just hot with the weather. It was hot with change, with happening, with beautiful black girls pulling up from every little dogtown and holler and city and shouting, "We want to be in pictures." Rafe Madigan could have any girl he wanted. He could have them any way he wanted: doggie-style, ass-backward, all happy to go down on him (black girls—happy to go down on him!), two at a time. No matter what he asked, he found some beautiful young woman willing to do it. Sometimes he'd try asking for the freakiest thing he could think of just to see if they'd refuse. But they never said no. Never. He was born and raised in Los Angeles and he'd been a good-looking, smooth-talking, heart-stealing black man all his life, yet he had never seen anything like it. Got kind of boring sometime. Just waiting to see if he could find somebody different. Somebody who might make him feel different. It was a great warm, wet sea of flesh after a while. Couldn't tell one from the other. A few sweet words, a mention of the movie business, and he was in. One more fuck.

That's what it was like when he met Angela. He was acting a lot. He'd been on the fringes of the business since '68 but somewhere around '71 after *Sweetback* and after Sam Arkoff and Roger Corman figured they could make some goddamn money fast off this game, he couldn't stop working. He just had to show up at an audition and the part was his. Never the lead, though. He was handsome, but he wasn't quite *something* enough for that. So he played his share of cops and bouncers and sweet kid brothers of the leading lady. He kept busy. And he was called in a lot to read with people—the audition traffic had never been heavier.

When Angela came in for her audition, Rafe wasn't thinking about anything in particular. He'd been idly checking out the girls as they came in—that one had a nice ass, this one pretty lips—but he didn't think much beyond that. Until she came in. There was something so sweet about her, that little bit of a southern accent that she was trying unsuccessfully to hide, the long, pliable neck with a hollow at the base that he couldn't help but think of kissing, breasts that looked as though they'd fit right into his hands. She was something else. Thing was, the producer saw it too. Rafe saw the whole thing happen—the card, the look between them, the hardness that came into her eyes. And he knew he'd have to wait until Kaufman was done with her to make his move. She walked right out past him without another word after the audition. No rap, no phone number, no nothing. He was out in the cold. He didn't worry about it long. There was always someone else. But she did have an elegant throat.

That's actually how he remembered her a year later when he saw her at Wilt's—that long neck. He came right up behind her and put his hand on the length of it and she still didn't remember him. She was pretty fucked up but still beautiful. She must have been smoking all night. More than that, she was getting that look people get when it's not happening. Rafe had seen it before. The parts don't come and the change doesn't come and the moment you moved out here for doesn't come and there you are. Your blood starts to turn to ice. He could see it in her eyes. He came with the rap anyway. Might as well get some.

But it was that last moment of softness he saw in her that made him give her his phone number. After they'd finished, when they were lying together on the bed, the last ripples dying beneath them, Wilt and that girl she knew just a few feet away, he could see her eyes in the half-light of the room. There were tears there. She looked about fifteen, just a girl. That touched him somehow, made him want to know her. So he slipped his number into her pants pocket after she fell asleep.

He didn't think about the fact that he'd left her there. These girls didn't ask anything of you. Except maybe that you help get them a part. They didn't seem to need to be courted or treated well, they didn't ask questions, they didn't mind if you didn't take them to dinner, or if you didn't know their names. They just wanted to be in those movies. They didn't know there wasn't a damn thing he could do about that.

It was a Sunday afternoon when she called him. Sundays were hard. You spent the morning getting over Saturday, either regretting or celebrating or trying to remember what you'd done and hoping it wasn't too fucked up. Then maybe you'd go out to lunch, but then there was the afternoon. Maybe a movie in Westwood, but that didn't last all day. Maybe somebody you knew from a picture was home, trying to decide what to do with himself too. Maybe you'd have to face the day alone, but that was to be avoided at all costs. He was grateful when the phone rang. He didn't care who it was.

"Hi, is this Rafe?" A girl's voice, southern.

"Sure is. Who's this?"

A pause. "We met the other day, well, night really. At Wilt's house?" She trailed off, silence yawning. He smiled. "Sure. I remember. We had a pretty good time. Angela, right?"

"Right."

He could hear the easing in her voice. What could she have said to further identify herself: that was me you were fucking at that party? "Well, Angela, how you been?"

"I been all right. Took me a couple of days to get over that party. You know."

"How well I do. It was some party." They fell into an awkward silence. "Well, Angela, can I ask why you called?"

"It's Sunday. My roommate's out. The light was making me sad."

"What?"

"The light was making me sad. Doesn't that ever happen to you? It comes in all orange and soft and it just feels sad. Like you gotta talk to somebody? I found your number." She stopped.

His heart tightened oddly at her words. "What are you doing now?" he said.

"Nothing. That's why I called," she said.

"Well, why don't you meet me at the Santa Monica Pier in about half an hour. We can do nothing together."

"OK." He could hear the relief in her voice. That made him feel a little sad too.

There had been a break in the heat—the sun was on his back was friendly, not a hammer, as he waited not far from the Ferris wheel. The distant shouts of children in the surf made a counterpoint to the music from the merry-go-rounds and Scramblers and everything else behind him. It made him think of how he loved coming here with his old man, the few times he'd managed to do it before his father died. The music made him feel hopeful. He was just listening and staring out at the water so intently that he didn't even hear her come up behind him. She put her hands over his eyes, laughing. He turned around, caught her wrists. "Girl, you don't know me that well yet." But he was laughing too.

"I don't know," she said, poking him gently in the belly. "I think I know you pretty well. Rafe, right? Don't like to waste any time with a girl."

"No, I don't. And my last name's Madigan. Just so you know."

"Mine's Edwards. Angela Edwards." She laughed. "Seen you naked and I still didn't know that. That is really something," she said. She leaned on the railing next to him and looked out at the sea. "Really something."

He felt, for the first time in months, a little uncomfortable about . . . well, about that. About balling a girl before you even knew her last name. This girl anyway. "So," he said after a while. "How long you been out here?" They both kept looking at the sea.

"Me? Mmm, I don't know. Two years, I think." She laughed again. "That's how you know it's getting to be too long. When you lose track. Where'd you come here from?"

"Me? Over in Watts."

"Really?"

"Really. You lookin' at a natchel-born colored man from Los Angeles."

She laughed. "I don't know if I've ever met one of those."

"Now you know one pretty well." He paused. "Well. He'd like to get to know you pretty well anyway." What the hell? He never said stuff like that. "Want an ice cream?"

She looked at him, her eyes never wavering. "I'd like that a lot."

"OK, then."

They each got vanilla and stood, meditatively licking them, not talking. Sometimes he shot little looks at her, watching her tongue play around the edges of the cone. She was totally unself-conscious, licking her arm when the ice cream melted down the side. He didn't know what to say. He remembered the sounds while they made love; the memory made his stomach tighten, heat moving across his belly. But now, as they stood here clothed, he didn't know what to say.

"So you're an actor too, huh?"

"Try to be."

"What you been in?"

"Oh, you know. Lotta Corman's stuff. Had a couple of lines in *Blacula*, was a bartender in *Cool Breeze*. I'm around."

"How'd you get into it?"

"How's anybody get into it? People told me I'm good-looking. I'm good at memorizing. I like the sets. I thought I'd get famous. All my troubles would be over. Now I'm used to it. You never know when something might break for you either."

She looked at him intently. "You don't, do you. That's what I always say to people. It could happen any time. You don't even have to be the lead. Somebody might see you, and then everything could change."

"Right." He was smiling a little. But it was easy to believe her. For a moment, it seemed not only possible but likely that they'd both make more of this than they had so far.

It was easier to talk after that. He found out that she was from Tulsa and that her parents thought she worked for a dentist until very recently. "The way they found out I'm acting is that my mother saw me dancing almost naked on a bar in *Street Fighting Man*. I swear, she don't even like that kind of movie. Somebody told her I was in it. That didn't go over too good."

"No?"

Her eyes closed briefly as though it hurt her to remember, then she looked straight at him. "No." He didn't ask any more; her look told him what he needed to know. So he went along when she changed the subject. She told him how much she loved LA, the drive of it and the smell of the drying flowers in the overheated air. Her skin made him think of the way paint looks as it's poured from a can. She used her hands constantly as she talked, touching the railing, knotting them together. As he listened to her, he realized that it had been some time since he'd talked to a woman. Fucked 'em all the time. But talked to one? It had been awhile.

Sundays were funny that way—made you think about stuff you hadn't done before, or hadn't done in a while. Back home, up until the riots in '65, Sunday was car wash day. Every family on the block that had a man to speak of—an uncle, a dad, a brother—would pull their ride out into the street, get the radio going so that all the songs became one song, one cry of loss and love and sweet soulful torment, and start washing. The washing had a very particular rhythm. You started with the body of the car, a slow, slow series of circles, kind of like you might make on a woman's body if you wanted to get her really hot. Then down to the rims, shining them so good that you could see your face in them, all weird and curvy but still recognizably yours. Then you did the outside of the tires—a little wax to make the black gleam. Then the buffing, the kids' favorite part, the car's true metallic color emerging, each its own shade, like a face. And then the best part, the ice cream truck coming down the street, the men all sitting with beers on the porches, their voices ping-ponging back and forth, the edges of their voices rough, sweat running down their faces, music lofting overhead. After his daddy died, Rafe always went over to his friend Joe's for car wash day. It wasn't the same, but it was better than nothing. Better than sitting in the house with the women, fussing with a chicken or a ham, listening to the sounds of complaint on their lips.

He hadn't thought of that in years. He didn't know why he was thinking of it now. Angela was standing very close to him, not speaking. "Hey," she finally said, "where'd you go?"

He laughed. "Thinking about Sundays when I was a kid. I don't know. You make me think, I guess. Don't do too much of that. I like to keep on the move."

She smiled. "Let's take a walk. I'll tell you what I did on Sundays when I was a kid."

She told him about a starched white dress so stiff it left marks on her legs when she sat down. She told him of hair pressed so flat it shone, of big white bows tied at the perfect angle. She told him about the Vaseline on her legs, the oil against the crinoline, the slippery way it felt between her thighs, the way it would melt and dust would stick to her ankles on hot days and the fans waving faster than fireflies all through the sermon.

She told him about the time she went to services with her friend Louann, who was Holiness born and raised and about the babble inside the church, the heat and the folks falling out, jabbering in tongues, their voices roaring from their mouths like poured gravel. The women falling backward into the gentle, strong arms of the men, the kids all sweating, watching the adults around them praise God with their bodies. She took his hand without seeming to realize she was doing it. People streamed past them all along the boardwalk. "It was like God put on a red dress and came down to wail with everyone. My church was so quiet. Everybody just prayed all to themselves, but there? There at Louann's church, I could feel God. He'd be loud, you know? That's why I like loud things. Big things don't tiptoe."

He looked at her, mystified and charmed. "You got a lot going on in that head of yours."

"I do."

They walked a little farther. "So should we go back to my place?" he said after a while.

"Yeah," she said. "Sunday's no time to be alone."

"Well, let's eat first."

They went to one of those little sandy seafood places in Venice and ate clams and laughed. She professed continued amazement at his boyhood in LA and at both their prospects for success. After a while, he said to her, "Do you remember when you met me?"

She looked down at her feet. "Well, we got off to a fast start."

"No, not then," he said. "I read with you at your audition for *Street Fighting Man.*"

She stared at him, then her mouth opened slowly, remembering. "That was you?!" she squealed. "I totally forgot!"

"I thought you forgot, but that was me." He lowered his voice. "You should have gotten the lead."

"Really?"

"Really."

"Well, that's sweet of you. That's really sweet of you." She smiled and he felt it all the way down his back. The air smelled of salt and heat, diminishing now. "Should we go?"

"Yeah, I think maybe we should," she said. She stood up and held out her hand girlishly. He took it, bent over, and kissed it. He'd never done anything like that before.

This time, back at the house, it wasn't wild like at Wilt's. They knew each other's names now. He hadn't kissed anyone this way, long and slowly on the sofa, one hand just barely moving up to forbidden territory, since he was in high school at least. She was shyer now but still eager to please, first up, then down, then sideways. They left the stereo on, Marvin Gaye of course. Afterward they talked and talked and she fell asleep with her head on his chest, her hair rough wool under his nose. He wondered what it would be like to see her on a Monday or a Wednesday, or all the days after that, how she'd look with her hair braided up or wearing pajamas, what she looked like as a girl in that church. Time was passing, this life getting tired. She made him think about other days of the week, what else there might be. He hadn't met anyone who made him think of that stuff in a long time. She snored a little and he rolled over to sleep.

She stayed all night and he didn't mind. That was different too. But in the late morning he had to ask her to leave. He had an afternoon call that day. They kissed goodbye, lingeringly, and he promised to call the next day. He'd be shooting well into the night and she had to work at the club. But he was whistling as he arrived on the set that day. "You look happy, bud," said one of the grips as he found his place behind a grubby old desk in the fake police station they'd set up. All the grips knew him. There was a small, tight fraternity of people who jobbed from film to film.

"I am happy. It's a good day."

"Look like you got some last night."

"Maybe I did and maybe I didn't." Normally he would have replied with something unspeakably crude. But he sort of wanted to keep a line around her. *Getting soft*, he thought. *You getting soft, my man. Girl better be worth it.*

Rafe was cast as a cop in this one. He couldn't remember the name of the movie to save his life. But Fred Williamson was in it, and Rafe, who had worked with him before, had a scene with him this time. He sat behind his desk, a toy gun strapped around his chest, ready.

Williamson strode onto the set and perched on the edge of the desk. Rafe sighed and Williamson turned to face him. "Hey, my man, you playing my partner?"

"Yeah, but I don't last long." Rafe paused then, feeling bold, added, "You oughta know that, my man. You the producer."

Williamson smiled slightly. He ran a hand over his face. "That's half the problem, trying to do all this shit myself. It's the only way we gonna ever get anywhere in this town, but damn." He slid a hand thoughtfully over the smooth handle of the gun holstered around his shoulder. "It's a bitch doing all this shit. You lucky you just an actor."

Lucky. Rafe didn't say anything. He just looked at Williamson's calm, prosperous back. He thought of all the auditions he'd been on, all the cops and bartenders and luckless younger brothers and nobly killed boyfriends he'd played. He didn't feel all that lucky. Just stuck doing something he'd be damned if he could see the way out of. But he didn't think about that too much. What was the point? "Action," called the director. And the scene began.

6

SHEILA JENKINS CAME TO LOS ANGELES FROM THE hard side of Chicago about four years before Angela did. She was eighteen and beautiful, although she barely knew it. It didn't take her long to figure out what to do with that once she got to LA. In Chicago, all she'd known was cleaning up her mother's vomit after yet another binge, and ducking when her mother threw things. As soon as she saved up bus fare from her summer job, Sheila got on the first Greyhound west she could, leaving Mom passed out on the cold kitchen table. She called a neighbor from a nearly deserted bus stop once she was safely away. "I'm not doing it anymore," she said to Miss Clarissa, their next-door neighbor and the author of the only kindness she'd ever known. "If I stay, she's gonna take me down with her." Miss Clarissa agreed to go check on her and wished Sheila the very best.

By the end of her first week, Sheila had given blowjobs to two minor producers and slept with a director. By the end of the second week, she had taken a hard look at her clothes and looked around at what the pretty black girls on the street were wearing and decided that she was gonna have to use some of the money from the parts she'd gotten as a result of those two blowjobs to start acquiring a decent wardrobe. So she did. By the end of her third week, she had been hired as a Bunny and had realized that those first two blowjobs were only the beginning. She didn't like it, but she steeled herself to do it. She'd been told all her life that she couldn't do shit, that she wasn't shit. This was her chance to prove that wasn't true.

But no one found her on a soda fountain stool and said, "You're the one." She didn't even like movies that much, that was the really funny thing. She just wanted to be someplace where she would be thought beautiful, found useful, not yelled at.

Once, after they had become lovers, she asked Angie why she had come to LA. "To be in pictures, of course," she said. But then Sheila pressed, "But really, why? We all want to do that."

Angela looked thoughtfully at the ceiling. She sighed and then scooted closer to Sheila on the sofa. "Did you ever see *Splendor in the Grass?*"

"Um, I think so. Is that that one with Warren Beatty?"

"Yeah."

"Oh, yeah. Damn, he was fine in that movie. He could do me any old time. You think we could get to a party with him?"

Angela sucked her teeth. "I don't know." Then she laughed. "I mean, if anybody could do it, you could. But that's not why I brought it up. I saw that movie when I was eleven with my mama. And well . . . I don't think I ever saw anything so beautiful."

"What do you mean, Ange?"

"I mean . . . it was like my heart stopped. When she was in the hospital after she tries to drown herself and she's muttering all crazy and he goes into the room even though the nurse is trying to stop him and he's in there for just a second and then he comes out and he goes to the corner of the hall and hides his face"— here she stood up and walked to the corner of the room and hid her own face for a second. Then she turned back around to finish her story. "Then he starts crying really loud and she hears him and . . . I could feel it all through my chest. Natalie Wood too.

When she looks at him. Or when she's talking to her mother and she goes under the water and she comes up screaming about not being 'spoiled'? I felt like I wanted to scream too. Like they knew how I felt all the time. Like they knew something I couldn't touch." She sat back down. "Guess I thought if I came out here and got in pictures, I'd find some way to touch it." She picked at a loose thread of the sofa, embarrassed now. Sheila looked at Angela's feet, which were twirling around in circles and bumping into each other the way they did when she was having trouble expressing herself. She reached out and rested her hand on one foot, stilling it. "Oh, Angie. I don't know how you're ever gonna make it here." She pulled her down to the sofa next to her and kissed her. "I swear I don't. I'm really gonna have to look out for you."

"OK," Angela said, a shy look on her face.

"OK."

Sheila knew the men were necessary. And she knew that what she and Angie were doing had to be hidden. Men loved to watch two girls get it on; Sheila had been in a couple of those scenes. But to feel the tenderness she felt for Angela, the desire to be with her all the time, the way you would a new and extra-good boyfriend . . . that was freakish. Dykesville. Uncool. So she kept it to herself. Lots of girls had roommates, after all. No one knew what they did after the lights were out.

Sheila found that being Angela's lover made all the men's greedy hands feel less offensive to her. Having someone to come back to who knew how to touch her, someone she longed to touch, made the men's eager sighs and lickings easier to manage.

Angela didn't talk about Rafe too much, even though they saw each other pretty steady. Sheila found it easier if she got high or made sure she was out when he came by to pick Angela up. She played it cool, though. Rafe was pretty nice. She and Angela both still talked sometimes about maybe meeting a nice guy and settling down after their movie careers were over, but more and more this seemed like idle talk. Sheila found that it was even beginning to annoy her when Angela brought it up. One time they were at Venice Beach on a rare day off together, their feet dug in the sand, the sound of the Temptations drifting over their heads, when Angie brought up the idea of the mythical nice guy again. "You think so, huh?" said Sheila.

"It's gotta be *some* nice guys in Los Angeles."

"Look like you got the last one—and he ain't even kinda talkin' about marryin' you, is he?" said Sheila.

Angela squinted a little "no." Then she looked at Sheila. "I don't know. I'm just talkin'. Don't know if I really want to get married anyway. I just like the idea of having somebody who could take care of me."

I'll take care of you, Sheila thought. How she wished she could embrace her right there on the sand. *If it wasn't dykey, I could,* she thought. And that thought made her sad. She moved her foot closer to Angela's. "We do all right together."

Angela looked at her lover, her eyes suddenly soft and considering. "Yeah. I guess we do." She looked back out at the waves. "We do."

7

THE SKIN WAS THE FIRST THING. THE SKIN ON THE back of his neck, where his hair was a little more closely cut. It was like a child's, downy and soft and then shading up into a mass of kinks. Angela loved to touch and kiss him there, thought about it when she wasn't with him. Or the way he kissed her, without ever asking, without ever checking to see if it was all right. He knew it was all right, that whatever he might do would be what she wanted. He never hesitated right from the first. He never hid anything from her, his hands frank and knowing, moving easily over her body, his tongue in her mouth like it belonged there, so she couldn't think of anything else or anyone else, just the sweet moments she was suspended in with him and waiting for them to continue.

She still loved Sheila too. Sometimes this confused her. Other times, she didn't see why she should have to choose. She and Sheila slept in the same bed every night she was home, curled around each other like cats, all but purring, their breath rising and falling together. Angela loved the smell of their skin together, the way they looked so much alike and could share clothes and eyeliner and make each other come without even thinking about it much. Like they were the same flesh. She loved that too. Was that possible? She was doing it. But she kept wondering.

She didn't lie to Sheila. No point in lying to each other. After all, the first time she slept with Rafe, Sheila was next to her. And they both slept with men regularly, for business and pleasure. A girl couldn't get anywhere in town without it. Angela would sometimes fleetingly wonder how far she was getting with it, but it didn't pay to think that way often. Just keep putting one foot in front of the other was the only way to keep going. Sometimes she thought of Rafe as she made love with Sheila, sometimes vice versa—a double exposure. She was aware of Sheila, of her affection for her, the life they'd built, with its rickety self, the pleasure they gave each other so easily and confidently. And she knew Sheila loved her too. Sometimes she saw her giving her a quick look in the mirror as they put on their lipstick in the morning, or the way she always seemed to want to be touching some part of Angela when they were sitting on the sofa. They didn't own each other. But they kept finding ways to be together. They both wanted that. Angela found it easiest if she just moved through it and didn't think too much. When she started thinking, she got scared.

They were both still Bunnies more than they were actresses. There were so many girls like them. The number of beautiful black people per square inch in Los Angeles in those years was staggering. Yeah, the real power was all white still, but the images on the screen were too black, too strong. Melvin Van Peebles beating down that white cop in *Sweet Sweetback*, *Shaft* ruling Manhattan, his leather coat flared out behind him, Ron O'Neal strutting so smooth in *Super Fly*.

Angela and Rafe loved to go to the movies together. (That was something she didn't share with Sheila, who got very nervous watching herself on screen and got bored watching most other people.) They saw everything that came out, especially all the black pictures.

It was after the movies one night, walking back to the car from a double feature, that Rafe first asked her, "What's up with you and Sheila, anyway?

"What do you mean, 'What's up?'"

"I mean 'What's up?' I mean, you remember how we were all . . . together . . . that night at Wilt's. I just wondered . . ."

Angela felt her face go still. "We're friends. She helps me with stuff. We both want to be in pictures. That's all. We ain't dykes, if that's what you're worried about."

"That's not what I'm worried about. I just . . ." He trailed off. They were sitting in the car now. "This is kind of special to me . . . you are." He drew a deep breath and laughed. "I mean . . . no strings or nothin'. But still. I was just wondering where we stand."

She took his hand, played quietly with the fingers. "I'm standing here right now. That's all I can say. I got . . . I got stuff I have to do to get work and stuff I want to do because I feel like it. But you do too. And we're together now, right? It is kind of special. I . . . well, that's all. I don't know what else to say about it. I'm with you now."

He took his hand away, looked at her for a long moment. "Right," he said. It was impossible to tell what he was thinking. He just started the car, his hands easy on the wheel. He began kissing her roughly as soon as they got in the house. Like he was trying to make a point. But Angela wasn't sure it was a point she wanted to see.

When Angela went up for her part in *Coffy*, she knew that something big was coming. Something really big. The audition was pretty much like any other. The look-over. The reading of a few lines of dialogue. The question: "Do you mind doing nudity?" By this point, Angela had had her clothes off in more movies than she cared to count. While she couldn't really say it *bothered* her, she sometimes felt like there had to be more to an acting career than pretending to be dead and taking off her clothes.

Then the call came, "You have the part of Jackie," the message on her service said. "Shooting begins Monday. You will be required on set for three to four days. Please come to the office to pick up your script." When she got it, she found that she had a long scene with Pam Grier, the star of the movie. Pam was a big, tough, luscious girl. She looked ready to do whatever she needed to do. And she really knew how to fight and how to handle a gun. Angela was comfortable with a gun too. Her father had showed her how to shoot when she was a little girl. She still remembered his words: "Any of them crackers feel like they need to come back down 'round here, you're going to show them what for." But she hadn't been asked to use those skills in a movie yet. The gunplay was all for the stars. Maybe if she did well enough in her scene here, Jack Hill, the director, would ask her if she knew how to handle a gun. "Yes, sir." she imagined herself saying, standing her straightest. "I sure do. My daddy taught me." No matter how hard she tried, she couldn't get rid of her accent. Sheila told her to stop trying, that it gave her a trademark, something for casting directors to remember her by. So she learned to smile broadly when someone said in what they thought was an accent like hers, "Well, where you all from, honey chile?" Learned not to flinch when people said briskly, "Well, yeah, she's got a great body, but what are we going to do with the voice?" Like it wasn't even her voice. Like she was just some disembodied, honey-dipped thing. Well. Now she had a few lines. She'd show them.

She worked harder than she thought it was possible to work to get ready. When she walked on set that day, she knew it stone-cold solid. She had even worked out a little story for her character, how she came to be the hooker she was, a little bit of her relationship with Coffy. She'd read once in a profile of Dustin Hoffman that he always prepared an elaborate history for each of his characters. Sheila sent her to the set with a kiss and a whispered "Go get 'em, girl." She felt like a million bucks as she started her car.

She murmured her lines to herself as she was made up, stuffed into a cheap, long, curly wig and poured into an ankle-length orange polyester number. The wardrobe woman yanked the front of it quickly, experimentally. Then satisfied, she blew a cloud of smoke into Angela's face and walked away. Angela caught sight of herself in the mirror and almost laughed. She looked like a whore. Her mother would have died. But she felt kind of excited, to be so completely not herself. She ran her hands across her body, giggled again. "You think so, bitch? Well, I'll show you," she said. That was her line to Coffy, just before they started ripping each other's clothes off. She wiggled in front of the mirror, then went down the hall to the hotel room that was the set for this scene.

Pam Grier sat a little behind the camera, smoking a cigarette and laughing at something one of the grips was saying. Stationed around the room, looking bored, were women all dressed like Angela. Beautiful, cheap polyester birds. Bright and inviting and not long for this world. They leaned against the wall, talked to each other in easy voices, until the director came on set. "All right, ladies, places, please," he said crisply. "Quickly, quickly. We've got to get this shot in thirty." Everyone hopped into place as though poked with a cattle prod.

"Hi, I'm Pam." A briskly extended hand.

"I'm Angela."

"You ready to do this?"

"You bet."

"You look good in that dress, girl. Too bad I gotta tear it." She smiled briefly. Angela smiled back. They took their places opposite each other. "Action," called the director. "You want something, bitch?" snarled Pam.

"I want you to watch while I kick your ass," Angela snarled back furiously. She felt herself ten feet tall, only rage.

"I think you'll be the one doing the watching."

"You think so, bitch? Well, I'll show you!" Angela lunged for the front of Pam's dress, suddenly feeling truly angry. Pam eluded her with one swift side step and just as quickly reached forward and ripped Angela's dress wide open. Her breasts sprung forward, swinging a little as Angela lunged for Pam's dress and tore it. Now all the girls were screaming and fighting, fabric tearing, shrieks. Angela felt her leg bump into the coffee table so hard that she knew instantly it was going to be bruised. Then she crashed to the floor. The cheap carpet felt scratchy underneath her back. Pam was tussling with someone else now. Angela felt an odd mixture of embarrassment and intense excitement. Her eyes were brass, her breath was coming hard. She felt no impulse to cover herself where she lay. The scene went on until a leggy blonde reached into Pam's wig and came away screaming with bloody hands. Coffy had hidden razors in her hair.

Finally, Mr. Hill called, "Cut. And print."

The screaming and rolling around stopped as suddenly as though a plug had been pulled. "Thank you, ladies. Very nice. Very realistic," he said. He shifted from foot to foot. "Next scene in fifteen."

Someone brought Pam a robe, but no one brought anything for Angela. She stood, nearly naked and starting to be cold for a minute before Pam turned to her and said, "Nice work. Hope we work together again soon." Then she went off, her robe drawn around her shoulders. She stopped to bum a cigarette from the cameraman. She suddenly looked a lot smaller. Angela shivered and drew her arms across her breasts. She went back to her holding area. Shimmied out of what was left of her dress and handed it to the wardrobe lady, who took it with a disdainful sigh. She skinned back into her street clothes without a word to her fellow actresses, took off the long, cascading, and now tangled wig. Unbraided her hair and picked it out. Used the communal jar of Pond's to clean the heavy make-up from her face. Changed back into her regular self. But she felt a little thrill when she thought of what it felt like to scream that line and then rip Pam Grier's dress off. Hot. That's how she felt. She felt hot.

She was still feeling that way when she pulled up to the bar where she'd arranged to meet Sheila. They were going to have a drink to celebrate. Her legs were long and perfect. She was smiling a little bit. Everyone turned to look at her as she walked into the bar. It was like they could smell her high. She saw Sheila and took the stool next to her.

"Hey girl, how you doin'?"

"I'm good. You look happy. It went good?"

Angela ordered a gin and tonic and then said, "Sheil, it was unbelievable. We were all screaming and rolling around and tearing each other's dresses." She paused and laughed into her drink. "I loved it."

Sheila grinned too. "What was your favorite part?"

"Tearing her dress off. Or maybe when she tore mine. I felt so crazy." She paused, sipped her drink. "It kind of made me feel like making love to somebody. All naked like that."

"Did it?" said Sheila, her eyes steady over the rim of the glass.

"Yeah. Maybe even two somebodies. I don't know. I just feel like I could do anything tonight."

"Well, let's see," said Sheila, grinning. She looked around the bar. "Have another drink first." So they did. Then one more for courage and a little trip to the bathroom for just one little toot.

After that, Angela was racing. She could hardly keep her own hands off of her breasts or away from the damp, comfortable space between her legs. She threw one leg over Sheila's—it was dark, no one would see, and leaned in, close. "I wish you could have been there to see it."

Sheila leaned in so close that Angela could feel her breath on her ear. "I wish I could have too." Angela stayed on the seat somehow, but Sheila's voice went all through her, settling somewhere between her legs and her stomach. She turned, brushing her lips across her friend's cheek and said, "Let's get out of here."

They drove home, kissing at every stoplight, too high to worry what people pulled up next to them might think. They fell on each other as soon as they were through the door, little agonized cries escaping them, not even taking the time to lock the door. Angela didn't think about Rafe. She was utterly consumed by Sheila's hands on her, Sheila's tongue in her mouth, Sheila's breath in her ear. When they were done, they lay on the carpet by the door, spent and laughing. They both jumped about a foot in the air when the doorbell rang.

"Who the hell is that?" said Sheila.

"How would I know? Let me go see." She was feeling so loose and hot and cheerful that she barely buttoned up her dress and didn't put on shoes or anything. She looked like a woman who'd just been fucking her brains out. Sheila rearranged her clothes and was on her way to the bathroom as Angela opened the door. It was Rafe, standing there with a bottle of wine and some flowers. She pulled her dress closed a little tighter, suddenly embarrassed. Nothing there he hadn't seen before, but . . . he could see it on her, what she'd been doing. Everything. She could smell it on herself.

He stood, looking at her for a minute. Seemed uncertain what to say or if he could speak anymore. Were there words? "Thought you said you weren't a dyke."

"I'm not."

He was silent for a long moment. "Don't look that way to me." More silence. "I don't know about this, Angie. I don't know about this."

She didn't say anything. A police car passed by outside, its siren blaring. They stood facing each other. Then he dropped the flowers on the floor, set the wine bottle down with an oddly delicate gesture, and turned and walked away. She watched him go, still holding the front of her dress. Sheila came out of the bathroom just as she closed the door. She came up behind Angela. "Who was that?"

"Rafe." She was still staring at the door. "I told him we weren't dykes."

"Well, we aren't." Sheila slid her arms around Angela's stomach.

"But what are we?"

Sheila turned Angela to face her. "We're very good friends." Then she laughed. "Damn good, if I do say so myself." Angela didn't laugh. She felt a headache beginning. She stood clutching her dress, suddenly unsure of herself. She'd been so sure just a little while ago, an hour ago, safe on the floor with Sheila. But now she didn't know. She didn't know what she was doing.

8

EVERYBODY KNEW EVERYBODY THEN AND EVERYONE was willing to do anything. Any drug you wanted, you could get. Any clothes you wanted to wear were fine. The longer your hair, the better. The fewer questions you asked, the better. And it didn't really matter, did it? I mean, everything was cool really. It was kind of a turn-on if you thought about it, the two of them together, their brown girl legs intertwined, their brown girl mouths pressed together, their brown girl hands moving over each other's beautiful brown girl breasts. Who wouldn't find that sexy? Who wouldn't find that a turn-on? Hell, he didn't know why he hadn't asked for it that first time. Well, yes he did. He wanted Angie for himself. It hurt to think of her with Sheila. He kept thinking of the light in Angie's eyes that time she told him about church when she was a girl. He wanted that light for himself. And he could see, that time that he went to her and she had clearly just finished making love to Sheila, he could see that some essential part of her belonged to Sheila. He didn't know if Angela was aware of it. But he could see it, and it made him want to cry.

He didn't call her for a few days after he walked in on them. He knew he was hurting her. She called his service over and over. In the end, when he called his service, he could hear the reproach in the operator's voice: "She's called at least five times, Mr. Madigan, and she says it's very important. Did you get our other messages?"

"Yes. I did." His voice was level.

"Well, good," said the voice emphatically. "We'd hate to see you miss out on an important message."

Why the fuck do you care, lady, he thought. But he said, "Right," and hung up. He dialed Angela's number, not really thinking about why. She answered on the third ring. "It's Rafe."

He could hear her rapid inhalation of breath, almost a gasp, and then she spoke. "I been calling you and calling you. You 'bout to run me out my mind."

He laughed in spite of himself. "I wasn't the one who came to the door half-naked." Getting right down to it. She went silent. For a long time. Finally, he spoke. "Look, it's cool. I just had to . . . well, it's a lot to take in . . . but you know, it ain't no thing but a chicken wing. We both grown. And we both free to do what we like. Right?"

"Right." She paused again. "I'd like to see you tonight. That's what I'd like."

He stretched his legs out. "Well, why don't you come on over here then, girl. I guess I wouldn't mind seeing you either."

"See you in twenty, then." She was there in fifteen. Standing on his doorstep grinning with her fine self. He buried his nose in her neck, inhaled her sweet musky scent whole. Who would have thought it was the beginning of the end?

In 1971, Melvin Van Peebles made *Sweet Sweetback's Baadasssss Song* for $500,000. It earned $14 million. That's how it started. Both major studios and small, scruffy independents like Samuel Z. Arkoff's American International Pictures started turning out cheaply made, bodacious, and hyperreal action pictures, starring black people, if not made by them, as fast as they could buy film stock. The most compelling of them, like *Sweetback*, with its mix of black power and misogyny, the thrill of watching a black man beat a cop to death with his own handcuffs (even though it took place out of camera range because it was just too expensive to make it look convincing), offered an evening of the score to those for whom the score had been so uneven for so very long. It was 1971, 1972, 1973. Martin Luther King, Jr., had been dead for four years, five years, six years, and peace had been given more than a chance. So to rise up in the theater, to look up in the theater and see yourself, no matter how manipulated and filmed and badly lit, and speaking crappy, unconvincing dialogue, to see yourself, to see your rage there for a minute—that was enough for a lot of folks. But then of course it all started to fall apart, almost the second it began. The flesh turned on the flesh. The NAACP called it out. The white people made all the money. The black actors got only dope and coke and cold fried chicken and pay that was less, far less, than union scale. And whatever the point had been got lost in a sea of Afro'd gun-totin' tough guys declaring war on the pushers and gettin' all the honeys. The honeys, as usual, had little to say. They got raped, they stood by their men, sometimes they stood up for themselves, but not without making their way through at least two to three nude scenes. The good times couldn't last forever. They never do. But Rafe and Angela didn't know that then, lost in each other's sweet embrace.

He pulled her closer to him, sighed. "What am I gonna do with you, girl?" he said. They were standing just inside his doorway, breathing each other's breath, trying not to fall away from each other. "I don't know," she said softly. "You know, with Sheila, she's always there, she's helped me so much. I really love her. But . . ."

"But you just a natural-born freak." He said it so softly and gently, smiling, that she couldn't hear the whip in the words.

"I guess," she replied. "What I was gonna say is that I wanna be with you too. I just wanna do what feels good, all right. That's all. That's what's been working for me so far—what feels good." Now her hands were working on his belt buckle as she looked at him steadily.

"Right," he said. She slid down onto her knees, a supplicant, as he leaned against the door and closed his eyes. "Well, you do know about that," he murmured. After that, there was nothing else to say.

In those days, for those films, there were no walks down the red carpet. Usually, there wasn't even anything you could call a cast party. Sometimes somebody brought some beer the last day of shooting and everyone would raise them for a sip after the last shot. For *Coffy*, however, things were a little different. Jack Hill decided to have everybody over the weekend it opened in LA. He'd been doing all right for himself and he had a pretty nice house in the Hills. There was room. And a nice big pool. Why the hell not? Everybody was always up for a party.

All the actors and producers sat together in the back of a movie theater in South Central, having entered, almost furtively, a few minutes after the show began so that there'd be no fuss and they could gauge the real audience reaction. It smelled of pee and mildew and spilled Coke. Pam Grier sat tensely in her seat, gnawing on the corner of a long manicured nail from the initial chord of the opening theme until the taillights of her car faded away under the closing credits. She winced at every shot fired and mouthed her character's lines along with her image on the screen. Angela was squeezed in between Sheila and Rafe. Rafe's was hand on her leg, Sheila's just an inch away. Sheila spent half the movie sneaking looks at Angela next to her. The crowd went insane. They gasped as Coffy's little sister lost her mind and then her life to heroin, then roared with pleasure as Coffy blasted her way to revenge against the evil pushers. "You want me to crawl, white motherfucker? You wanna spit on me and make me crawl? I'm gonna piss on your grave tomorrow," she bellowed. The crowd went wild. Hill smiled just a little bit. He had worked hard with Pam on that line, on her delivery and attitude. He could see, at the end of the row, Sam Arkoff, the producer. He wasn't looking at the screen at all. His head was swiveled around and he was looking at the audience with pure cash-money joy on his face. Once he had said to Jack, "You know, that goddamn Van Peebles was onto something. We've got to give these people what they want. People, black or white, will pay good money for that." Hill knew he was right. He did the best he could and tried for as much integrity as possible with a minuscule budget, a ridiculous script, a cast that by and large had never set foot in front of a camera before and an order from on high that there had to be at least three to five nude scenes for the women. He did what he was told. And the audience loved it.

When the fight scene came up, Angela's toes curled right up inside her shoes. She couldn't believe it, couldn't believe that was her up on the screen, fake hair flying, rage sparkling in her eyes. The camera work was shaky, her mascara was smeared, she was half-naked, the cheapness of the room they were in and the carpet they rolled around on was apparent. But it didn't matter. She looked magnificent. She'd seen herself in the movies before but always in the background. Here she had a line, was visible for at least five or ten minutes. Sheila gave a little squeal of excitement and squeezed Angela's hand. Something joyous expanded inside her. Just the way it had the day that she shot the scene. She felt herself *in* it, fully *in* that cheap, stupid moment. She didn't feel cheap and stupid. She felt like Jackie, her character. Jackie who had been a cheerleader in a little town outside of Fresno and through a series of bad breaks had found herself in this brothel, forced to act this way. She felt all of Jackie's anger, right down to her toes. Couldn't anybody see how Jackie had suffered and worked? "Go 'head, Coffy. Give that heifer what for," said a rough voice from the audience to general laughter. She was the heifer. But she didn't care. There she was on the screen. Real. Bigger than life.

She loved watching the audience get so excited. There were parts of the movie where people screamed out loud in the theater. When Coffy took down all the dealers, a couple of people stood up and applauded. It was like at Louann's church, all over again. She was sanctified by the frenzy all around her. Rafe leaned over and murmured in her ear, "You looked mighty fly, baby. Congratulations." She smiled and kept looking at the screen.

Afterward, everyone piled into cars to make the drive to Jack Hill's. Rafe and Angela and Sheila went together, companionably passing around a joint as they drove. Since almost walking in on them that time, Rafe had taken a distant, what-he-didn't-know-wouldn't-hurt-him attitude toward Sheila and Angela's involvement. He treated them like they were just buddies. They cooperated by acting like buddies. Their jobs, or the hope of getting any jobs, demanded that they pretend an interest in the men around them that had nothing to do with their true feelings. So they were used to acting like nothing was going on between them. In a funny way, nothing was. They were lovers because they loved each other but also because they were both willing to do anything they felt like doing. He ran his hand around and around the inside of Angela's thigh in small circles as he drove.

She really cared for him, she thought. Just like Sheila. It's just more love. She leaned her head back against the seat, pleasantly high now. They were pulling into the driveway.

A lot of other people were there already, the music banging, joints out, shoes off. As they walked into the house, Angela looked through the glass doors and saw a couple of people splashing around in the pool, fully clothed. Pam Grier sat on Jack Hill's lap.

"Is this the best little actress in the world?" he said loudly to no one in particular. She beamed and kissed him behind his ear in a friendly way, then got up to get a drink. He smacked her butt as she left, and she laughed. "The best, I tell you," he said again.

As Angela turned away from the bar, holding her drink, another girl from the fight scene came up to her. She was draped around a short white guy with long sideburns and a nervous smile. "That crowd was really something, huh?"

"Yeah," Angela agreed.

The man spoke. "I think you ladies are in a massive hit. People were really groovin' on it."

"I know," said Angela. Who was this guy anyway?

"Well, I'm Cindy here's manager, and I think she's going all the way with this." He paused. "Who's your representation, anyway?"

"My what?"

"Your representation?"

"Oh . . . nobody. I mean, myself I guess. I just go on a lot of auditions."

"Well, if you ever feel you need someone to represent your interests." He took his business card and jammed it right into her bra so that just the corner stuck up. It scratched a little. "Jack Rosenstein is the name. I love you girls. Work with a lot of you. Gonna make Cindy here a star." His hand moved rhythmically around and around on Cindy's butt as he spoke. She just kept smiling blankly. "Thanks. I'll think about it," said Angela, slugging the last of her drink and moving off to get another.

"Never Can Say Goodbye" eased out of the speakers, and people huddled next to one another in the conversation pit, doing coke and laughing excitedly. Angela sat down next to Sheila. Rafe was at the bar. "How you feeling, sweet?" said Sheila. Their legs were almost touching. "I'm all right. I think the movie's really gonna hit. I can't believe it," replied Angela.

"Girl, you got that right. Did you hear that guy behind us when Pam got up there with that gun? Wham, bam, thank you, ma'am! He was losin' it. I couldn't believe it. People are ready for this shit." She took a swig of her wine and then squealed as the music changed to Sly Stone's "Everybody Is a Star." "Oooh, I love this song. Let's dance." She grabbed Angela's hand and ran over to a corner of the room. No one else was dancing, but she didn't care. Watching her, neither did Angela. They were laughing, eyes closed, hip to hip, until they were both suddenly aware that someone else was with them. Rafe had sidled up to them, grinning. Sheila threw her arm around him first, then around Angela without a word, and they kept on dancing, loving one another. "Thank you, ladies," Rafe said when the song ended. He kissed them each on the neck gently. Sheila and Angela smiled, their arms around each other. "Oh, yeah," murmured Sheila. "That's a real fine brother you got there, Angie. I hope you know that."

"I do." In that moment, she loved them both. She loved everything. Her heart beat in time with the world. The sun would never stop shining. Sly Stone would never stop playing. No one was ever going to die again. Nothing would ever be lost again.

By this time, a lot of people were in the pool in various states of undress. Their voices were high and tinny. In one corner, a well-known white producer and a young black actress kissed hungrily, their mouths wide open. Angela and Sheila and Rafe came out the door together, undressed, and dived in. The blueness pressed against Angela like a live thing. She swam around and between arms and legs, some naked, some not, until she had to come up, gasping and laughing, for air. When she came up, Rafe and Sheila were leaning against the side of the pool, kissing, Rafe's hand resting on Sheila's breast. Her heart tightened so much that she had to put her hand against her chest and press down. She breathed deeply. Once. Twice. Another time. She walked through the water to them. There were no words in her head. But this is what came out of her mouth: "What the fuck are you two doing?" They both looked at her, stoned and befuddled with arousal, genuinely surprised. They didn't say anything. Tears mixed with the chlorinated water on Angela's face—tears she was surprised to be crying. She loved them both. She'd been so happy just a few minutes before. Water dripped from her mis-shapen hair down her back. She sloshed up to Rafe and stood before him for a minute. Then she slapped him. He hit her back, wordlessly. Sheila screamed once. Then they all just stood there, looking at one another, the shrieks of the party going on all around them. Somebody fell into the pool. Stevie Wonder was playing on the stereo. Something broke inside Angela and she started sobbing, running awkwardly toward the pool's edge, Rafe behind her. Angela snatched her clothes off the chaise longue where she'd left them and ran into the house, yanking open doors in search of a bathroom or an unoccupied bedroom. She finally found a bedroom with nobody in it. Rafe had disappeared behind her. Maybe he had lost interest. She sat alone, yanking on her clothes, thinking of Rafe's hand on Sheila's breast. While they were kissing, neither of them had been giving her the slightest thought. It scared her terribly that she could be forgotten by the only people she loved in Los Angeles. She pressed the heels of her hands into her eyes. She thought she might throw up. They were free to do what they wanted, all of them. There was a knock on the door. She straightened her clothes and yelled, "Yeah."

The door swung open to reveal a startlingly handsome young man with hooded eyes and an even, smooth, café au lait face. He was still except for the anxious, constant wiggling, twisting, of the fingers of his left hand. His eyes bore the fixed, buzzed stare of the coked-up. He looked a little familiar to Angela. "Who the fuck are you?" he said in a high, squeaky voice. Suddenly Angela realized who it was. She sucked her breath in, startled. Huey Newton. She'd heard he came to a lot of these parties, but she hadn't expected to see him here. "My name's Angela." She stood up, wiping quickly at her eyes. "Angela Edwards. What are you doing here?"

He laughed, a high, rapid laugh. "I love a good party. These pigs throw the best ones, sister." He paused, looked rapidly around the room, yanked at his pant legs a quick moment, fast enough for Angela to see that he had a gun in his sock. "Were you in the movie, sister?"

"I was." She blushed. "Did you see it?"

"I did." He laughed again. "It was something else. Revolutionary."

"Really?"

"Oh yeah. We still got to seize the means of production, but yeah, the message was right on. Taking back our streets. Sticking it to the pigs. That's what it's all about." He looked at her breasts, wiped quickly at his nose. "You here alone, sister?" Angela sighed. She didn't feel like playing the game right now. "No. I'm here with my . . . my boyfriend. I was just going to look for him in fact."

"All right then, my sister." He reached down and with a rapid, nervous gesture, touched the gun, then looked up. "You have a beautiful day. Keep the faith."

"I will," said Angela. She went to walk past him—he had never moved out of the doorway—and as quick as a cat, he caught his arm around her neck and kissed her, wetly, on the lips, using a lot of tongue. Angela wrested her head away. He grinned. His pupils were nearly as big as his irises. She wiped at her mouth with the back of her hand. "That was the same old shit, my brother," she said. He just kept grinning. She shook her head and pushed past him out the door. He made no move to stop her.

Jesus Christ, will they all act the same come the goddamn revolution? Sometimes she wished she had a gun herself—she could think of a few niggers needed shooting. White ones too. All the slimy, grinding tongues that had been in her mouth that she allowed there for . . . because she didn't know how to say no? To get a part? For fun? Even Rafe wasn't what he used to be. Like all the men were. They all stopped being fun eventually. She still laughed with Sheila, though. She sighed deeply.

Suddenly, unbidden, her father's face appeared in front of her, looking the way he did, with his eyes turned hard, whenever he saw white people in Greenwood. When Angela was about five, she asked him why. "They no better than mad dogs, baby girl," he said, his eyes narrowed and still blackened with something remembered. "You don't never walk near a mad dog iffen you can help it." He paused. "And if you do, you keep your gun ready. But don't let 'em see it. They'll kill you if they see it." He took Angela's hand, touched her head once, briefly, with his calloused hand. She had thought she might cry then. Just the way she thought she might cry again now. But instead, she made her way to the bar. It was past time for a drink. "Let me have a Long Island iced tea," she said, lowering her voice to a sexy purr out of habit. "Coming right up, miss." The bartender smiled at her. She smiled back, no happiness in her heart. Sheila came up behind her. "Hey, baby girl." Angela spun around. Sheila was standing so close behind her that she couldn't move. "You never call me that in public." Sheila smiled, her eyes soft and stoned. "I know. But I'm sorry, baby girl. He was looking really good today and he seemed interested and you know . . ." She trailed off.

"What do I know?" Angela said, her voice full of ice.

"You know who's gonna be home with you at the end of this."

The ice started melting despite Angela's furious resolve. She reached around and picked up her drink. Swallowed, feeling it all the way down her insides. Sheila gazed at her steadily. No one was looking. Angela took Sheila's hand, just for a second, and rested it on her stomach. "OK. OK. But not in front of me, all right?"

"Oh, baby girl, not again. There's plenty of other brothers that'll do me more good—and some that ain't brothers." She nodded slightly toward a little hubbub at the door. Bert Schneider, who ran BBS, the company that had produced *Easy Rider*, had just come in with a small phalanx of followers, mostly white. Schneider was busy giving Huey his best soul brother handshake, his face flushed with effort and booze. The music was even louder—"I'll Take You There" now. She could see Rafe trying to get close to Schneider, felt Sheila's steady gaze upon her. Whatever would happen would happen. She finished her drink and said, "Let's go." And they both sashayed toward the knot of power in the room's center.

Bert Schneider was tall and handsome in a glossy, overworked way. His face had the leathery texture and orangey glow of a man who owned a tinfoil tanning tray and wasn't afraid to use it. He wore pink-tinted aviator glasses, and his hair was feathered and swept carefully away from his face. He reminded Angela of a weasel. The look he gave Sheila was that of a man who hasn't eaten in a week and just sat down at a feast. Angela felt a stab of defeat under her ribs, but she turned quickly to the man Schneider was with, her smile large. She could see Rafe looking at her, but she didn't look back. He knew how it was any damn way. They'd talked about this. So she just went on. She'd be with him later.

Schneider's friend was better-looking than he was, with a gentle, feline face and soft, dark hair. He smoked rapidly and his pupils were wildly dilated. He introduced himself with a pronounced Brooklyn accent that didn't go with his face. "Todd Jameson here. I work with Bert, making pictures. And who might you be?" From behind her, Angela could sense Sheila's gradual encroachment on Schneider, the slow easing into his space. It was getting late, the lights going down, the music shifting to a slower groove, Bill Withers and Marvin Gaye. Angela suddenly felt very tired. She had an image of simply resting for a while in Rafe's arms or in Sheila's. But she owed it to that girl on the screen, herself larger than life. She owed it to that girl to get another part. "I might be free for a little while, Todd. If you get me another drink," she said silkily. "My name's Angela Edwards. I'm an actress."

9

IN 1973, CHEAPLY MADE ACTION FILMS STARRING black actors, which had commonly come to be known as blaxploitation movies, earned millions of dollars. So much so that it was widely said around town that blaxploitation was keeping certain studios afloat. Only a tiny percentage of this money ended up in the pockets of black people in the industry; almost all of the producers and directors were white. That year, Angela Edwards earned $7,000, and that was mostly through Bunny work. Sheila earned $10,000, but she kept on fucking Bert Schneider, hoping it would lead to a part. It didn't, but she explained her continued relationship with Schneider this way: "You know, Ange," Sheila said one night as she eased her shoulders under Angela's gentle hands. The breeze coming through the window smelled of car exhaust. "I actually kind of like the guy. He scores great coke and he makes me laugh." She paused. "And he loves going down on me. But he doesn't do it as well as you do." They both smiled. Angela gave Sheila's shoulders a little squeeze.

Angela was getting tired. At first, she'd thought that small parts would lead to bigger ones, more fucking would lead to less fucking, or at least the room to be more discriminating. With Rafe it was good. With Sheila it was better. With everyone else it was something to do, a way to score coke or relax or try to get a part.

But she looked the tiniest bit used up. It wasn't even that much fun anymore. Her eyes felt like smooth black rocks. She had thought acting would be a way to get inside the glow she always used to feel at the Dreamland. She thought that this work would let her make something real, be seen for someone real. But now she'd been doing it and doing it and it turned out that there was only one thing they wanted to see. And so she was hard-pressed to keep her clothes on in a scene, let alone speak.

Since the high of *Coffy*, that glorious fight scene, that glorious party, that glorious day, her life had fallen into an unvarying rhythm. She kept working at the club, so most of her days were free. She auditioned four days a week (got her hair and nails done on Fridays). She read *Variety* and *The Hollywood Reporter* religiously. Nights before work, she went to Rafe's on Monday, Wednesday, and Friday (unless he was shooting late), and spent Tuesday and Wednesday with Sheila. The weekend nights were for producers, the days spent with Sheila. Sometimes she came to Rafe or Sheila after a producer and he or she, depending, would hold her while she cried, or get high with her. Sheila was going through the same thing. She'd been a little bit luckier, but not a lot. They were both on the pill. They had to be careful to get different color cases so they didn't start taking each other's. Sheila's case was purple, Angela's pink. One day, in the bathroom, after carefully applying her false eyelashes and lipstick, she picked up her pink case, her mind completely blank, as it so often was these days, and opened it. There were her pills for the last two days. Sitting in the case. How the fuck did that happen? Her throat constricted. What happened if you missed two days? She hadn't missed two days fucking. She'd been with Rafe last night and the Friday before that—no producer this week. Christ. She took today's pill, her heart pounding. The two untaken rested in the case, looking at her like stony white eyes. She drank more water. It burned her throat. She looked at herself in the mirror. Beautiful. She was always beautiful. Why was she so scared?

Sheila knocked on the door. "Come on, Angie, get a move on."

"Coming." She ran a hand over her flat stomach. "Coming."

Sheila didn't notice anything. They were going to a premiere and she was giddy and high with the moment, plus a little speed. She talked nonstop. Angela didn't say anything, only looked out the car window, seeing those two pills nestled accusingly in their slots. "Do you have a joint, Sheil?"

"Sure. Look in my bag."

Angela looked around, found a small half-smoked one, pushed in the cigarette lighter. Waited.

"You OK, Angie Bangie?"

"Yeah. I'm fine. Just a little tired, though." She inhaled deeply, tried to let the joint do its restful work. But her stomach stayed knotted. She could feel small dark claws tearing at the inside of her head. But she tried to ignore them, smiled and took Sheila's hand.

Of course, she was pregnant. Remarkably, it had never happened before. But she knew it, even though she tried to act like she didn't. She missed her period, her breasts started hurting all the time, she felt like crying half the time. One night she got in the car and drove the streets, looking for an open fried-chicken joint. She had to have some chicken that minute or die trying to get it. A couple of days later, she started throwing up.

She kept going to work. She could still fit into the costume, still do the required Bunny dip when serving drinks, was still able to stand all night, only resting on the edges of things. She still glowed, beautiful, some nights, but not every night. Not the way she used to. Sometimes, after her shift, she lay in bed, her breath shallow, her hand resting on her stomach, wondering what would happen to her when she could no longer lean, do the Bunny dip, hide her belly or the motherhood to follow. What would she do when she was no longer herself alone?

It would have been easy to have it taken care of. It was 1975. It was legal now. One or two phone calls or a shy admission to Sheila, who freely admitted having had two abortions and being more than ready to have another should she ever need to. Days went by. She didn't say anything. She felt sick all the time, though she didn't tell anyone. The girls were always talking in the locker room about who was best to take care of it. Somebody was always pregnant or getting over having been pregnant. Angela didn't have to tell them about herself.

"Well, you know, Doc Finkelstein over on Wilshire? He'll fix you up just like that. Uses that, what's it called?

"Vacuum?"

"No, girl, that little spoon. Damn, what is it? It's some letters."

"D and C?"

"Yeah, that's it. You don't bleed at all hardly. You can be back at work in two days."

"Mmm. I remember when that stuff used to damn near kill you." This from Becky, one of the oldest Bunnies. "My friend Sarah got so messed up she won't ever be able to have children." The room went silent. "But now it's all different," Becky said after a while. "You can just walk into a clinic and take care of it now." Becky had worked for Playboy so long it was hard to imagine her taking any interest in the world outside these flocked velvet walls. She'd given up trying to make it as an actress. She just worked her shift, did her thing, and went home. She violated the no-fraternizing rule as much as she could get away with, but none of her regular dates had become sufficiently infatuated with her to get her out of the business yet. She was thirty-two years old. Angela had to sit down as the conversation ended. No one said anything to her. Sheila gave her a sharp, appraising look but then finished squeezing into her shoes without comment.

That night, on the way home, Sheila said, "So when were you gonna tell me? When you went into labor?"

"What?"

"Angie, I know you're pregnant. Think I ain't seen you running to the bathroom all hours?" She made a face. "Or heard you throwing up?" Sheila looked quickly away from the road at Angela. "You can hear that shit, you know."

Angela crossed her arms over her stomach and ducked her head to hide her eyes, which were suddenly full of tears. She let them fall. She could just barely feel the warmth through her jeans. "I thought if I didn't . . ."

"Didn't what? If you acted like it wasn't happening, it wouldn't be?"

Angela was silent.

"Look. I've been where you are. We can take care of it. It's not no big thing, just like the girls said it's not."

Angela tightened her arms across her stomach. She looked out the window of the car, still crying. She had a sudden memory of being in church, her mother's firm shoulder next to her, Mrs. Hamilton's square brown neck and head, topped by a black straw hat, in front of her. All the things she'd done—slept with all these people, been Sheila's lover all this time, all these things. She was afraid of being a mother, but she was more afraid of what might happen to her if she didn't have the baby. Maybe she'd have to keep begging for something she was never gonna get. Maybe she'd be punished. Maybe she was being punished now. What if she died trying to have an abortion? And it might be nice to have a baby: Someone she created. Someone she could always hold. A reason to stop auditioning. She was so tired. "How much does it cost to do it?" she said, her voice flat.

"Usually it's about two hundred dollars. I've had it done a couple of times."

She had that much socked away. Not a whole hell of a lot more, even with all the tip money. It just seemed to go in and go right back out again. She always looked good. But that cost money. Everything cost money. "Sheil, I could come up with that kind of money, but . . ." She drew a shuddering breath. "I just don't know. I don't know if I can do it."

They were almost home now. Sheila spun the wheel confidently. "You'd be giving up everything, you know. You ever seen any pregnant Bunnies? Or pregnant girls in these movies out here? And do you think Rafe wants a baby? I doubt it. He's out here trying to get his break. Just like the rest of us."

Angela drew another breath. "I know." They were in the parking lot now. Sheila turned off the car but didn't open the door. Angela's stomach leaped and rolled, but she knew things had changed. She wasn't going to throw up anymore. She was just going to keep this slime at the back of her throat. "But what if I went ahead and kept going like this . . . and that break never comes? Maybe I'd be sorry."

Sheila pulled out a cigarette and lit it. "Well, girl, you better decide. You don't have long. What are you, about six weeks along now?"

"Yeah, that's what the doctor said."

"OK then. You can't go to the clinic after twelve—too dangerous. You need to make up your mind." She blew a stream of smoke out, her eyes narrowing. Angela didn't say anything. What was she going to say?

One night when Angela was about sixteen, sometime after she lost her virginity, her father came home looking shadowed and beaten. Angela was setting the table slowly. She hated setting the table. She was thinking about Warren Beatty, which she spent a great deal of time doing. Her mother continued her usual efficient progress around the kitchen, from stove to counter to table. "Hey, Johnny Lee. Supper be ready in two shakes. How was your day?"

"My day?" he said, his voice heavy. Mother and daughter both turned to look at him, startled by the rawness of his voice.

"What is it, Johnny Lee?" her mother asked. Angela didn't dare open her mouth. Her mother stood still, a casserole dish in her hand.

"I had to help Doc Taber with the Montgomery girl today. Lord have mercy. What a mess."

Mildred put the casserole down on the table, went to her husband. "What do you mean, Johnny Lee? Help Doc Taber do what?"

He sat down, heavily, wiped his sweating face. Angela suddenly felt very aware of the smell of meatloaf cooking. "Well, I guess I might as well tell this in front of Angie. She gon' hear it 'round town anyway. And it's something a girl like her oughta know. Hilda Montgomery was in the family way."

Mildred drew a sharp breath. Angela didn't say anything, her mind briefly full of images of herself and Bobby Ware making love every chance they got. Hilda was the same age as her— she went around with Henry Wright. She always had his letter sweater draped over her shoulders. Her father was still talking ". . . so she tried to take care of it herself—must have been six or eight weeks along. She used a knitting needle." He trailed off, was silent for a short while. "God almighty, what an unholy mess."

"Well, Johnny Lee, what'd the doctor need you for?" Angela's mother asked, her voice shaking. She set down her spoon and folded her hands in her lap. Angela had the sense that they were shaking too.

"Needed something to stop the bleeding. Nothing in his bag was workin'. Sent that boy, that Eddie that lives next door to him, over to get me from the store with some cotton wool and some alum. He used up every damn thing he had in his bag. But wasn't nothin' gonna save that girl." He stopped again. "I ain't never seen so much blood. Not even in the war. She musta bled out right there on the floor." A harsh, sudden sob escaped him. "There wasn't nothin' we could do. Not a damn thing. You hear that, Angie?" Angela stood in the corner, gone to stone. "Couldn't do a thing. Folks'll be talkin', but I want you to know what can really happen if you start messin' around. You can end up dead. You understand me?" Suddenly he rose, and in two strides, stood directly in front of her, his face so close she could smell his grief-soured breath. "Dead. You got that?"

"Yes, Daddy." Her voice a whisper.

"All right, then." He left the room without another word, silence lying between mother and daughter. They never talked about it. But it lay between them. They sat together at Hilda's funeral, her mother's arm around Mrs. Montgomery's heaving shoulders. When Angela walked up to Hilda's coffin, she thought about how she'd known that girl all her life. Her face looked gray and waxy under the make-up. She had none of the beauty she used to possess. There was nothing of Henry's in the coffin with her. She was wearing her best churchgoing dress. Angela stood there until the breath of the next mourner was on her neck. But Angela didn't stop making love to Bobby. She just made damn sure he had a condom on every time he came anywhere near her.

And now, here she was, pregnant by her own stupid mistake. She sometimes thought she should have just kept on with Sheila, and stopped with Rafe. Then nothing like this ever would have happened. Time went by. One week, then two. Sheila didn't say anything, but Angela could feel her counting off the days, watching. Three months. It was too late now. Her pants were getting tighter. She could hardly fit into her Bunny costume anymore. One afternoon, a hot afternoon kind of like the one when they had cut their hair all those years before, they sat on the sofa, watching TV, legs entwined. "So you're going to keep it," Sheila said, her eyes not leaving the television screen.

Angela didn't look away either. "Yeah. I guess I am."

The room was quiet except for the yammer of the television for a moment. "Gonna tell Rafe?"

"I guess I'd better."

"I guess you should. Let me know what he says." Sheila sat up and rubbed Angela's feet experimentally. Then her belly. "Well. My Angie Bangie a mama. How about that?"

She went over to Rafe's one night after this, maybe thirteen weeks along now. He'd been away on location for three weeks (his first location shoot), so she'd been able to avoid this moment. She had to pull over to the side of the road once to throw up for the first time in weeks. She lit a cigarette as she mounted the stairs to his apartment. This was a new habit. She never used to buy them, just take hits off the other girls' cigs. She buzzed, walked in, but as Rafe went to kiss her, she turned her head away, afraid of what her breath must smell like.

"What's up, baby? You ain't seen me in three weeks and you can't give me a little sugar?"

"Just not feeling sweet tonight, I guess." She pushed past him to come in. He scowled but didn't say anything. She went straight to the couch, picked up the wine he'd poured, drank. "I mean, I missed you and all, baby. I just had a bad day."

"Still, I ain't seen you in three weeks and you're all . . ."

"All what?" She couldn't stop the evil tone in her voice.

Rafe closed his mouth, drew his lips into a tight line. Angela could almost see him deciding not to talk. She'd loved him so much once. "I don't know, you just seem a little upset."

Angela leaned back on the couch, closed her eyes, and pressed her fingers into them until she saw the orange-red blood pulsing through. Nausea overcame her again. She leapt up and barely made it to the bathroom, leaving Rafe astonished on the couch. When she came out, shaky, angry, embarrassed, Rafe stared at her. "That's right. I haven't had my period in thirteen weeks." She almost screamed it. "Damn you. I don't want your damn baby. I don't want anybody's damn baby." She crumpled to her knees like a soul singer, the sobs she'd been keeping to herself suddenly pouring out. Rafe did not get up from the couch. He stared as her ragged voice filled the room. "Fuck you. All right, fuck you. I'm an actress, not a mother. I'm an actress." Now she was screaming. Her eyes hurt. Her head hurt. She wanted Rafe to put his arms around her, but she thought she'd never ever be able to get up from the floor again if he did. She stopped screaming, looked right at him. He loved her, she knew suddenly. But not enough. And she didn't love him enough either. He sat on the couch as she continued to kneel on the floor, scrubbing at her eyes with the heels of her hands like a child.

Finally, he leaned forward, years older than he had been when she walked into the apartment. "You're keeping it," he said finally.

Angela continued to kneel on the floor. "Yeah."

"Why, for God's sake? Nobody gotta have a baby these days if they don't want to." His voice cracked, broken.

"I just . . . I don't know. It ain't anything wrong with having an abortion, but . . . I'm scared to have the operation. I couldn't decide. I been feeling like nothing's gonna happen for me in the business anyway. Like maybe it's time to make a change . . . I didn't mean for this to be the change I made, but . . . sometimes stuff just happens."

He stood up and went to the big window that overlooked the parking lot. "Yeah, stuff happens. But this . . . I'm not gonna be a daddy. I'll tell you that right now."

Angela eased up off her knees but not off the rug. She pulled her legs up under her chin, fetal position. "I didn't think you would be. I wasn't even sure I was going to tell you. Sheila thought I should."

"Sheila." His back was still to her.

"Yeah."

"Well." A long silence fell. Rafe continued to look out the window. Angela finally rose from the floor. The room smelled faintly of vomit and cigarette smoke. "I guess that's it, then," Angela finally said.

Rafe turned around. His eyes were dark and sorrowful but not giving. The moon shone behind him like a streetlight, so bright. "Yeah. That's it, then. You take care, baby." He turned back to the window and looked out of it until she gathered her things and left. He never once touched her.

10

S HE LOST HER BODY. IT WAS UTTERLY CHANGED, not her own anymore, not that long-legged, tawny shape that had elicited so many looks and made her feel so magnificent. Gone now. Now was swollen ankles, constant indigestion, elbows and knees poking her every which way from inside every time she moved, a jiggly butt, saggy breasts with huge, round, flat nipples. She couldn't imagine ever wanting to have sex again. She was so disgusting. Who would want her now?

And she had to go back to Tulsa. She'd tried to stay in Los Angeles. Dear Lord, she'd wanted to stay. But once she started showing, the Playboy Club sure as hell didn't want her and she couldn't temp looking the way she did and auditions were out of the question and Sheila wasn't earning enough money and she needed to eat more, not less. Pregnancy made you so damn hungry. She'd never thought so much about food in her life. Finally one day she stared into the refrigerator thinking she *had* to eat something *right now* and all that was in there was a quart of milk (milk, she hated milk, but the doctor at the clinic told her she had to drink it), an old carrot, and a half-eaten can of tuna fish. She had $152 to her name. What she had managed to save had vanished in the last few months. She was six months pregnant. And she was so hungry. She burst into tears. Sat down at the kitchen table and sobbed like a child. Why had she gone ahead with this?

What was she doing? Then she did something she hadn't done in nearly three years. She picked up the phone and called her mother.

"Mama, it's Angie."

"Angie." The voice on the other end of the line broke into a million shining fragments. "Angie, is that you?"

"Yeah, Mama. It's me." She was clutching the phone so hard her hand hurt. She heard her own breath, the growling of her stomach.

"I ain't heard from you in so long . . . I didn't know what to think. You still in them pictures?"

Angela pressed her free hand to her temple, hard. "No, Mama. I ain't been in a picture for a while."

"Hmm. Well. I know you wanted to be in pictures, but you know I didn't raise you like that. I'm glad to hear you ain't doin' that anymore. I couldn't hardly hold my head up."

Angela's own head was starting to pound. "Mama. I got something I need to ask you. I'm . . . Mama, I'm gonna have a baby. In just a few months. And I want to know . . . I want to know if I can come home to have it."

An absolute silence followed her words. Angela listened to the faint, sublunar hum of the telephone lines. The silence probably lasted five minutes. "You got nowhere to go?" Her mother finally said.

"No, ma'am"

"And the man?"

"He's gone."

More silence.

"Well. I can't have my baby outdoors. You best to come on home. We'll think of something to say to people." She paused. "Or we won't say nothing at all."

Angela started crying again, soundlessly this time. "Thank you, Mama."

"That's all right. You just get yourself on home."

Angela borrowed the money from Sheila for a bus ticket. Sheila saved more than Angela, even though she seemed to smoke just as much dope and dress as well. She got money from men often. They had stopped making love, but they still slept together and Sheila braided Angela's hair for her every night and helped her blow it out in the morning, her hands moving slow and gentle across her head. Sheila didn't claim to understand what Angela was doing, but she braided her hair. She could do that.

The night before Angela left, Sheila took the night off from the club. All Angela's goodbyes had been said. The Bunny dip was part of her past now, though she still laughed at the stories Sheila told her after work in the morning. So this night, she sat, a glass of wine next to her, a cigarette burning in the ashtray, between Sheila's legs on the floor, just as she used to sit between her mother's legs to get her hair combed. Sheila's hands worked quick and deft to cornrow tight, flat braids. "Oww. Damn, Sheila. Don't pull on it like that."

Sheila rapped Angela's head smartly with the comb and laughed. "Girl, how many times have I combed your nappy head since you came out here?"

Angela took a long draw on her cigarette. "I don't even know. A thousand? Two thousand?"

"Something like that. And every time I yank one of your naps, you say that mess. Think you ain't never had your hair combed before." Her voice softened, her hands moved quickly through Angela's hair. They were quiet for a time as Sheila finished her work. "I'ma miss your nappy head and your evil mouth," Sheila finally said. She lowered her hands to Angela's shoulders. "And these shoulders." Her hands moved still lower, to Angela's tight globe of a belly. "This too. I'ma miss you, girl. I miss you already." Angela put down her cigarette and wiped her wet face. She moved the ashtray aside and turned to face Sheila. Kissed her the way they hadn't kissed in months. "I miss you too. You're my heart. You know that, right? You saved me. When you walked in that office that day. You saved me."

"I know." She slid her hand across Angela's cheek. "You haven't been so bad yourself." She grinned. "Even with this nappy hair." They sat awkwardly for a long time, holding each other. Then they went to bed. They did not make love. But they lay spoon fashion all night, their breath making all sounds and no sounds, the small, soft sounds of union.

The bus ride back to Tulsa was many hours long and many hours uncomfortable. Angela cried a lot of the way. People on the bus studiously ignored her. When they pulled up to the bus stop in Tulsa, Angela looked around. It had not changed a bit in the five years since she had left. The largely unpaved parking lot still swallowed departing cars in a cloud of red dust. The lone clerk's radio still played tinny soul music — Earth, Wind and Fire now instead of the Supremes. Angela looked like a bird of paradise come to roost in a sparrow's nest. Even at six months along, her Afro was meticulously maintained (she'd made a quick stop in the station bathroom to get it together after she got off the bus). She wore a loose-fitting bright red Indian-style dress that hung to her ankles, red lipstick to match, and enormous silver hoops. Silver platform shoes added to her height. Most pregnant women in Tulsa wore tentlike gingham tops with bows and blue or black maternity skirts of modest length at the knee or below. Usually, they wore hats on their neatly straightened hair if the day was sunny. One woman in town — the librarian, Joan Harris — wore a modest Afro of the sort Cicely Tyson wore in the early seventies. But, people always said to each other, "She ain't from around here." (She had grown up in Boston and married a Tulsa man.) Angela stood in the bus station, looking for her mother, drawing all the light in the room to her. Small children waiting with their mothers stared openly.

Mildred looked more or less as she had when Angela left. Her hair still shone like wet silk, pressed hard and pulled back into a neat bun. It was shot through with gray now and her skin was slightly more lined but still clear and mellow brown, severely lovely. She wore a navy blue shantung dress with a wide white collar of the kind she had worn for the last twenty-five years, and she smelled, faintly, of lavender water. She walked toward her daughter, slowly at first, then with quicker steps. "Angie," she finally said. The glorious apparition turned toward her. "Don't you look something, girl. Looks like you learned to put mascara on out in Hollywood, even if you didn't learn how to keep your legs together. You look good, Angie. Real good. Different. But good."

"Oh, Mama." Angie folded into her mother's arms, crying again. "I can't believe I'm home."

"That's all right, baby. That's the place you go when you've got nowhere else to go. You know that."

They walked home. Angela's mother didn't know how to drive. Angela would have killed for a cigarette but didn't know how to tell her mother that she smoked now. Folks Angela didn't recognize nodded and smiled at her mother and stared at her openly. "This my daughter, Angela," Mildred offered with a polite smile and a wave of her hand to anyone who asked. Angela smiled the way she'd been taught to as a girl, surprised to find her Tulsa manners coming back unbidden. But she could feel in the sway of her hips, her expanding belly, the itch of her fingers for a cigarette, the itch of her ears for some noise, how she had changed.

At home, there was no banner on the door, but there was a quiet acknowledgment that this was not an ordinary return. All the fancy china was laid out, the table laden with her mother's best cooking. Her father stood, massive, still wearing his pharmacist's coat, home from work to welcome the prodigal. "How you doing, gal?" was all he said. He held her tight but then appeared unable to look at her. He didn't say anything about her pregnancy. Her brother, Otis, was there in his overalls, his three girls running around the front yard, kicking up dust. Her sister, Jolene, pregnant with her fourth, sitting on the weathered front steps in a faded flowered cotton dress, a man's work boots on her feet. She'd married a farming man from a little ways out of town—a good man, but a little low-class, Mildred thought. How her children did scatter. Angela looked like nothing she'd ever seen. Beautiful but so bright and hard, like a pile of red rhinestones and rubies thrown in a bowl, dazzling, some valuable, some not. And she was so jittery, washed out, nervous. She drummed her fingers against the side of her thighs through the whole meal or against her big new belly. Mildred didn't want to know what she'd been doing since the last time they'd spoken, all that time ago. She'd never been able to forget the look on Angie's face in that movie: happy. Blank and happy to be standing up on that bar with no clothes on, dancing. Now she looked at her daughter's head, bent over her plate, laughing at something silly Otis was saying, or turning to smile at her father, never looking at Mildred. Who was this exotic creature they now welcomed into their home? At least Angela looked up from her chicken leg to glance at her mother. Mildred smiled at her, and Angela smiled back gorgeously, unexpectedly. For a minute, she looked almost like a movie star.

During the welcome-home lunch the only comments made about Angela's clothes and her burgeoning pregnancy were "You look good," "How you feeling?" and "Hopin' for a girl or a boy?" Jolene expressed her opinion that boys were too much trouble, always breaking stuff. But after the last corncob was picked clean, the last long hug exchanged, Angela and her mother were alone in the kitchen, and Mildred gestured toward a chair for her daughter. "Go on, girl. You can sit down and help me dry from there. I know you must be tired."

"Thanks, Mama. I am pretty tired." Her hands ached for a cigarette, but she busied them with the dishtowel she was handed. She was going to have to go get some smokes soon, though. She couldn't take much more.

"So, Angie. How's it feel to be home?"

How's it feel to be home? Home with the dust already filtering into her oh, so careful hair, with the silence easing into her ears, and walking slowly, slowly, behind the people on a deteriorated Greenwood Avenue. Home where the way she dressed now made people think she must be crazy, where no one looked anything like her and she was trying to figure out how to tell her mother that she smoked. Home where she couldn't even in her wildest dreams imagine telling anyone about half of what she'd done, to get parts, to have fun, for reasons she couldn't even explain. They wouldn't understand. They couldn't. Sitting around the table with her family for the first time in five years, she knew it. It came on her like a stone, filled her mouth and her eyes. They didn't know her. They couldn't know her. But where else could she go? "Feels all right I guess. I . . . I wasn't sure how you'd feel about having me home like this Mama."

"Well. I ain't gonna lie. You made your bed, you got to lie in it. I ain't raisin' this baby." Her hands remained busy in the sink. "But sometime everybody need a hand up. Everybody does something they ain't so sure about sometimes. And you my daughter after all. What am I gonna do, leave you and my flesh and blood in the street without a dime to your name?" She walked over to Angela and handed her a glass, her hands slick with soap. "I don't pretend to think you been right. Don't go thinkin' that. Me and your daddy don't think you been right. But like I said. We can't put you outdoors. Wouldn't be no better than dogs if we did that. Would we now?" She looked Angela straight in the eye.

"I guess not, Mama." She dried the glass slowly. "Mama?"

"Yes, Angie."

"I'm just dying for a cigarette. When I'm done with this, I'ma go on down to the drugstore and get some."

Mildred's back stiffened. Her hands stilled in the water. But just for a moment. "Don't you smoke in this house," she said finally, scrubbing around and around a cast-iron frying pan. "You do that out back. Where folks can't see. And don't you get them at your father's store. What would folks think? You go on down to the newsstand."

"Yes, ma'am." Angela closed her eyes. The baby shoved an elbow into her kidney.

That night, Angela lay in her narrow old bed. It had the same mattress from five years ago. She could almost smell her old self on it. She couldn't find a comfortable place to put her stomach, her legs, her brain. She'd braided up her hair herself, laboriously, as her mother darned socks by the gooseneck lamp that she had always darned socks by. But it was 1975—who still darned socks? Where was she? She missed Sheila's hands in her hair. She had to keep lowering her arms to rest as she got to the back; it took forever to finish. She'd had one cigarette out back, just under the kitchen window, feeling simultaneously fourteen and ninety-five years old. Hiding like a kid even though she knew so much more than anyone else in this damn town.

She rolled over to her side, shoved her pillow under her stomach, belched uncomfortably. The baby rotated again. Angela's eyes filled with tears. She ran her hand over her stomach, now so huge and alien. What would she do when the baby was born? Right now she felt as though she was going to be a beach ball forever, no matter how she tried to gussy it up with interesting Indian-style dresses. She fell asleep crying. If her mother heard her, she didn't come in.

11

ATER, WHEN HE THOUGHT ABOUT WHAT HE regretted most, it was that he hadn't told her the rest. He never told her about the way he gazed at her when her back was to him, maybe doing the dishes or lighting a cigarette. He never told her that it took every ounce of his will not to go to her when she knelt on his floor in tears. That it took every ounce of his will not to walk to her and lift her up by her elbows and cover her face with kisses and say that he'd love her and the baby forever. If she'd just be with him. But he saw what Angela couldn't see. He saw that they would fail each other in the end. It broke his heart in two. He couldn't explain how he knew it. But he knew it the way he knew his name. And so he left her to sob on his floor, alone.

So now there would be a child in this world who bore his blood but not his name. How he had hoped never to do that. He thought about it for a long time. For an ocean of not calling and a mountain of not getting in his car and driving to her house to see her and a continent of being away from the sweet back of her neck, but seeing it before him every time he closed his eyes. Then one balmy Sunday when the weather was kind of like that day they'd spent eating ice cream at the Santa Monica Pier, he went to her apartment.

He sat out front in his car for a long time, smoking and looking at the small window that she and Sheila shared. He thought about the way Sheila's tongue had felt in his mouth that one time at that party when they were all so drunk and happy. He couldn't explain it to Angie or anyone, but he thought now that he'd been trying to understand, by kissing this girl that his girl loved so much. He thought that if he tasted her, he might understand what made her so special. He thought maybe he could take it in. But later, at that same party, when he'd seen them sitting with their thighs almost touching, laughing into each other's faces about nothing before they went to the men who mattered, their bodies like sacred offerings, he knew that he had failed. That whatever it was stayed between them. They couldn't even tell him about it. He took one last drag on his cigarette, flung it out the window. "Fuck it," he said. Then he got out of the car. The air smelled of smog and lilacs.

Sheila answered the door. She was wearing a bright green halter top and white shorts. She looked tired and, Rafe realized, she was getting a little old and hard-looking. She wasn't going to be able to pick up work much longer. She must be nearing thirty. He sighed. Fewer calls had been coming in for him too. It was tiring to even think about it. "Hey, girl," he said.

"Hey." She didn't seem particularly surprised to see him.

"Can I come in?"

Sheila stepped aside without a word. Rafe walked in. The apartment looked the way it always looked. Beat-up gold sofa with an Indian print throw over it. Bras and lacy panties strewn over every surface and hanging from every doorknob. Copies of *Variety* and *People* and *The Star* underneath takeout cartons on the table. The smell of smoke and perfume and Ultra Sheen in the air. She was listening to Aretha Franklin while a cigarette burned in the ashtray. "Sit down."

Rafe sat uneasily, lit a cigarette. Sheila sat across from him in the battered rocker she had found on the street. "Is she home?"

"Angie?"

"Yeah. I know I ain't been around, but . . ."

"She's gone."

He put his cigarette down so that he wouldn't drop it. "What?"

"She's gone. She went back home about three weeks ago."

"Back to Tulsa?"

"Where else she gonna go?" Sheila picked up her cigarette, took a drag, narrowed her eyes. Rafe thought it might be to keep from crying.

"Why'd she leave? Why didn't she tell me? Why didn't you?"

"Like you said, you ain't been around. I . . . I wanted her to stay, but I ain't even working enough to keep myself fed hardly. And she eating for two." A bark of a laugh. "She'll be all right. Her mama and daddy took her back in."

His ears were ringing. Gone. She was gone. "Well . . . well . . ." He trailed off, took a drag of his cigarette.

"You mattered to her, you know," Sheila said after a time. "You know that, right?"

He nodded. He was afraid that if he opened his mouth, girlish sobs would escape. Faggy. None of that. Not in front of her. Sheila took another drag, got up, walked to the window. "I miss her too. I miss her a lot," she said.

Now he could speak. He could offer her that. "I know. I know you do." They sat in silence, separate, smoking their cigarettes, as the city aged all around them, as the work they were permitted to do faded away, as they realized nothing lasts forever. It was 1975, and everything was about to change. It was just as well. They were awfully tired.

12

FTER A FEW WEEKS, ANGELA BEGAN TO SEE that sticking close to home was the best course. She couldn't walk downtown without engendering comments both whispered and audible. She felt like a freak rather than a lovely LA girl in her big 'fro. And her bright dresses and platform shoes, which she kept to even as they hurt her feet and got harder and harder to put on, well, nobody dressed quite like that here either. She could see the high school girls looking at her with wonder and envy, and some fashiony types (her mama called them "fast") wore dime store versions of her clothing. But she stood out, pregnant, alone, lonely.

They ate meals together. The clinking of silverware on plates often made the only sound. Silence seemed to have completely overtaken her mother. Sometimes her father chatted, in a general way, to both of them, about events at the store, signs of life in the Greenwood section, which had been nearly abandoned throughout the 1960s and early 1970s. But he never looked at Angela's face. His drugstore, which he'd been running for nearly thirty years, was one of the few old businesses standing. When she went in to pick up something for her mother, she sometimes saw customers who'd known her as a girl. The women's eyes slid slowly across her; she didn't exist. The men stared frankly and briefly, usually at her glorious hair or her breasts, despite her pregnancy. Then they'd look away, afraid Johnny Lee would see what they were thinking. After a while, she stopped going down to the drugstore unless her mother absolutely insisted, which she rarely did.

Angela was about eight months along and had been home for two months when she finally said it. Another silent dinner had almost ended when the words jumped out of her: "Why won't you talk to me?" She addressed both parents, but primarily her father, who probably hadn't spoken to her directly more than five times since her homecoming.

Johnny Lee looked up, his dark face stern and comprehending, "What you mean, gal?"

"I mean y'all took me in, but you been treating me like . . . like one of those gals you all talk so bad about. I mean I came back to this godforsaken, boring-ass town with nowhere else to go and y'all treat me like trash." She stopped. A sudden memory of standing next to Sheila that long ago day on Venice Beach stole her breath. This wasn't home. Why had she left her home? Her parents looked at her like figures in a painting, their silverware suspended over their plates.

"Like trash, huh?" said Johnny Lee. "I see you eatin' our food, sleepin' under our roof, 'bout to have a baby with no man in sight after doing God knows what all in that city you been living in. And you upset we treatin' you like trash." He paused. "Girl, you gettin' better than you deserve." He went back to his meal.

Angela was on her feet before she knew it. Her mother looked at her, her fork frozen halfway to her lips. She ran upstairs, her mother's steps behind her.

She lay on her side in her old bed, sobbing. Her mother entered hesitantly. "Angie."

Angela's only answer was another ragged sob.

"Angie. Listen. Your daddy . . . well, he had harsh words for you, but he wanted you here too." She sat down on the edge of the bed, something she hadn't done since Angela was a child. Tentatively, she rested her hand on the middle of her daughter's back. "I don't . . . I don't pretend to understand what you done. And you know how angry I was. But now . . . well, you making your own way. You went off there to that city and made your own way. Ain't a person alive that ain't made some mistakes." Here she stopped talking for so long that Angela rolled awkwardly over to look at her. A sorrow Angela hadn't seen in years colored her mother's face. But now she was listening. "Lord knows, we all made 'em." She drew a deep breath. "But don't you think that steppin' out and tryin' to make your way was one of them. I was mad at you. Lord, yes. But I didn't raise you to die here. I'm glad you didn't hide." Tears were running down her face now. The room was so still that Angela could hear the hum of the universe, the one she always stood on the landing trying to hear. The women sat together for a long time.

After this, Angela came to know that her child had to be born in Los Angeles. When she thought of who she loved most, who she felt least alone with, it was Sheila. Sheila's hands in her hair, Sheila's hands on her belly. She remembered looking at Sheila one time as she drove, her hand easy on the wheel, talking about something funny and laughing. They were both laughing, and Angela looked at her and thought, *Now I am perfectly happy. Right now.* She thought about that moment for a long time, the way they touched each other, how alive she felt at those moments. And then she knew what to do. She picked up the phone. "Hi."

"Angie? Angie, is that you?"

"Yeah."

"Well . . . well, what's happening?"

"I can't do this."

"What?"

"I can't do this."

"Can't do what? Can't stand living with your folks?"

"No."

"Can't have a baby?" Sheila laughed shortly. "Too late to decide about that one."

"Yeah, I know."

"So what can't you do?"

"I can't do this without you. I can't live here. I can't . . . I can't have this baby without you, Sheil."

Sheila was silent. For a few minutes. Then, her voice shaking, she said. "I didn't think you could." She went silent again. Their breath blended through the receiver. Finally, Angela spoke. "Can I come home?"

"Yes. Yes. I want you to."

They both started crying at the same time. Sheila was able to speak first. "You know we're gonna fuck this up."

"I know. But we'll do it together."

"You got bus fare?"

"I can get it."

"I'll see you soon then."

"Soon then, Sheil."

Her parents expressed no surprise when she thanked them for taking her in and said that she had called her old roommate, Sheila, who was willing to have her come and live with her until the baby was born and maybe after. "I'll get a job, Mama. A real job. I know that acting ain't gonna feed this baby," she said.

"Well, that's something," said her mother.

The night before Angela left, as she squeezed and shoved her few belongings into her suitcases, just as she had not long before to come back, her mother came into the room holding a yellowing photograph. "Angie?"

"Yes, ma'am."

"You remember when you was a little girl and you found

this?" Her mother extended the photograph to her. It was the beautiful woman her mother wouldn't explain.

"Yeah, Mama. I remember. You wouldn't tell me who it was."

"Well, I think you should know now. This is your grandmother, my mama. She died in the burning in 1921. I was just a little girl." She closed her eyes. "I don't want to tell you no more than that, so don't ask me. But I think you ought to have this picture now. It belongs with you."

Angela couldn't speak but took the photograph her mother held out and carefully slid it into the outside pocket of her suitcase. She swallowed and said, "I'll take care of it, Mama. Thank you."

"Take care of yourself, too."

"I will."

Her mother took a step toward her. "You better. You about to be a mama." Their embrace, when it came, was long and awkward. Angela thought of Sheila's mouth on hers, how her mother would never understand. The baby kicked between them, a live thing. But silent.

Foxy
Brown

1974

Here's the scene everybody remembers from *Foxy Brown:* Pam
Grier emerges from a biplane and stands in a field with two
strong black men wearing headbands, their muscled arms glint-
ing in the sun. The light is brittle and cheap. Her strong features
are set, the eyes shards of obsidian. She's not going to do it herself.
One of the men pulls out an enormous knife and says, "He's
ready, sister." She is wearing black leather. She nods. The men
take the nervous, narrow-hipped white pimp—an actor whose
name is forgotten even as Pam's lives forever—and pin him up
against his long, lean, luxe Thunderbird. It is white, too. They
pull down his pants. He is screaming. He screams, "You're crazy,
Foxy. You can't do this." He is wearing skintight blue underwear.
She does not speak, just stares. Then the men begin to cut below
the belt, out of the camera's view, and the man shrieks. Shrieks
the scream of a thousand black men lynched, a thousand women
raped, a thousand children's heads bashed into walls, brains
staining the wood. But this time, the white man screams and
screams. Later, she will present the penis, in a pickle jar, to the
white man's evil paramour. The film is too cheaply made to have
a prosthetics budget, so the white woman's horror will be suggested, dependent on the convincing shrieks and hysterical cries
of the actress. She will convince. For now, as the white man
screams, Pam Grier does not look away. The sweet blood of
vengeance drips to the ground, out of sight.

Part II

MILDRED

13

NGELA WAS BORN IN 1950 INTO A CITY WEDDED
to a myth. Lies whispered from the faded red-brick buildings, hung in the dust-scented air, hummed along with
her mother's sweet voice in the mornings. There was the myth
that the streets flowed with oil—they didn't. All the oil that had
led to Tulsa's prosperity lay in the vast fields to the west, which
were separated from the city by the Arkansas River. Sheer will—
and the willingness of the city fathers to offer whatever a working-
man might need (legal or not) within its confines—led to the
wealth of Tulsa. And that included the riches of Greenwood, the
black section of town, where she lived. There was the myth that a
man could come out to the wild land of the west and make whatever he wanted of himself. That had been true for some, but
those days were long gone by the time Angela was born. There
was the myth that everyone was happy with the way things were,
that Tulsa was the magic city it claimed to be, an honest, decent
place. But Angela's mother, Mildred, knew that wasn't true. She
kept the pact, she didn't tell her children about what she knew.
But she'd known it since the last day of May in 1921.

That morning Mildred knew something bad was happening.
It sat over her shoulder on its haunches, its slick teeth gleaming.
Her mama didn't even play the Victrola as she went about her

housework, and she shushed Mildred every time she opened her mouth: "Girl, I ain't got time for that today. Can't you think of nothing to do on your own? Go on out in the yard. Or go 'round to Vernella's. I can't have you underfoot today." Her daddy had gone as silent as the moon. After her mama chased her out to the yard, she saw him cleaning his gun out back of the house, apparently having finished his work hours early. Had he even gone to work today? Why was he home? Why did his gun need to be cleaned? It wasn't hunting season. She knew better than to ask any questions. She went to Vernella's. Vernella was sitting on her front step, knees drawn up under her chin, drawing in the dooryard dust with a stick.

"Hey, Vern."

"Hey, Millie. What you know good?"

"I 'ont know. My mama fussing something awful today."

Vernella looked up, relief and fear at war in her eyes. "Yeah. My mama too. I heard her telling my daddy something happened down to the Drexel building yesterday. Something with some colored boy and a white lady. Then she saw me listening and told me to get on outside." Vernella returned to drawing in the dirt, a look of elaborate boredom on her face. But her hands were shaking. Mildred's stomach tightened. Everybody knew what happened if you messed with white ladies. Mildred sat down next to her friend, found a stick, and started drawing her own patterns in the dirt. Her patterns were more ornate and nuanced than Vernella's. She loved the feel of the silken dust beneath her feet, the sense that she might make an image there. Always had. She thought of the colors she might use if she could somehow get them into the earth. Another time, they might have gotten up and gone to look for worms in Vernella's mother's lush vegetable garden. But today neither of them spoke. They were eight years old.

All over Greenwood that afternoon, the air was molten lead. Maybe nothing would happen. Maybe the boy—his name was going 'round town now, Dick Rowland—would be forgotten. Or maybe he would be the only one who would pay. The old ones didn't think so. But the young ones could hope. So Greenwood tried to live normal that afternoon. Teenagers got ready for the prom that night. Mothers hummed a little faster than usual and prepared dinner. Folks made plans to go down to the moving pictures or out to walk the avenue in the warm Tuesday air. But it didn't last long. The guns were loaded, the torches lit.

Mildred's parents sent her to bed early that evening. No explanations. And from Mildred, no protests. She kissed them both and her father put one arm tight around her, something he didn't usually do. She smelled his bay rum and gun-oil-scented skin. Her mother kissed her gently behind the ear and brushed her hair back with her hand. They both gave her long looks before she went off in her white nightgown and careful braids, her feet brown and elegant against the floor.

The next thing Mildred knew, her mother had materialized in her room. The first day of June had just begun. Her mother's voice was thick and fractured. "Millie, you got to get up, get up, get up. We got to get out of here now."

Mildred knew that the terror had come. Her mother, who rarely raised her voice above a cultivated whisper, except to laugh, was sweating and crying. She ran her hands over her face. Her eyes bulged dangerously. "Millie, I said we got to go this minute. These white folks done lost they minds. I told your daddy we should have left last night!" Her mother grabbed her arm and yanked her out of bed.

She fell onto the floor and her mother dragged her back up. She hurriedly shoved her feet into her Sunday school shoes, the first things that she saw. No socks. No stockings. No dress. Mildred heard explosions outside, things breaking, the occasional scream. It was already hot and her feet felt peculiar in the stiff shoes without lacy white socks. Her mother held her hand so tightly she could feel each bone. "Come on, girl. We got to go now." Her palm was slick with sweat.

Mildred wanted to ask where they were going, but speech eluded her. It seemed as though she ought to ask a question, but she couldn't think what it might be. Her hip hurt where she'd hit the floor. She finally thought of the question. "Where's Daddy?"

"He's gone down to the Dreamland with his gun. They trying to hold 'em off down there."

Her mother dragged her out the front door. They were both running as fast as they could. Once she was outside, Mildred thought she might never speak again.

Across the road, flames leapt from Vernella's small house. The step they had been sitting on the day before had been obliterated, orange flames horrifying the morning. The garden was torn up, destroyed. Pieces of wood, shards of crockery bowls, what was left of a rag rug, and one of Vernella's dolls littered the street.

Mildred had heard gunfire before in her life. Her daddy shot cans out back sometimes and she liked to watch, to feel the startle in her bones at each blast. But then it was contained, not a threat, not like this. The air crackled with electricity and smelled of smoke and faintly of burnt flesh, like a Saturday-afternoon barbecue. For a long time afterward, she couldn't eat without remembering that smell. "Mama, what's happening?" she screamed over the flames.

"White folks done lost they minds. Your daddy told me to stay in the house, but I just couldn't. Wanna try to get over to Mount Zion. It might be safe there. They burning down every house they find." Mildred didn't know why her mother thought the church might be safe. Was God closer there? Where was God? The girl and her mother crouched down and ran low, porch to porch. But not low enough. The men were in front of them before they even heard their approach. Their faces were bright red, and they stank of sweat. Their guns were held down in front of their thighs.

Mildred stared at them, words lost, and then felt the warm, sudden wash of urine down her legs. "Get up, nigger. We're taking y'all down to the courthouse. And iffen you don't come"—he made an airy wave with his gun toward a dust-covered body, maybe an old man, not fifty yards from them, his head at an odd angle, his flesh the color of a plum—"that could surely be you lyin' there. So git up. Git!" Mildred's mother screamed but didn't move. She continued to kneel in the street, clutching her daughter's hand. Mildred scrambled to her feet. Her legs were wet and sticky. Her mother still knelt, screaming. "I said, nigger bitch, get up!" There were two men. The cords in the neck of the shorter man stood out in furious relief, like they might break through the skin. Mildred's mother didn't rise. Mildred took an unconscious step away, sobbing, screaming, "Mama, Mama," the only word she knew anymore. When he fired the gun and her mother fell backward into her own blood, she felt as though she'd been seeing that moment all her life. Mama, Mama. Her mother jerked once, the blood bright against the ground, then lay motionless. Mama, Mama. The taller of the two men poked her in the back with the rifle, almost knocking her down. "Come on, you little coon bitch," he said. "Don't stand here crying for your mama 'less you want to end up like her." Mildred stumbled along. The only things she could see in front of her were her mother's wide-open eyes, gazing at the blue sky starred with orange flames. Her hair was streaked with dust and blood and was wild around her head.

As hard as she tried—and after a while she stopped trying—she never could remember the rest of that day. How her father found her or where they went after. How she got blisters on her feet that got so badly infected she couldn't walk for a week. How she got scratches all over her face. What she said to her father about what had happened. The day was a hole. A hole the size of her dead mother's skyward gaze.

It was about two days later that she and her father went back to the remains of their home. They stood there for perhaps an hour, not speaking, the sun wounding the backs of their necks. Mildred didn't know what her daddy was thinking. He had used only the words he needed to—words like "eat," "sit down," "I don't know"—since that day. She wanted to take his hand, but she was afraid to. Then she spotted the only painting they had ever had in their home. It was a hand-tinted postcard of Leonardo's *Last Supper*. Mildred knew the occasion represented, of course, but she didn't know anything about the painter. She just loved it. Even though the colors were muddled and guessed at, she was always obscurely moved by the positions of the figures, their stern and sorrowing faces. She stepped forward, heard a black crunching under her feet, bent down, and picked up the picture. She held it gently, not wanting to damage it further. Miraculously, it was only slightly blackened on the edges. She also found the metal plate from their old Victrola, where Mama would put on Scott Joplin and they would dance together for a few minutes when their work was done. Until Mama would laugh and say, "Girl, we got to cut out all this foolishness. What would your daddy say?" And Mildred would laugh and say, "I don't know, Mama." And her mama, Anna Mae, would say, "He'd say we gone plumb crazy." Then she'd smile and give Mildred the biggest hug she knew how and get ready to start dinner. Mildred picked up the plate too. Kept it. Her father said nothing. Nothing about how they were dirty or what was she going to do with that old stuff. He let her pick up what she needed. The only thing he kept was a picture of Anna Mae that he'd stuffed into his shirt the night of the shooting, as if he knew it would be all he'd have left of his wife. It curled from the sweat of his chest.

On her wedding day, he gave Mildred the picture, along with these words: "Time you had this now. You know your mama would have been proud of you." He looked out the window, clutching Mildred's white-gloved hand tightly. "They no better than dogs. Killed that beautiful woman. I spent the rest of my life trying not to hate 'em. You try not to hate 'em either. But be mighty careful before you trust one of 'em. They no better than dogs." Mildred nodded. She kept the steel plate and *The Last Supper* and the picture of her mother. Sometimes, once she had a family of her own, she ran her fingers over the smooth surfaces. But she couldn't find the words to speak of what she'd seen. It was a blindness in her heart. She passed the photograph on to her boldest child. She remembered the colors: the brilliant blue sky, the black smoke, the orange flames. And she remembered the smell. Ash and burnt flesh. That she carried with her until the day she died.

14

I N 1954 *CARMEN JONES* WAS RELEASED AND DOROTHY Dandridge became the first black woman ever nominated for a best-actress Academy Award. She smiled from the cover of *Life* and *Ebony*, adorned in the finest designs, her skin the color of desire. The magazines praised her beauty and poise, her elegance and modesty. They didn't write about the failed marriage to Harold Nicholas, the autistic daughter banished to an institution, the back doors she was forced to enter and the dining rooms she was not permitted to eat in, the pills, the sorrow that would eventually consume her. They wrote only about the exquisite surface. The week that *Carmen Jones* played at the Dreamland, Mildred walked to town every day while the children were in school and Johnny Lee was at work. One day, she asked a neighbor to take Angie to her afternoon kindergarten and then went to the early show and saw it twice. She didn't tell anyone and the ticket taker figured it was none of his beeswax what she did. She sat there, barely breathing, watching the brilliant colors swirl about the frame and Dandridge sashay with the glory of the blessed through the center of the screen. Mildred cried every time she saw it. It was like being at church when everybody was singing and she couldn't catch her breath. Like the dirt under her hands as she worked in the garden, the sun on her neck as she hung out the wash. Like the flowers by the roadside that made her long for a way to scoop the color up and keep it inside her.

She'd learned, after that day in 1921, that there was no time for dreaming or wondering, no time for listening for the fairies only you could hear scampering across the earth around you. You had to keep moving on, had to keep yourself in check. Keep everything neat. It couldn't keep the terror away, but it kept your hands busy and your body busy so you didn't just lie down in your sadness and not get up. So you didn't fall into the sky, never to return. So she gave her family what she could, gave her husband, Johnny Lee, her order and affection, her children her presence and the occasional smile. But none of them knew that she was a person who would go see *Carmen Jones* six times in a week and cry every time. They didn't know about the colors. And she didn't know how to tell them.

A Sunday morning at the Edwards house. Mildred bustles around the stove, stirring oatmeal, shifting sizzling bacon. Unlike many women on their side of the tracks in the 1950s, Mildred neither has to take in washing nor go out to clean or cook for a white family. Johnny Lee is the only black pharmacist in Tulsa. He studied and saved and suffered to get there. But he's there. His prosperous family shows that he's there. The children are seated. Otis, Jolene, and Angela. Ten-year-old Otis seems suited to where he was born. He is serious and quiet, an average student, handsome and stolid. He has a beautiful smile and large hands that he will grow into. Jolene is eight. Her favorite thing to do is to play house with her dolls and help her mama out in the kitchen. She is always bossing around the other children, much to their annoyance. It's important to her that things are done correctly. She once cried for an hour and a half over a B on a spelling test, the first grade below an A she ever got. Angela is five, in kindergarten, and in love with the world. Her hair ribbons are always untied, her knees are always dirty. She wants a witness to all she says, does, and thinks. She never stops talking. Mildred's ears ring with it, the sweet maddening chimes. "Mama, Miss Arthur says that I can be line leader on Monday." "Mama, when will I have homework?" "Mama, you gonna sing in church today?" Mama, Mama, Mama.

Mildred makes distracted affirmative noises toward her. They are trying to get to church, always an ordeal. The neat braids to be made, getting Angela into her stiff white dress and then getting her not to spill anything on it for the half an hour before they go. Making herself presentable. Answering Johnny Lee's questions about where his tie was. Her head was aswirl with detail. Finding everything and herding them out the door, clucking and fussing like a hen. Johnny Lee walked behind her after closing the door. "Lord, woman, we gonna make it in plenty of time."

"Just barely."

"Well, the Lord will wait on us." He grinned. "Really, Millie, we gon' be all right. You don't need to take on so."

Mildred sighed and didn't answer. Angela ran pell-mell ahead of them, kicking up dust. "Angie, don't you get your good dress dirty!" Mildred yelled. Then sighed again. "That child like to kill me. Just can't keep nothing nice."

"Well, you know how she is. Just got to do what she want to do. She been like that ever since she was born," said Johnny Lee.

"I know. I just hate to see her come into church all dusty."

"Well, the Lord won't mind. Maybe you could let it go too." He looked at her, steadylike. Mildred didn't know what to say and they were just about at the church anyway. So she didn't say anything.

Pastor Tyson was in fine form that day. Mildred let his voice roll over her like a river. What she liked best about church was the chance to sing. She poured everything in her into each hymn, letting the words buoy her up. She didn't have a particularly good voice. But she loved to sing. Just like her mother had.

After church, folks stood in little knots talking, heads inclining toward one another and then away. The children pelted around, happy to be free in the warm spring air. The women's voices were like music.

"Pastor Tyson surely preached the word today, didn't he?"

"He sure did. Lifted me right up"

"Well, it's some folks around here could use some lifting. You hear about that old Della down off of Archer?"

"What about her?"

"She ain't fed them kids in more than a week. City come in and took 'em away. They puttin' 'em all with different families."

"Mm-mm-mm. Some folks just don't know how to do."

Mildred cut in. "Well, you know she ain't got no man to help her and what's she got . . . six kids?" She ventured a little laugh. "Seem like you might just forget to feed 'em sometime." Shocked looks. "Oh, not really, I know you got to feed your children, but you know them kids must have just run her 'bout out her mind. Kids can be more than a notion. Y'all know that."

The sisters looked at her, no rueful smiles of acknowledgment on their faces. Then Constance, the most upright of them, spoke. "Children are the Lord's blessings."

Mildred felt chastised. "I know . . . but sometimes I just get so tired. You know. Don't you? I ain't saying Della was right but—"

"Well, Millie, you got to just take it to the Lord, then. Lean on His arm. Just like Della should have done. He don't never give us more than we can bear. And folks around here would have helped out."

Mildred sighed. "I know that's right, sister." Johnny Lee came up to her, nodded to the ladies, and said, "Millie, I'ma run over to A.J.'s and take a look at this old heap of his. He need some help getting it running. You be all right, huh?" He kissed her on the cheek and walked off. She took her leave of the ladies, wishing for the thousandth time that she had one true friend among them.

She took Angela's hand, called to Otis and Jolene, and headed home. Angela was fretful on the walk home. She was angry at having had to leave off playing with her friends and she cried, her voice piercing and sullen, for the whole long walk. Her feet scuffed up little clouds of dust. Otis followed a few feet behind, talking quietly to himself, and Jolene walked along, for all the world looking like a smaller version of the righteous Sister Constance. Mildred didn't speak to any of them. She didn't let go of Angie's hand but nearly dragged her along. Her own eyes stung, but her pace didn't slacken. There was still Sunday supper to get, some mending to do, quiet Sunday chores. Her head was pounding. Once inside, she helped the children change out of their meeting clothes and told all three of them to get on outside. Once they were gone, she sat stiffly on the edge of the bed she shared with Johnny Lee, her legs pressed tightly together. Then, suddenly, as though slapped by a giant hand, she was howling, crying, hysterical. A wind tore through her heart. The only words in her head were *I can't bear it, I can't bear it, I never should have had these children. Never should have married this man. I can't be nobody's mama.* She sobbed and moaned and gasped like that for a long time, the happy shouts of her son and daughters floating in through the window. But outside, no one heard her cries. When she was done sobbing, there was still Sunday supper to get. And she was still alone.

She noticed him first the following Saturday under the triangular awning of the Dreamland. She'd heard that there was a new projectionist down there. Eddie Jones, who had been the one to shut off the film the night of the burning and tell folks they better head on out, had died after many long years in that small room in the dark. Especially after the riot, he kept to himself. No one ever hardly saw him in the daylight. But this new man stood outside, leaning against the front of the theater, long legs braced to prop him up, his face turned up to the sun as folks filed into the theater. He held a cigarette in one slim hand. He happened to lower his head and open his eyes just as Mildred, Otis, Jolene, and Angie walked up to the theater.

The old Dreamland had not survived the burning, but the new one was built in 1929. People still came, as regular as rain, but just walking across the threshold was no longer a magnificent experience. In the old Dreamland lobby, the carpet hushed beneath your feet, the chandelier sparkled overhead, there was never a crumb on the floor or the smell of oil anywhere. Now there were fluorescent lights and a glass candy case that marred the open, generous space, and the replacement carpet wasn't replaced often enough. Though it was vacuumed regularly, it held onto just the least little bit of the grit from people's shoes and the kernels of dropped popcorn. Just enough to make it begin to feel run-down. But they still had the pictures. There were different stars now, different stories, but they were still such a joy to Mildred, her salvation. She went every weekend with the children—Johnny Lee had little interest, though he went once in a very great while. Paid their money and sat in the warmly gathered dark, looking at Bette Davis and Katharine Hepburn and Cary Grant and Marlon Brando and John Wayne and Judy Garland. Always white people. Sometimes there was Lena Horne, smoothed against a pole, her face bearing no traces of pain. And there was Dandridge. But mostly these beautiful others. The children knew to be quiet during the pictures. They grew to like these times. Their mother seemed content at last.

It was right that she met William at the Dreamland. It was there that good things in her life happened. He tipped his hat ever so slightly as she guided the children in. His skin was a warm, dark brown. His cheekbones so smooth and angled that it looked as though he spent time in the morning polishing them. His eyes were like no man's she'd ever seen; they were true, true black and so kind. In that minute between them, she had the oddest feeling that he was seeing something about her that no one else had ever seen. He looked at her face for a long moment and then smiled. He did not look at the children, the way most people did. Nor did he say anything about their goodness or beauty. He just looked at her. Mildred swore she heard her heart beat, just once, in her chest. She nodded and led her children into the picture show. Katharine Hepburn today. Her favorite.

Not long after this, she was out hanging wash on a Monday. The children were at school. The sun was out and the air was quiet. Something calm had been in her since early that morning. Her hair had been braided up under a scarf, but it had gotten so hot that she took it off and now her hair slowly came unraveled. She shoved rumply wisps out of her eyes as she hung the heavy, damp sheets and overalls. She was singing quietly to herself—"His eye is on the sparrow"—and not thinking anything in particular. All of a sudden, a man's voice, a sweet tenor, joined hers, causing her to start and drop the sheet she'd been trying to hang. A short shriek escaped her: "Who is that?" She bent to pick up the sheet and found herself looking up into the black eyes that had studied her so just the other day. He was smiling, looking right at her.

"Sorry, Miz Edwards, it's only me, William. William Henderson from down to the Dreamland. You sounded so lovely I just had to join in."

"Well, you scared me 'bout half to death." He looked at her so intently that she suddenly felt very aware of her hair all awry, the wet sheet heavy in her hands where she'd gathered it up. "What you doing out here anyway?"

"On my way to work. Here, let me help you with that." He hopped the fence in one nimble movement and took one end of the sheet from her. She'd never seen a man touch a piece of laundry in her entire life. He took some clothespins from her and said, "Well, go on. You do your end." She did, then picked up her scarf, lying forgotten on the ground, and tied it back over her hair as quick as she could. "Thank you. I . . . thanks."

"Happy to do it, ma'am." He stood, looking at her, until she felt she had to speak.

"Can I offer you some lemonade or something, Mr. Henderson?"

"I'd greatly admire that. You know what else?"

"What?" she said.

"I think we're gonna be friends. So I think it might be all right if we were on a first-name basis. That is, if it's all right with you . . . , Mildred." His eyes never left her while he said this last. Mildred's face grew hot as she said, "I think that would be all right . . . , William." This man hadn't even lived in town a month, come from somewhere back east. New York City, folks said. And here he was talking to her like this. How'd he even know her name? Must have been asking folks. So fresh. Anybody would have said he was being fresh. Why didn't she mind?

"Good. Then where's that lemonade?" He followed her up to the house as she went and got it but waited outside politely as she brought him a glass, then went back in to get one for herself. He was already drinking by the time she came out, one foot resting on the front step. She stood behind the screen door, watching the muscles in his throat. When he finished, he looked straight at her and said, "Whyn't I help you finish up all this wash and you come on down to the Dreamland with me? I gotta open up." His voice as soft as baby's hair after a bath. What could she say? The kids were all gone to school, the house straight, Johnny Lee down to the drugstore on the other side of town. She opened the door. "You really want to help me finish up?" she said.

"If you'll accompany me down to the theater, I will. I expect you'd like to see the projection room."

How did he know that? She had never been in a projection room, but she'd always wondered what made the films glow in front of her. Sometimes, if it wasn't such a good movie, she'd turn her head a couple of times to look at the square of light that the image emanated from and try to figure out what was up there. What made everything happen? When she was little, before her mama died, she was always trying to take stuff apart to figure out how it worked. Her mama told her it wasn't ladylike. And then her mama was gone and there wasn't anyone to stop her. But by that time she couldn't get herself to care. What was the point of trying to understand? None of this went through her head at his words. She just knew a wild willingness was on her. "Well, let's finish up, then. I believe I will join you," she said, sliding a hank of hair back into place under the scarf. There were no questions in her mind. Every proper thing she'd ever been told, every proper thing she'd ever done, seemed to have utterly left her.

They finished the laundry together, William keeping up a steady stream of chatter, asking her what her favorite pictures were and who were her favorite actors and actresses. He had opinions about just about every movie actor there was. His favorite was Errol Flynn—though he confessed to great affection for Harry Belafonte too, which made Mildred squeal a little and confess her *Carmen Jones*–going, something she'd never told anyone else. He smiled at her gently. He worked with a cheerful will Mildred had never seen in a man, asking her for clothespins and moving swiftly around the clothesline just the way a girlfriend might have if she'd had a girlfriend to speak of. When they were finished, he said, "Let's go," and they went out the gate—he let her go first—and walked down the dusty road to town. Mildred found herself questioning nothing, just going along to see what would happen. "So, Mildred," he said, "I've been talking a lot and you've barely said a word. What are you thinking, Miz Edwards?"

"I'm thinking I've never met anyone from New York before. What's it like there?"

William's eyes clouded over. "Tall. The tallest place you ever did see. With people rushing all around wherever you go. Did you ever see *His Girl Friday*?" Mildred nodded. "People talk like that. Just that fast. Even the colored folks."

Mildred was shocked. As much as she liked Cary Grant, she'd had trouble following that movie, the language spilled by at such a speed. "Really?" she said. "I didn't think folks could talk that fast. Not real folks. Ain't that something." She paused. "We must seem kinda country to you then, huh?"

William laughed. "Country? Hell, yeah."

Mildred blushed. She'd never been walking alone with a man who swore before. She kind of liked the way he dragged out the ll's.

"Oh, pardon my language, Mildred. But, yeah, it seems country to me here. But my mama and daddy left me a little bit of a place. They come here in 1930, didn't socialize too much with other folks. They liked to stay off by themselves. Anyway . . . it was time I left New York."

"Why?"

He looked up at the sky briefly. "Did you ever see a blue like that before? Like being under a teacup. Couldn't never see a sky like that back east. I come to miss that after a while."

Mildred looked up at the cobalt bowl over their heads, then back at William. "Yeah," she said, her feet slowing into an easy lope. "I could see how you would miss that. But is that the only reason?"

"Well, that and a broken heart," he said.

Mildred drew in her breath.

"Oh, don't look like that, Mildred. It's a few broken hearts in Tulsa, I bet. Gotta go a long way to get away from that. One way or the other. I need to see what I need to see every day. A sky like this. Don't nobody understand that here. But that's OK. I'm paying my bills. The rest will take care of itself in time." He drew a deep breath. "Hard to find that kind of time back in Harlem. That's the one thing it's very hard to find enough of." He leaned to the side of the road and pulled up a long blade of grass. Stuck it between his teeth. "I like to see a sky like this. A pretty ol' gal walking with me."

Mildred giggled. She felt . . . well, she plain didn't know what she felt. Except that she'd never been with anyone that she felt she could talk to about the way the sky changed from blue to silver to orange back to blue, depending what time it was. Who had time for such foolishness? But she felt that if she shared her thoughts with William, that he would listen. That he was the kind of person who exulted in the colors of the sky too.

They fell quiet as they approached the theater. Without speaking, Mildred began to lag a few steps behind William, trying to make it seem as though they weren't walking together. When he came to the theater, he unlocked the door, looked quickly both ways. No one passing. He beckoned her in, a wicked grin on his face. She scooted in behind him, laughing.

The theater was hushed and black inside. It smelled slightly of popcorn, the carpet gritty underfoot. She stood uncertainly just inside the door, until William stepped toward her. "No one's gonna come in." She just looked at him. He extended his hand, kept his gaze steady. "Here," he said quietly. "It's up this way." He led her up the stairs, so easily and quickly she didn't even have time to think about it. Her hand was right where it ought to be.

The projectionist's booth was tiny and airless and warm. It was lit from overhead by a bare bulb, casting harsh shadows. There was one tall stool, a huge machine with many sprockets and gears that Mildred supposed was the film projector, a small, thin shelf on which rested copies of *Ebony* and a few heavy books. On the walls were movie posters of every sort, Gable and Garbo and

Lena Horne. But what really made her stop was over in the corner, the most beautiful thing of all: a painting. She walked over to it as though pulled. "What's this?" she said, never looking away.

"It's a poster from an art show I saw back in New York. There were something like sixty paintings in that show. All about going up north. The painter lives right in Harlem. Colored man. Dark as you please. His name's Jacob Lawrence."

"A colored man painted this?" Colored people painting pictures? Pictures about going north?

"Yeah." William came and stood just behind her, so she could feel the warmth of him. "It's something, ain't it?"

It looked like church. A wide flat pew ran up the middle of the painting, the floor various shades of brown and gray and white. And then people sitting on either side, wearing bright yellows and reds and blues, their dark brown faces suggested by swatches of color. A door was at the front of the painting. But you couldn't tell where it led. Outside or just into another part of the painting. It made her eyes hum, her heart tighten in her chest. The way the colors lay so close to one another but never together. And people like the ones she'd always known. The ones who lowered their eyes when white people came through town and held them up so proudly the rest of the time. The ones who lay in the streets dead all around her all those years ago. She hadn't thought about that before she came up these stairs into this strange room, with this man she didn't know. But she felt something slide into place in her chest. She touched the back of her hair. William's breath warmed her neck, but she didn't move away from him. She just gazed into the image, so familiar, even though she'd never seen it before. "It sure is something," she said.

"It looks like my dreams," he said. She turned, laughing a little with the strangeness of his comment. But when he looked away from the painting and then down at her, the laugh died away. She could hear her heart in her ears. She stepped backward away from him and toward the painting, and he reached out and touched the side of her face gently. "I thought you might like it," he said quietly. "That's why I wanted you to come up here." He smiled a little. "You smell like lavender. That's what all the ladies around here use."

"Yes, I guess I do." She didn't move away, but she couldn't have said why. He dropped his hand back to his side.

"I thought you'd like the painting. You're the only one around here I've showed it to." They smiled at each other, and the feeling of a kiss about to happen fled the room. But they both knew it had been there. Mildred looked at her feet for a moment, then turned back to the painting. The long hallway that Lawrence painted with a dark doorway at the top of the frame was almost something she could walk through. She could imagine the texture of the floor underneath her shoes. William breathed quietly behind her. Neither of them spoke for a long time. After a while, he said, "So this is where I spend my time."

Mildred looked away from the painting, feeling bold. "Can I see the rest of the booth?"

"That's why I brought you up here. I see you come in with your kids every Saturday." He paused. "I wanted to show it to you. Do you have time?"

"Yeah, sure. A little bit. They at school 'til three." She looked at her feet quickly, then up, and she stepped over to the projector. "So how's this here thing work?"

William smiled and then proceeded to talk her through every detail of the projector: how the film threaded through it, how the pictures were broken up into tiny frames that gave the illusion of movement. (Twenty-four frames to the second, he told her. "Really?" Mildred said. She plain couldn't believe it.) He let her load the heavy reel onto the projector, allowed her to touch the glossy celluloid leader. She'd never been so freely invited to touch ma-

chinery she was curious about. As she got more and more interested, her awkwardness fell away. She asked a thousand questions,
until, finally, William said, "It's almost time for the first show."
Nearly two hours had passed. "Oh, my Lord," she said, clapping
her hand to her mouth. "I've got to go."

"OK," said William. "But promise me you'll come back."

She looked at him steadily. Something was starting. "I promise." And then she left.

That night, cooking dinner, she let the rice water boil clean away,
nearly burning her good pot. She forgot that Otis and Jolene liked
string beans but Angie didn't so she always got only one. Angie
cried for five minutes at the indignity of having a pile of green
beans on her plate. The hair stood up on the back of Mildred's
neck as she listened to her child's sobs over this tiny, tiny matter,
but she drew four deep breaths and took the other beans onto her
plate. Johnny Lee talked about something that had happened at
the pharmacy earlier that day. She wasn't sure what. When she
was still for a moment, she could still see the smoothly machined
angles of the film projector, feel the celluloid under her fingers.
And she could almost taste the reds and blues and yellows of Lawrence's painting even though she might not get another chance
to see it. She felt a little easing, a sense of contentment. She was
interested in how things worked for the first time in a long, long
time.

The next morning, she woke up happy. She couldn't think why
for a minute. She stared at the ceiling, as Johnny Lee's warm, familiar bulk breathed next to her and the children's sleeping
breath filled the house. Then she remembered. She felt a slight
twist of guilt at being alone with a man like that, but then she re-
called the gentle, respectful way he'd showed her all that machinery and let her look at the painting and she didn't care how scan-

dalous it was. She curled her toes. Johnny Lee woke up with a sigh. "You up, Millie?"

"Yeah, I'm awake. How are you?"

He rolled over and rested his arm across her chest. "I'm all right. You?"

"I'm all right. Couldn't sleep." He grunted and started moving his hand experimentally around her nipple. She felt her legs starting to shift around, that feeling gathering between them. She embraced him with a little sigh. They made love with quiet pleasure, like always. But as she came, William's name floated into in her mind. She wondered what his breath would feel like on her neck. She closed her eyes, embarrassed and guilty to be thinking such things. Johnny Lee asked if she was all right. She said yes, it was good, that she loved him and it was good. He kissed her throat, murmuring, and she held the back of his head. She imagined it was William's. Tears gathered behind her eyes, but they did not fall.

A week went by. Two. The days were long, longer, longest. It was getting to the meat of summer. Mildred couldn't stop thinking about that painting, about the time that William had taken with her, the way his hands moved over the film projector. She'd be washing the dishes or sweeping the yard and she'd find her mind had wheeled entirely away, was entirely with William. Finally, the third laundry day, she found her feet walking down to town of their own volition after she'd hung the wash. *I've just got to see that picture again*, she thought. That was all she let herself think. When he greeted her at the door, his eyes dark and pleased, she was thinking about the painting.

He had acquired a small cast-off love seat for the room and wedged it into a corner. A book called *The Migration of the Negro: A Catalogue* rested on it. She sank onto the seat without thinking, her hand caressing the glossy cover, which showed another painting. Black people again. "Oh, William. Where'd you get this?"

"At that show I told you about. Before the war. Want to look at it?" But she had already opened it and was gently thumbing through the pages.

She looked up again, the book on her lap, her hands resting on it. "How'd you know I was gonna come back?" she asked.

"I'm a patient man," he said. "And I missed you. I knew you musta missed me."

"How'd you know that I missed you?"

"I know all about you. I know you ought to be making something with those beautiful hands of yours. I know how much you love these paintings. I know you should have left Tulsa a long time ago and if you was a man and didn't have your family to take care of, you surely would have. And I knew you'd come back."

"I did miss you." It was almost a sigh at first. "I did miss you. I had to come back." He was sitting next to her now, so close she could smell him. She didn't see him leaning toward her. But it was happening, at last. His tongue was in her mouth. She put her hand on the back of his neck, felt the muscles of her face relax. She was herself at last. No one's mother. No one's child. No one's wife. She was only herself.

She shifted her legs apart, opened her mouth a little wider. Thought nothing. There was nothing to think. His hands were on her waist, now on her breasts, now gently pushing her dress up. She wasn't wearing stockings. She never wore stockings on laundry day. When he touched the inside of her thighs, she gasped and he stopped. "Is this all right?"

"Yes." She breathed. "It's just fine. Don't stop." So he didn't.

She left the book with him. He said he'd keep it for her.

After that, being with him was all she could think of. He was the air she breathed, the words she said, the light around her. They couldn't meet often; everybody knew everything in Greenwood. It was so easy for people to talk. But they met when they could. Mildred felt guilty. She looked at Johnny Lee and thought, *He is so good, so kind, I love him. How can I?* But William was a new life for her, one she'd never imagined, one with *her* mind and *her* heart at the center. While she felt guilty, she didn't feel wrong, which surprised her down to her shoes. Being with William was inevitable. She needed to see him periodically in order to keep breathing. When she was home, she talked to the kids, made love with her husband, did the wash, ran the house, but when her mind was at rest, it rested on William, on something he'd said, or the curve of his throat or the way the back of his head looked as he walked up the stairs. Or the feeling of his tongue in her mouth, his mouth on her breasts. The feeling that she would never need another thing.

On Sundays the longing stretched before her, a featureless plain. The snap and chase of getting the kids ready for church distracted her for a while. It wasn't until Mildred sat in church, Pastor Tyson's voice rolling over her, that she gave herself over to that endless distance.

She sat, tears like needles behind her eyes, praying to be delivered. When she closed her eyes, voices rising all around her in song, she saw only the base of his throat, that small, sweet depression in his skin before her, the taste of salt. She saw her mouth resting there. There was no deliverance. She was not to be set free.

All day, every day, her lips moved soundlessly saying his name. William. William. William. Her tongue rested on the syllables, they caressed her teeth. William. William. She lay her hand on her stomach where he'd lay his hand, she felt her tongue in her mouth where his tongue had been. No one saw her but he. At last she was comprehended. At last she comprehended someone else. She hadn't known she was missing that until he brought it to her, a feast she could not enjoy, a blessing she could not celebrate, a gift only partially hers, water in the desert. His name was her prayer, his touch her church. But no one knew.

One time when they were entwined in their small dark space,

he took her head in both hands, ran his thumbs over her closed eyelids, and whispered, "Look at me. I'm here. Look at me." She opened her eyes. Even as she came, crying out the words he'd given her, she didn't look away. Neither did he. She took up the words. "I'm here. Look at me. I'm here." And with him, she was.

15

SOMETIMES THEY DIDN'T EVEN MAKE LOVE. THEY played checkers or just sat together and looked at the Lawrence book. William talked with her about the colors he used and why he might have chosen them. She helped him thread the film through the projector before showtime, and he complimented her when she did it well. William told her all about New York and Chicago and other places he'd been. He showed her paintings he'd made. He sketched her once. She'd never even seen a black man hold a pencil for anything other than writing. She sat as still as a stone as William looked from her to his pad, to her again, his face beautiful and intent. When he showed her the sketch, she started crying. "Oh, I don't look like that," she said, pushing at her tears with the heel of her hand.

"Like what?" he said.

"That pretty. Like . . . I don't know. I don't look that pretty."

William smiled. She had to go in a few minutes. "No. You look prettier." His face turned serious. "I wish . . ."

"What?"

"I wish that I'd met you a long time ago."

Mildred was silent. Her head was pounding. What was she supposed to say? "I wish I'd met you then too. I mean . . . I love Johnny Lee too, but . . . I don't know . . . things. Things can't change so easy. You know? Sometimes they just can't."

"I know. I know. But . . . Listen. You might see me 'round with somebody else. You might hear some stuff. I'm just a man. But you need to know this. I'm here if you want me. If you ever want me. I'll be right there." They stared at each other for a long time after that, not even touching. What else was there to say?

Johnny Lee said to her once, "Girl, your head been in the clouds a lot lately." She smiled at him and said, "Naw, I'm right here. But you know I got a lot to do around here. I get distracted, that's all." It went on only another few weeks after that. Only until the day she came home a bit later than usual from her stolen time with William and found Angie and Johnny Lee at home, Angie's face tear-stained, a large new plaster cast on her arm. They were both sitting at the dining room table, Angie drinking a chocolate soda from the drugstore. Her father must have made it special. At first Mildred's voice seemed to have stopped working. Johnny Lee just looked at her. Angie blew bubbles into her glass but was otherwise uncharacteristically silent. Johnny Lee rose to his feet. He seemed taller than he'd ever been. "Woman, where the devil have you been?" he said.

"What?"

"I said, where the devil have you been? In case you ain't notice, your daughter broke her arm running 'round the yard at school first thing this morning. They been calling and calling you from the school. Finally had to come down to the store to get me so I could sit with her at the hospital. You been out this house since nine-fifteen and I don't see no groceries or no signs no how that you been doin' nothin' you supposed to around here."

The sink was full of pots and pans, the yard unswept, the breakfast dishes not put away. The smooth surface she'd worked so hard to maintain was gone. She'd kept it up a month, then two, then three, keeping it all going, doing the housework double-time. But now her baby sat with a broken arm and those big eyes fixed on her, asking the same question her husband was. "Yeah, where was you, Mama? I was on the highest bar, higher than even Pookey can climb. But I fell," she finished wistfully. "Where was you at, Mama?"

Johnny Lee stepped right up to Mildred, his face a few inches away. "Who is he? Who the hell is he, you goddamn whore?" His hands, hands that had always been so gentle with her, were balled into fists. Suddenly, he turned away from her and swept the kitchen table clear of dirty dishes. Some of them shattered on the floor. Food went everywhere. "Clean that up," he said in a murderous voice. Then he strode out of the house, never looking back. Mildred still hadn't said a single word, feeling wet between her legs where she and William had just finished making love, the heat of his eyes on her, the killing look in her good Johnny Lee's. She couldn't move. Angie was silent. Tears ran down Angie's face. Then she stood up. "I'll help you clean up, Mama."

"You'll do no such thing. Sitting there with your arm broke. It's my job. You go on upstairs and lie down."

"OK, Mama." She went obediently out of the room. Mildred knelt before the mess on the floor. She knelt for a long time before she collapsed forward, smearing her hair with her family's morning food, sobbing harsh, animal cries. Her daughter must have heard her. But she stayed upstairs as she'd been told. They were separated by the floor, the wall, the slow knowledge of what could happen if you broke the rules. You might be happy. But the price would be high.

16

WHEN JOHNNY LEE EDWARDS HAD BEEN BACK from the war for about a week and a half, he was walking with Mildred on the other side of the tracks, running an errand. He was feeling good. His wife was pregnant with his first, he was back from serving his country with honor, he was getting back into the saddle at the pharmacy, the delicate work he had trained so hard for. They were walking along a narrow sidewalk when an old white woman came tottering right down the middle. In passing her, Johnny Lee brushed her coat sleeve with his elbow.

"Watch where you're walking, nigger," she said. Didn't even look up. Didn't miss a step. Just said it as they always did. Mildred and Johnny Lee had both learned since they were children not to respond, almost not to hear. But this time, he felt his face turn into a fist, his hands tighten into weapons. Mildred stepped quickly to his side, seeing that he was close to lashing out, with his mouth or his hands, and knowing that to do so could get them both, could get them all, killed. She lowered her head, and her voice became servile. "Sorry, ma'am. He wasn't lookin' where he was going. Sorry."

"Well, you ought to be. Damn lazy niggers." She was too old, had done this rant too many times, to give it full vigor. She went on her way. Johnny Lee's head pounded. Mildred looked up at him, and he could see fear in her face. She tried to smile. "Johnny Lee, you all right?" she asked. "You know how white folks is. That's one thing that ain't changed a bit while you been gone." She laughed a little. But he didn't. He couldn't.

"You know, in France, I was never once called 'nigger,'" he said. "Not one time. We went into this one village and this girl, this *white* girl, cried and hugged me like I was Jesus Christ come down from the cross. I'd come to save her village. That's all she cared about. Everybody, crying and hugging us. And now I'm back here . . ." They had stood together in the middle of the side-walk, speechless.

He never thought he would feel that kind of fury toward the woman who stood by his side that day. But he'd never have be-lieved she could do what she'd done. He loved her. He loved the curve of her hips and buttocks under the modest dresses she fa-vored, the sound of her laughter. Most times she was as orderly as any Tulsa housewife could be and he loved that too. But he also loved having a woman with a heart. He didn't claim to under-stand it, but he knew it was there. He was a lucky man.

After he left home that morning, he walked. He walked and walked. He didn't even know where he was going. His hands were fists, his eyes blind. He must have walked for nearly two hours, maybe longer, a little past lunchtime, before he got so hot and dizzy that he had to stop. He stood in the sun for a few minutes, trying to get his bearings. Then he realized that he wasn't far from Frank's. Frank's with its cool interior and sawdust-covered floor and cold beer and strong whiskey. He walked that way. He didn't care who saw him go in, and plenty of people did. People who knew him. People who knew Mildred. He didn't care.

The interior of Frank's was dark and comforting and at this time of day, nearly empty. A bartender made sleepy circles on the bar with a damp rag. From the jukebox, Muddy Waters offered a good morning to a little schoolgirl. The stools offered respite. Johnny Lee sank onto one gratefully and ordered a beer and a shot—something he'd never done in daylight in his entire life. But in the sweet darkness of Frank's, no one would ask any questions he didn't want to answer.

He sat there a long time, drinking and stewing, the liquor softening the day around him. People came, people left. The kind of people who would go to Frank's during the day were the kind of people who didn't talk to one another much. They were just there to drink. That's why he was startled when he became aware of a presence at his elbow. He turned and found Mabel Littlefield sitting next to him. Johnny knew her from the store. He knew everybody from the store. She came in a lot for various headache remedies and was never seen in church on Sunday. She had the kind of beauty that is mere months from being lost to drink and despair. But she was still just barely young enough and hungry enough for affection that a man could find some solace in her arms. "Why, Johnny Lee Edwards," she said, her voice bright and insinuating, "I declare, I ain't never seen you in here. This place is only for bad girls like me."

"Aww, Mabel, you ain't so bad. Don't look so bad no way."

"Listen to you." She laughed and leaned into him. "Ain't you sweet?"

Johnny Lee turned back to his beer. He felt something gathering in him, through the haze of anger and sadness and liquor. Then he turned back to Mabel. "I 'on't know. You wanna find out?"

She smiled. "Buy me a drink and see what you can talk me into."

An hour later, they leaned on each other, giggling and trying not to fall down, all the way back to her small room. She walked up the stairs ahead of him, trying to sway her hips seductively but too drunk to pull it off. Once they got inside, she went into the bedroom, giggling some line about changing into some-thing more comfortable. He stumbled to the bathroom, mutter-ing, "Just give me a minute. I'll be . . . I'll be right wish you." After he'd finished urinating, he looked at himself in the mirror. His eyes were bloodshot, his skin a clear dark brown. He pressed the heels of his hands into his eyes to push back the tears that threat-ened. He took a deep breath and went out to the woman who awaited him, the woman who was not his wife. She lay on her bed, her legs spread a little, wearing a cheap lace camisole. She gazed at him. Her eyes were full of hope. Her breasts were loose and sagging. Johnny Lee stood and looked at her. Then he groaned and shook his head. Shook his head and went out her door and stumbled back to Frank's. He thought he could hear her crying as he went down the first couple of steps. But he didn't worry about it. He was going to get drunk enough to forget.

The bartender brought him home when his shift ended. He smelled like three distilleries and was nearly incoherent. Mildred accepted his foul-smelling arm around her neck with a brief word of thanks to the bartender, who nodded. She walked him up-stairs. He kept talking. She didn't know what he was saying.

She helped him lie down in the bed, knelt to remove his shoes. As she took his foot in her hand gently just for a second be-fore she moved on to the next shoe, the sobs he hadn't cried all day tore out of him with staggering force. Mildred sat stock-still for a moment. But then sat him up and pulled him toward her. He allowed it. He cried for a long time and when he could finally speak, he said only one word. A clear one this time: "Why?"

"Oh, J.L., I . . . I didn't want to hurt you. I didn't want this to happen, I just . . ."

"For God's sake woman, why?"

"Because I loved him. That's why." Her hand stilled on his back. The truth was out, unalterable.

"You loved him."

"Yes."

"Do you still?" A long silence. "Don't lie to me," Johnny Lee finally said.

"Yes, I still love him."

"Can you tell me who he is?"

"I don't want to." Another red surge of anger, but he couldn't sustain it. He just needed to hear their voices interweaving for now.

"Are you going to leave?"

"No. I love you too. And the kids."

"Ain't no reason I shouldn't beat your ass black and blue and put you out the house for good."

"I know."

Johnny Lee lay back on the bed, tears still leaking out of his eyes. The room whirled desperately. He had a vision of Mabel's stretched-out, worked-over body splayed out on the bed. He felt as though several foul animals had died in his mouth. What was he going to do? Mildred had broken his heart. But he still loved her so. He lay on the bed, her hand moving on his forehead, his fists at his sides. He got up to vomit, horribly and long, and then stumbled back to bed. She wet a rag and wiped his face and then resumed her gentle stroking, never saying a word. He fell asleep like that. He had no idea what the morning would bring.

17

TWO MONTHS HAD PASSED. BEFORE HE LEFT FOR the store, Mildred said to Johnny Lee, "I'm doing the wash today and then gonna work in my garden for a while if it's time before the kids get home. Constance usually out at the same time, she'll probably see me out there." He nodded. Since he'd found out, Mildred had begun volunteering information on what she was doing every day, whether he asked or not. At first he asked, but then he stopped and she kept on telling him anyway: an offering. He could tell things had changed by the dutiful way she moved about the house, the sad silence beneath her every movement, even as she spoke to him or the children, but he still accepted her offerings.

He was in the back mixing up something for the Foster baby's colic when he heard the bell. He went out front and sighed when he saw who was there. That old busybody Joe Moore. He was just like a woman, way he had to know every single thing that went on, who said what to who and when and what for. Seem like the man just came into the store to see who else would come in, not because he needed anything. Fool needed to get a job. He'd sit at the counter nursing a Coke all day and trying to pry stuff out of him. But Johnny Lee kept his mouth shut. That's what people valued about him. "Hey, Joe," he said. "What can I do for you today? Anything different than I do any other day?" He laughed.

"Hey, Johnny Lee. I'm all right. Think I'm gonna have my usual. And gimme a pack of Sen-Sen and a copy of the paper. What you know good today?"

"Same as yesterday, my man, same as yesterday." He busied himself getting the Coke and Sen-Sen and newspaper. Joe settled himself with a great rattling of paper and a lot of sipping and commenting on the stories there. Johnny Lee made noises of agreement. Didn't need to do much else for Joe. He just liked to know that he had half an ear.

The morning passed in its usual, quiet rhythm. Joe had another Coke, Johnny Lee dispensed medicines, cigarettes, advice, a friendly word, to everyone who came in. Around noon, the bell rang and a man Johnny Lee had seen only a few times came in. Sometimes he came in for cigarettes, but he never had much to say. Johnny Lee didn't share his wife's love of the pictures or he might have known it was the projectionist. "What can I get you?" Johnny Lee said.

The man looked at him quickly, then away. "Pack of Kools."

"Anything else?"

"Nope, that'll be all." He seemed nervous. Johnny Lee couldn't figure it out. The man was the kind that a woman would find good-looking—smooth and polished. His skin had a kind of glow. He sounded like he wasn't from around here. He paid and then went on his way. He gave Johnny Lee a quick, penetrating look before he left. Johnny Lee's stomach knotted. But he didn't yet know why.

Once he was gone, Joe looked up from the paper he'd been studiously examining while the man was there. He whistled long and low. "They say that William Henderson's been getting around."

"What? That cat that just left?" Johnny Lee still felt unsettled. A knowledge was coming to him.

"Well, you see what he look like, don't you, brother? You think a cat like that—they say he used to live in New York City too—

ain't been pulling down whatever he likes?" Joe laughed low in his throat. "Shoot. That dog could teach us all a few new tricks." He laughed again. The words were out of Johnny's mouth before he even knew it: "Joe, I need to run down the street for a minute. I can trust you to help out anybody who comes in, right? Just don't go messing with the medicine. Anybody needs a prescription, tell 'em I'll be back in about ten minutes."

Joe looked surprised, but then understanding floated into his dark eyes. *He knows,* Johnny Lee thought, suddenly so sad he had to close his eyes for a moment. *Dammit. Who doesn't know?*

"Sure, man. You know I got you covered. Take as long as you need."

"I'll only be about ten to fifteen minutes," Johnny Lee said firmly.

"Right," said Joe, sliding off his stool and stepping behind the counter.

Johnny Lee moved quickly through the streets. People greeted him with a nod of the head or a wave of the hand. Same as always. He knew everyone and they all spoke to him. He spoke right back. Never had it been uncomfortable before. It always reminded him of how necessary he was here, how at home. He had been made to look foolish in his home. He yanked the door of the theater open in a fury and ran up the stairs.

The man was bent over a large machine—Johnny Lee supposed it was how they showed the movies—fiddling with a large wheel with loose stuff on it. Johnny Lee acted before he thought. He stepped forward and shoved him as hard as he could into the machine, which was so heavy that it swayed but didn't fall. The large spoked wheels fell off with a clatter. It was a cheap shot, but Johnny Lee, who usually wasn't that kind, didn't care. "What the . . . ," said the man, wiping at his now bloodied mouth.

"What's your name? You been fucking my wife. Least you could do is tell me your name."

He stood up slowly. Johnny Lee thought he'd never seen a man look sadder. "My name's William Henderson. I . . . I'm sorry about your wife."

"You sorry. You sorry. You bet your smooth-talkin' ass you're sorry. What the hell. What the hell."

William said nothing for a minute. Didn't raise his hands except to wipe briefly at his mouth again. "I might as well tell you. I'm leaving here. You won't have to worry about me and her again."

Johnny Lee took a step forward, his hands still in fists. Why didn't he defend himself? How was he gonna hit a man who wouldn't raise his hands? He couldn't. His heart contracted again. He was going to have to live with this forever. There would be no satisfying punch-out, no shaking it out of him, no making it unhappen. "I want you gone by next week."

"I will be."

"Don't come around her again."

"I won't."

Johnny Lee left. He didn't feel any better. He stopped in the alley next to the theater where no one could see him and spent a few minutes sobbing as he hadn't in years. Then he pressed the heels of his hands into his eyes. He had to get back to work. He couldn't leave Joe in charge. This had to end.

He was back behind his counter in a matter of minutes, polishing, polishing. Joe sat at his stool, nursing his Coke and carefully not speaking. The marble surface of the counter gleamed. It needed no more effort. But Johnny Lee kept polishing. It was easier if he kept his mouth shut and never stopped moving.

18

BY THE TIME ANGIE WAS FOURTEEN, MILDRED couldn't do anything with her. All she did was fight with Jolene and Otis and stay up in her room doing God knew what for half the day on the weekends. That is, when she wasn't trying to go down past the ice cream parlor and switch her little fast butt past all those no-'count Negroes that hung out by the pool hall. It wasn't like Mildred didn't have enough on her mind. It wasn't like she didn't know what happened when you let things get out of hand.

It had been seven years now since she'd said goodbye to William. She'd chosen what she knew was right. Johnny Lee was broken in two, but he didn't leave. And he didn't beat her. And he didn't make her leave. He was a good and loving man. Mildred hung onto that for her life. For a long time after that first night, he slept on the sofa; they told the children he wasn't feeling well. He went to work early in the morning and came home minutes before dinner every night. He talked very little and the children looked from one parent to another at the dinner table with the hunted look of young fawns, Angie especially. Only once, not long after the scene she witnessed, had she ventured to ask about that day. "Mama, where was you that day I broke my arm? Why was Daddy so mad?"

"I did some things I wasn't supposed to do, punkin. That's all.

You know how me and Daddy get mad when you don't do like you're supposed to do. That's how Daddy felt. Just mad, that's all."

Angie studied her seriously. Mildred knew her daughter didn't believe her. "Well, he sure was mad" was all she said, though. Mildred watched her daughter skip off, her arm still tethered to her side. Wasn't slowing her down none. But her mama hadn't been there.

That's what she told William when she told him that she had to end it: that she'd failed her baby. She was so terrified making her way to him for the last time that she thought she might faint. When she saw his face and considered what she had to say she thought she might die. Could words be so hard to say, that you'd die saying them? That day she wondered. The look on his face. "So he found out?"

"Yes, he did, William. And I . . . you know I love you, but . . . I got the kids and he's a good man. I love him too. And what folks would say . . . the kids." She had trouble making sentences. He looked at her steadily. Not touching her. "Did you tell him it was me?"

"No." For some reason she couldn't fathom, Johnny Lee had not insisted that she tell him who her lover was. She was baffled but grateful. William nodded.

"I guess we gonna have to go on with our lives from here," he said.

Her chest hurt so much she could barely speak. "I don't know if I can." She was crying now. William stepped to her and took her hand. "You can. You have to. I will too." There were tears in his eyes, but they didn't fall. "You go on now."

"William . . ."

"Go on. I love you." He gave her a gentle push toward the door. Before she knew it, she was on the other side. She left the theater and walked up the street as bold as you please. Johnny Lee was at work and she had nothing more to hide.

She sent the children to the pictures without her for a while.

She thought she might die between missing the pictures and missing William, but somehow she went on. After about the seventh or eighth time they innocently reported that the man who used to always be out front before the pictures was gone. "You know, Mama, the one who goes upstairs and shows them. Mr. Henderson," said Jolene. Mildred nodded. Johnny Lee just kept eating. She thought she might have seen a brief movement from him, a look in his eye. But later she thought she'd imagined it. The next day, after everyone was gone to work and school, she found a package wrapped in brown paper on the doorstep with her name on it. It was William's copy of *The Migration of the Negro*, with a note inside. *This belongs to you. So do I. I couldn't see no way to work it out. But I meant what I said. You live in my heart. And if the time ever comes, I'm yours. I'm yours. Love, William*. Lord, how she cried as she hid that book in her wedding chest. Johnny Lee never ever looked in there for nothing. Every now and then when she was in the house alone, she'd get it out and stroke the cover. It still felt like silk under her fingers.

Keeping everything in wore her out. It was like having a light on in the basement all the time; the drain on her energy was slight but constant. She would have liked to tell everything to a girlfriend, but she really had only church-lady friends. She could not have said what was in her heart, especially since they all went to the same movie theater where her lover had worked and bought their menstrual pads and aspirins and stomach remedies from the man she had betrayed. Sometimes she cried. Hard. She missed the sparkly conversations, the shooting-star feeling of being with William. She and Johnny Lee found their way to a bruised truce: not much sex, not much talking, but a hard-edged communion that she took as her due. Sometimes she caught him looking at her over the dinner table with shattered wonderment, and she knew that it was right that she'd stayed but also that he'd carry the pain she'd caused him to his grave. And she had to live with that. But usually she was all right. Except where Angie was concerned.

Today Jolene came home from school and said that everybody was talking because they'd seen Angie out back of the school kissing on Calvin Wiley. "And, Mama, my friend Clara said that they go back there every day and she seen him feeling on her titties! What you gonna do, Mama?" Jolene had to know anything bad that was going to happen to Angela. She almost seemed, in her prudish way, to relish it.

Mildred dropped the sponge she was using on the dishes into the sink with a sigh. "Me and her daddy will talk to her, Jolene. Now I know you got some homework to do and them chores to get to. So whyn't you go on. You bigger than her anyway—you got enough to do."

"I know that, Mama. That's why I don't spend my time kissing boys in back of the school. You know, if you got on her more, she wouldn't be so fast."

"I'll thank you, miss, to let me talk to her as I see fit. Ain't nobody made you the mama around here, last I checked. Now get on."

Jolene stomped up the stairs. Mildred sighed. *I wish I liked her better,* she thought. *Must be a sin not to like your own child.* She wondered what she would say to Angie. Nothing she said seemed to work.

The door slammed, announcing Angela's arrival. She had never in her life entered a room quietly. At fourteen, she was all legs and arms and shockingly pretty. "Hi, Mama." She threw her books down on the kitchen table.

"Put those away, child. And get upstairs and get to work on your homework." Not yet. She wasn't ready yet. She went back to washing dishes.

• • •

The Edwards family sat down to dinner at 6:30 that night, as always. Johnny Lee led the prayer and then they all tucked in to their food. Otis never had much to say. At eighteen and in his senior year of high school, he was already engaged to a nice steady girl from his class and had plans to get a job out in the oil fields outside of town—they were hiring coloreds occasionally now. Things were changing. If there had been any farming left to do, it would have suited him well. But there wasn't. And he was turning into the kind of man who would happily take what he could get. Jolene took precise, fussy bites of her food, dabbing at her mouth delicately. She sat up very straight. Angie ate eagerly and talked a blue streak, until Jolene said, "Did Mama speak to you yet, Angie?"

"Speak to me about what?"

" 'Bout how you actin' out back of the school."

"What?" said Angela. Her voice went up in a nervous squeak.

Johnny Lee stepped in. "What's she talking about, Angie? Do you know, Millie?"

"It's not something I want to talk about at the table, J.L. Let's you and me and Angie talk later."

"What'd I do?" said Angela with the indignation of the caught.

"Yeah, Mama. She didn't mind having everybody looking at her. Ain't you gonna say nothing?" Jolene again.

"In God's name, woman, what is this child talking about?"

In the face of her father's persistence, Angela suddenly changed tactics, jumping up from the table. "I was kissing a boy, OK? That's what Miss Priss here is so upset about!" Looking right at Mildred, she shouted, "It's not like you've never done it." Then she ran from the room. Mildred and Johnny Lee didn't even look at each other. Then Johnny Lee stood up, and said, "My God, woman. My God." He pushed roughly back from the table and walked out the front door. Otis kept eating. Jolene sat without moving; the look of terror on her face made it clear that this had gone further than she's intended, that she was on the verge of knowing things she didn't want to know. Mildred rested her head on her hands, moaning. Then she got up and went to speak to her youngest daughter.

Angie was face down on her bed, sobbing. Mildred came in but stood only just over the threshold. Somehow, she couldn't go any closer. "Angie? Angie, why are you actin' like this?"

She rolled over. "I kissed him, yeah. He asked and I kissed him. I didn't even like it that much, Mama."

"Well, me and your daddy, we're just worried that you're gonna get taken advantage of. That . . . well . . . that you'll get to like it or you'll get with some boy who likes it and you'll be writing a check you can't cash. We just don't want to see that happen."

Angela wiped the tears off her face and looked at her mother fiercely. "I know why Daddy was so mad at you that time. I know now."

"Angie, it's things between a man and a woman that a little girl just can't understand."

"Well, I know. And I'm not so little. I understand more than you think I do."

"Oh, child, you think you do. That's how it is. But you don't know. Not yet."

Angela looked at her, her eyes hard. "I know what I need to know."

Mildred looked at her daughter and saw her slipping away. Not a thing she could do. She'd lost the right seven years ago in William's arms. "Well, just don't be out back of that school with any boys anymore. I ain't having that in my house. You understand."

"Yes, ma'am."

As soon as she left the room, she heard the tinny sound of the record player being turned on. Some of that Motown music Angie liked so much filled the air. Mildred stood alone on the other side of her daughter's door, and listened. But she didn't understand.

19

A NGELA WAS TWENTY. SHE HAD FINISHED HIGH school and started secretarial school. She was the best typist in her class. She never stopped shocking her mother. She had long curvy legs and a neck you couldn't help but think about and hips that came straight from Mother Nature and invited some man to touch them. Mildred was her mother, not someone aspiring to be her lover, and even she could see how beautiful her daughter was. It scared her. She could see how this one was bound and determined to make her own way, and that her way wouldn't be in Tulsa. Otis and Jolene had been grown and gone since Angie was sixteen. They each had children of their own and Angela was still here. She walked down Archer Avenue as though it were her personal property. And Mildred couldn't do a thing to stop her.

"Mama, you better get down here. We gonna be late."

"I'm comin' girl. That picture ain't going nowhere."

"Yeah, yeah, yeah. You said that last week and we was late. Come *on*, Mama. It's Katharine Hepburn." Sometimes it seemed like their love for movies in general and Katharine Hepburn in particular was all they had in common. Today they were going to see *The Lion in Winter* down at the Dreamland. They still went every Saturday afternoon, even though the theater was dirty and smelled of rancid oil and the part of town the theater was in was not the safest and the movies had often been playing everywhere else long, long before they got to the Dreamland. It kept them together, though. They didn't talk about it, but they both valued that.

Mildred didn't really understand *The Lion in Winter*. Oh, Kate looked good like always, her voice the sound of royalty and her face glowing, even with her hair all messed up. But everybody kept talking so sharp and brittle in sentences that no one would ever really use. And then that boy turning out to be queer and with the king of France no less. Pictures weren't what they used to be. She expressed as much to Angela as they walked out into the evening sun. "Oh, Mama, you've got to change with the times. Everything's changing. Can't you see that? That movie was supposed to be funny. And when those two guys—well, some guys are like that. So are some girls. You know that."

"Sure I know that. But that don't mean it got to be all up in your face in a movie. We don't got to see every crazy thing people do in this world, do we?"

"Mama, you so old-fashioned."

"Just got good sense, it seem to me. Seem like most folks done lost it. Don't nobody know how to act anymore."

Angela was silent. "Well, I liked it," she said after a while. "They was kind of crazy, but I liked it."

Mildred eyed her daughter speculatively. "You would."

As beautiful as Angela was, the only thing Mildred had ever said to her about sex was "Keep your dress down and your panties up." Even after their confrontation over Angie's first kiss, Mildred still couldn't find a way to talk to her daughter—even knowing what she knew about loving a man, or loving two men. How could she explain that to her baby? She couldn't. So she didn't. She didn't say anything. Mildred could almost see the wheels turning, see Angela working things out in her mind.

· · ·

Angela had been a fairly good student her senior year of high school. She was president of the Dramatic Society, had a solid B–average (didn't want to be too smart, scare off the boys), and spent plenty of time helping the sick at Greenwood Baptist like her mother before her. Since the kissing incident when she was fourteen, she'd appeared to lead the life of a modest girl. But Mildred couldn't help but remember that and, going back further, remember the way her eyes glowed like candles when they saw the revival of *Carmen Jones* together when she was ten and how that child pestered, pestered, pestered to be allowed to wear a flower behind her ear and a red skirt until Mildred lost all patience and shouted that no daughter of hers was going to walk the streets of Tulsa dressed like a common whore. Angie's eyes got big and filled with tears and she never asked again. But Mildred knew that Angela had never forgotten the easy power in Carmen's walk, the sway of joy in her hips; even if she did get her comeuppance in the end. She had so much fun before it came. So when she finally heard about Angie going too far with Bobby Ware, she wasn't entirely surprised. She knew she had to put a stop to it—but she wasn't surprised.

At first she'd been happy when Angie started keeping company with Bobby a few years before. He was a nice boy with a good family. But then she started hearing things; just little things at church first, but finally Jolene (of course) confirmed the whispers. Folks had seen Angela going down in Bobby's car to the edge of town, where it was well known that everyone went to park. She'd been seen emerging from his car with her hair mussed and her eyes shining. "Everybody knows about it, Mama. Folks talking all over town," said Jolene.

So she waited in her daughter's bedroom after school that day, as she should have done long ago, for her daughter to come home. But this time, resolve was in her heart. This time, she'd be strong—the way she should have been all along.

"Angela, I've heard tell that you've been seen all over the

place with Bobby Ware and not just keeping company. You've been down where folks go to park and under the bleachers with him. I've been hearing things. Are they true?"

Angela didn't say anything.

"Young lady, I am speaking to you. Did you hear my question?"

"Yes, ma'am. I heard it."

"Well, then I expect an answer and I expect it now."

Angela looked straight into her mother's eyes. Her back was that of a soldier on parade. "Yes, ma'am. To tell the truth, I broke up with him two weeks ago—not that I told you. But before that, I've been with him in his car, under the bleachers, every chance I get—for years. That surely was me."

Mildred covered her heart with her hand like Anne Baxter in *All About Eve* and sank onto Angela's bed. "What on earth were you thinking, acting like that with that boy?" she gasped.

"Mama, believe me. You don't want to know," she said.

Her mother looked at her, transfixed. "What. Did. You. Just. Say."

"I said that you don't want to know what I've been doing with Bobby Ware. But I'll tell you—it's been good." Her eyes were unwavering.

Her mother got up and moved forward one step, then two. Her hand, when it hit Angela's face, made a dull, flat crack. "I will not have a whore in this house," said Mildred. She did not raise her voice.

Angela touched her cheek for a minute, but she didn't cry. "You didn't raise a whore, Mama." She turned away.

Mildred spoke to her back. "That's fine you broke up with him. If I hear another word about you behaving this way with anyone, you can pack your bags. You old enough to make your own way. It's time you do it if that is how you're going to act. I will not have a slut in my house." She turned and walked out without another word.

She did not stop walking until she had reached the backyard. Once the floor was no longer under her feet, she stopped and dropped to her knees. The ground was moist beneath them. The palm of her hand still stung. She had never slapped her daughter before. Angela's eyes had been so murderously cold. But there was something else in them too. A departure. In that moment, Mildred knew that Angela was lost to her. That sooner rather than later, her daughter would be gone and she'd be left with her husband, who was kind to her, and the ashy taste of her memories and the dull glitter of her movies, and that would be the end of it. She knelt in the dirt, grateful no one could see. She knelt in the dirt and cried.

Angela sat at her father's right hand, her mother at his left. He led grace. "Lord, bless these gifts we are about to receive. For this and all the fruits of Thy hand we are humbly grateful. Amen." Amen, the two women echoed. The room was still with anger. Johnny Lee must have felt it, but he just started talking about how crazy old Etta Atkins came in to the drugstore today looking for her long-dead husband, something she did once a week. Both women laughed, like always, but there was ice between them.

Johnny Lee didn't need to know about what had happened this afternoon between them. He would talk to Angela about woman stuff; he was easier about it than most men. But this? Mildred hadn't seen any need to drag him into it. She understood her daughter well enough.

Her stomach dipped, remembering William walking up the stairs of the Dreamland in front of her. She knew how you could get. So that you'd do anything to have those hands on you again. But she knew what Angela didn't—how it ended with you crying alone in the dirt. She ate a small, ladylike forkful of her mashed potatoes.

Angela sat, eating, not talking. She was so beautiful, Mildred thought, so beautiful. When she was a little girl she always had one ribbon untied, her knees dirty, the look in her eyes she had now, as if she were seeing something you couldn't see. Angela didn't look like a girl who'd been arguing with her mother. She looked like a woman who'd made a decision. Mildred longed to touch her hand, to feel her daughter's skin next to hers. But she didn't reach out. She just laughed at the funny part of her husband's story. The same story she'd heard a thousand times. And continued to eat.

Angela made the first move. That night before bed, she kissed her father, then her mother. She said to Mildred, her voice almost inaudible, "I'm sorry, Mama." Mildred gave her a sharp look, then took her hand. "You know I only want what's best for you, Angie. I don't want you making mistakes you can't fix."

"I know that, Mama."

"You go on to bed now, girl. I'll see you in the morning."

"OK, Mama." Angela stood stiffly for a moment. "I love you, Mama."

"Child, I know that. I love you too. Go on to bed now." Her daughter made her way up the stairs, an angel ascending.

In the morning, they found a rumpled, empty bed, this note on her pillow. "Dear Mama and Daddy, I know you want the best for me and you think that if I finish secretary school, that will be the best for me. But I need something bigger than that. Times are changing and I know I got to change with them. I will be safe. I have money and will find a place to stay. I'll write when I'm settled. Please don't come after me. I'll tell you where I'm going once I'm there. I'm grown now and I'll be all right. I know what I'm doing. Love, Angie."

20

THE MORNING THEY FOUND THAT NOTE, JOHNNY Lee stood, holding the schoolgirl sheet of notebook paper with its ripped spiral-bound edges and read it over and over, as if reading it closely enough would make it say something else. After a long time, he turned to Mildred and said, "Did you know she was gonna leave like this?"

Mildred thought of her daughter's resolute back going up the stairs, the feel of her soft cheek recoiling under the slap. "No. How on earth would I know that?"

He didn't move. "Well, now what we gon' do? She ain't nothing but a baby. We don't even know where she's gone."

"She's over eighteen. The law say she's a woman. We can't get her back. Just got to hope she call."

He crumpled the note. His shoulders drooped in on his chest. He seemed to have aged since they came into the room. "What's our girl gonna do out there alone? People gone crazy these days."

"No crazier than they ever been," she said.

He stared at her. Shook his head slowly, bearlike. "You ain't the woman I married. You done got so cold. Your own daughter gone, and you just as cold as ice."

But he was wrong. Her heart was crushed to dust. Again. She couldn't even tell him. It had been so very long since she had really talked to anyone. William took her voice away with him. For years now, her heart had been dust in her chest. The only time she felt alive was at the movies. Or looking at the book William had left her. And sometimes at night, standing in the yard while Johnny Lee slept, looking up at the riot of stars overhead.

It started on a night like that. After Angie left, she rarely slept more than three or four hours. She roamed the house like an old ghost, drinking warm milk and trying to sleep. Often, she found her feet leading her out to the backyard. Johnny Lee never woke up. He slept like the dead. She stood, sometimes for an hour at a time, gazing overhead, looking at the sky unobscured by smog. She remembered her mama's face looking up at the blue sky, her eyes wide and sightless. She remembered the way her daddy clutched her hand on the day he died. Each knuckle was as big around as a walnut. His hand felt like a claw, his eyes rimmed in navy blue around the dark brown. He said, lying there on his deathbed, "Don't you never trust a white man. They ain't never to be trusted. Never." Those were his last words. No matter how hard he tried to forgive, the last thought he ever had was how much they had hurt him. But sometimes Mildred didn't think at all. Just gazed heavenward, the air resting on her like a caress.

One night, on a whim, she went to her trousseau trunk and picked up the Lawrence book, brought it outside with her. There was a full moon, bright enough that she could see the paintings fairly well when she opened it. They had a silvery, mysterious sheen and seemed to rise out of the darkness at her. She sat for a long time with her favorite, the one that could be a church but that William had told her Lawrence said was a train packed with migrants. She sat, gazing at it, until she felt herself almost within it, breathing the colors, tasting the fried chicken from home on people's laps, their sweat rolling down her face in the hot, enclosed space. She sat so long that she didn't really feel like herself when she got up and went into the small work shed that Johnny

Lee used to use before Angela left, still holding the Lawrence book. She pulled a rickety stool up to the rough-hewn table he'd made and picked up a board he'd left there. She ran her hands over it for a while, knowing the wood. Coming to know it. There was an old can of red house paint on the shelf. She opened it, stirred it, found a skinny brush and made her first strokes across the wood. She didn't know what she was doing. Didn't have a plan. But it felt right. She took off her nightgown so she wouldn't stain it. Piled it onto the stool for padding, sat naked, painting, thinking of nothing but the colors in front of her, the flat, rough wood in her hand. She found some more paints, yellow, a blue she especially liked, a little white. She worked awkwardly, slowly, using the wide, difficult brushes until the light began to change and she knew she'd better get back into the house. Johnny Lee'd be up soon. She looked at what she'd done, the sprawled colors. It didn't look like much. But her heart felt just a little bit less like dust. The taste of ash was gone from the back of her tongue.

Carmen
Jones

1954

When Dorothy Dandridge makes her entrance in *Carmen Jones*, your breath stops like glass in your throat. It is the Negro division of a military base. There has been all this pseudo-operatic singing in the scenes before. It is ridiculous. But at the same time it is so thrilling to see all those brown faces together talking and laughing, the center of the image. Then, swinging in from the right side of the frame, a small, sure smile on her face, is Dorothy Dandridge. She looks like life itself. She looks like sex itself. She looks like she will never apologize for anything, never have anything to apologize for, bring only pleasure. You cannot see the way the world will hurt her. You can see only her splendor—those long legs, a butt you'll never forget wrapped in a tight red skirt, a sweetly sexy black V-necked blouse, and a red rose in her hands. She strides into that false cafeteria like it's a Michelin four-star restaurant. Every man in the room tries to talk to her, earn her favor. She just laughs, the rose spinning between her fingers. Then she looks straight at Harry Belafonte, her black eyes promising him every joy he has ever dreamed of. She opens her mouth to sing. And she is beautiful. There is no denying her. There is nothing ridiculous here.

Part III
TAMARA

21

I LOVED WATCHING MY MOTHER AND SHEILA GET ready on Oscar day. To the rest of the world it takes place at night, swathed in burnished flesh, glitter, and tulle. But for those of us who lived where it really happened, it was Oscar afternoon, Oscar day, the holiest Monday of the year. It still doesn't feel right to me that the Academy moved it to Sundays.

The day began early, always, with my mother making a call to my school saying I was sick. I could hear her through my door: "That flu just keeps going around, doesn't it, Miss MacGregor. Well, I certainly will make sure she gets some rest." She always laughed hard in her piping girlish way once she hung up the phone. Then she and Sheila started in on preparing Sheila's special-best strawberry pancakes, made from a recipe her neighbor Miss Clarissa gave her when she was a little girl. The making of the pancakes was one of the very few references Sheila ever made to having had any kind of life before her adulthood in Los Angeles. Oscar day was the only day of the year that Sheila and my mother cooked. The rest of my childhood, I survived on microwaved this-and-that and takeout food. They fussed around in the kitchen together, getting flour everywhere and giggling like they were little girls, not women past thirty. Sometimes it would get suddenly quiet. I figured that's when they were kissing. They did that a lot in front of me but told me to tell everyone they were just roommates and that Sheila was a big help with the rent. I obliged. I did whatever my mother asked.

It would have been easier, I think, if she hadn't asked me to lie. If she hadn't been so busy trying to lie to herself. I mean, who cared about a couple of middle-aged black lesbians or bisexuals or whatever they cared to call themselves in Los Angeles in the early 1980s? No one, that's who. They had no power. They had very little money; Sheila was the manager of the Avis office at LAX, and my mother was the receptionist for a plastic surgeon, for Pete's sake. Their lives didn't matter to anyone but me. They were the only parents I knew. But not being able to talk about who they were, acting as if it wasn't happening, that was the hard part. My mother was never a big one for the truth, and Sheila wasn't much better. She always seemed a bit shocked to be helping to raise me anyway. And the truth? The truth can be way too nerve-wracking.

I lay in bed, pretending to be asleep. They set great store in waking a surprised me up to a beautifully set table with a platterful of pancakes and slightly burnt bacon set in the middle of it. I usually woke up between 6:00 and 7:00 every morning, and Oscar morning was no exception. But to please them, I hid in my room, reading Archie comic books and issues of *Seventeen* and *Essence* that my mother bought for me. "A girl's never too young to start thinking about how to look good," my mother informed me grandly when she got me my own subscription to *Essence* when I was five. So I learned a lot about being a proud and beautiful and lissome soul sister from a very young age. Not too much of it took, though. My hair stayed unruly, fuzzy braids sticking up all over, even though my mother applied gallons of Ultra Sheen to my head, her hands like music in my hair. My dark legs stayed ashy no matter what combination of creams my mother attacked them with. My disposition stayed ungirlish, despite my mother's determined effort.

Anyway, after a while, they came in to get me, hands floury, wearing aprons they'd gotten from who knows where. My mother always had her earrings on by this time, her fade carefully picked out into squared-off perfection. She looked good even when she was cooking. "Come on, Tam. Oscar breakfast awaits!" I laughed and went out to the kitchen and was appropriately noisy in my appreciation of the many pancakes and the beautiful table. I always ate a little more than I wanted so that my mother would not feel her work had been wasted. But not so much that she'd say, "Dag, Tam. You better watch that. You don't want to blow up the way some of these girls out here is. You only a little girl, but you don't wanna get fat now. You'll never take it off." Gauging the correct number of pancakes to get the pleased reaction without the censure took some doing, but by the time I was seven I'd figured it out. Four and a half pancakes was just right. My mother and Sheila smiled at me.

Once we'd finished breakfast, at about 10:30 or so, it was time to get out the magazines. *People, Variety, Vogue, Essence, Seventeen.* They spilled around our tiny living room in glamorous profusion. Sheila and my mother settled down on the sofa and read each other occasional little bits and showed each other dresses they particularly liked for about forty-five minutes. I read my Archie comic again, twirling my feet, still wearing my pajamas. Then suddenly, always, as though it were a surprise, Sheila or my mother would squeal, "Damn, we gotta get ready." Then Sheila would jump up and put on some Earth, Wind and Fire, and they'd grab my hand and we'd dance around in a grooving, hip-shaking circle to "Serpentine Fire," and then my mother would scurry off to the bedroom to change while Sheila got out the tote bag that we always carried our Oscar-day picnic lunch in. I liked to go to the bedroom with my mother and try to figure out just how she did it. What magic lay in her pots and brushes and glossy tubes to make her so, so beautiful? She never minded me watching. She never focused on me too much anyway. I lay on the unmade bed she shared with Sheila, watching her work on her face. "Mama?"

"Yeah, baby?"

"Who you think's gonna win Best Picture this year?"

"I want *Tootsie* to win. But they don't always give it to funny movies. Dustin Hoffman was great in that, though."

"Mmm," I said, then grabbed my foot and stretched it over my head. "Yeah, it was funny, but I want *E.T.* to win. I like Henry Thomas."

"He was all right," she said absently. My mother would have loved to have a real house herself, but she didn't share my weakness for stories of suburban longing. She'd been living in the same small, battered two-bedroom with Sheila since before I was born. My affection for cinematic suburbia dated back to Oscar year 1980, when I was five. *Ordinary People* and *Raging Bull* were both nominated for Best Picture that year, and Mama had a rule that we had to see all the major nominees before the awards. I loved *Ordinary People*, even though I didn't quite understand it. All that repressed aching and those giant, clean rooms. *Raging Bull*, on the other hand, gave me nightmares for weeks. But I never questioned my mother's decision to take me to everything. How could I at five? I just went and let the pictures wash over me and learned to have opinions about them all. The night after night after night that I woke in terror, Robert De Niro's bloody gray face before me, I accepted as the price I had to pay for the reward of climbing into bed between my mama and Sheila and sleeping with Mama's languid arm thrown across me: "It's all right baby, it's all right. It's just a movie. Mama's here." Her sleepy voice soft in my ear. When I was older and in film school, I had to concede that *Raging Bull* was the better film, but I maintained a bone-deep fear of it that never left me.

She turned from the mirror, grinning, "But you know what it's really all about this year?"

"Louis Gossett, Jr!" We both shouted at the same time. She finished her face, and I started jumping up and down on their bed. "Cut that out, munchkin," she said, but like most of her attempts to discipline me, it was without force. I didn't require much discipline, though. When things bothered her, she just eased by them like they weren't there. I didn't want to become one of those bothersome things she glided past. I jumped two more times to make a point and then hopped off the bed. My eye fell onto the old-time photograph of a brown-skinned woman she kept on her bureau. I rarely entered her room without looking at it. "Mama, do you know *anything* about your grandma? You keep that picture there, but you won't never tell me anything about it."

"Girl, I done told you a million times, it ain't nothing to tell. She died before I was born. I just like it. My mama gave it to me, and it's about the only thing I got from back home. It wasn't *all* bad. And I like old-timey stuff sometimes." She concentrated on her hair.

"She looks like you," I said.

She looked at herself in the mirror for a long minute. "I know." She took a deep breath and then was all briskness. "Listen, you, so full of questions—go on and get dressed. Sheila must have that picnic about ready by now. We're leaving soon."

I ran into my room and put on the first things I picked up off the floor, a pair of jeans and a relatively clean pink T-shirt. I got my little Brownie camera too and brushed my teeth for two seconds. My hair was all right. Mama always rebraided it the night before the Oscars and made me sleep in a stocking cap so it was as fuzzless as it was ever going to get. When I came out, Mama was on the goldish-grayish sofa, smoking a cigarette and looking at the ceiling. She was wearing a short, tight, shiny lemon yellow dress. Her toenails and fingernails painted a gleaming bright red. She had on a pair of yellow strapped Candies. She looked at me absently. "You ready, munchkin? Good Lord, is that all you could find to wear?"

"Yep," I said.

She sucked her teeth. "Honestly. I don't know when you're gonna start caring about this kind of thing. It's *important*." She sat up, stubbed out her cigarette. I was used to her fussing. I sat down on the sofa next to her, knowing she'd be satisfied, or at least lose interest, after she'd tightened two or three of the beaded balls that hung from the ends of my braids. Once she'd done that, she grinned at me and put her feet up on the sofa, inviting me to entangle my legs with hers. She got out another cigarette. "Ooooh, blow some smoke rings, Mama," I squealed.

She laughed and made a few, her lips a perfect O as she sent the cloud-soft circles of smoke to the ceiling. I laughed too. Her legs were warm underneath mine. Just as the fourth ring drifted toward the ceiling, Sheila emerged from the bedroom, wearing skintight jeans and a low-cut purple blouse, her hair sleeked back into a chignon. She looked at my outfit quickly but didn't say anything. She went to the door and lifted the picnic basket.

My mother smiled at Sheila, her eyes softening the way they always did when she looked at her, the way that made me feel as though I was in the way of something. "Put that basket down, girl," she said, her voice a purr. "We need to get in the right mood first." She shoved my legs off her and went over to the small boxy record player. I loved playing with the latch on it, almost as much as I loved putting pencil holes through the smooth gold fabric that covered the speakers. She rooted through the albums and pulled out an old Michael Jackson. She put on the record and the music crackled to life: "Ben." She extended her hands to Sheila, and they started dancing.

Sheila and my mother slipped into an easy rocking rhythm together. I could hear cars passing by on the street outside as I lay and watched them. They never asked me to dance with them at moments like this. I don't know if they would have minded if I had just gotten up and joined in. But I wasn't that kind of kid. I wanted to be asked. They swayed through the room, laughing into each other's breath, forgetting I was even there. I closed my eyes for a minute and imagined I was with them, feeling my hips swaying, Michael Jackson's sweet soprano pouring into my ears like cream. But when I opened my eyes, my mother and my other mother were laughing and bumping hips, their arms around each other's waists, and Sheila said, "Girl, remember that time when . . . ," and my mother said, "I ain't never gonna forget it . . . ," and Sheila said, "Remember how he . . ." and trailed off with a quick look at me. And my mother said, "Yeah, I remember," and dropped her arm from around Sheila's waist and looked at her in a way that I somehow knew I wasn't supposed to see and danced slowly over to the ashtray to pick up the cigarette still burning there as the song trailed off. She looked at me and said, "Come on, Tam. It's time to go." Sheila picked up the picnic basket briskly, looking a little past me, the way she always did. "Yeah, little bit. It's time to go." I walked out of the apartment ahead of them, alone.

When we got to the Dorothy Chandler Pavilion, there were already a lot of people there. There were bleachers all along the red carpet. Quite a few people came from out of town and slept overnight under the scanty shelter. And then starting at about 8:00 in the morning, the real fanatics, like Autograph Al with his three bulging shopping bags of signed autograph books, arrived. My mother told me once that he had the signature of every best actor nominee going back to 1960. This seemed unimaginably long ago to me. Al looked every day of it, his hair gray and frizzled, his pale face scrubbed but still looking like a paper bag someone had crumpled and then flattened out, his coat a thousand miles of rutted road. As bad as he looked, the actors always obliged his nervous requests for a signature. It was considered bad luck not to give him your autograph. He was always glad to see us. "Look how big she's getting," he said every year, patting me on the head. I never understood it. Why was growing such a big deal to grownups? Hadn't they done it?

We found our places on the edge of the red carpet with the same little gang of people who came every year. I even had Oscar friends: Tessie and Bessie, blond twins from Omaha who came with their Goldie Hawn–ish single mother. We played Uno and Old Maid and pestered the grownups for drinks of water for the endless hours before the arrivals began. Around 12:30 when we got there, the security was pretty light. I liked to pretend that I was one of the nominees and walk up and down the sidewalk waving and blowing air kisses and pretending to be interviewed by Army Archerd. Mama usually just watched, laughing, but one time I got her to come out onto the path. It scared me, though. She looked like she was going to cry. She walked a few steps toward the hall, then stopped. I took my mother's hand. "You all right, Ma?" I said.

"I'm all right," she said, her voice a little ragged. "Just feels funny to stand here. All these people all around. Makes you think what it would really be like." She drew a deep breath. "I'm gonna go sit back down, all right, baby?"

"OK." I heard Tessie calling to me. "I'ma go over here, all right?" I asked my mother.

"All right," she said.

At about 3:00, everything changed. The carpet was rolled out. Large men in sunglasses and tight, dark suits with earpieces and hidden weapons began patrolling the area. All the people who had come to watch were pushed rudely to one side where the bleachers were. The limos began to arrive. And the din began.

Every year it was the same. Always so loud that the sound seemed to be inside me as much as it was outside. Always the long, long cars discharging their passengers, more angel than human. Mama held tight to my hand as though I might get swallowed up by the sound, and Sheila, who rarely touched me, kept her hand on my back the whole time. Because I was small, I could usually squeeze through to the front of the crowd to see who was coming in. My best spot so far was the year before this one; I saw Warren Beatty coming in when *Reds* was nominated. Unlike so many of the movie stars Mama and Sheila and I had seen, he was quite tall; so many of them were really short. He was beautiful. Mama had squeezed in just behind me and she gasped and tightened her grip on my hand as he passed within a few feet of them. "Girl, if you could have seen him in *Splendor in the Grass*. Good Lord," she murmured. I couldn't take my eyes off Mama's face. She looked the way a person might if she'd seen God. We stood, holding hands, staring at where he'd been for a long time after he left.

My mother especially liked actresses who weren't afraid to show off their bodies and wore a lot of sequins. "That girl really knows how to work it," she'd say in a satisfied, soothed tone after a particularly nice outfit came by. And this year, we had something extra-special to wait for. First was Richard Gere, whom I adored beyond all reasoning. I had been changed forever by his surly, sweet face in *An Officer and a Gentleman*. I saw only the back of his tux as he hustled by, but even that made my teeth ache with joy. But also, this year, thanks to that same movie, we had to look out for Lou Gossett. He was the first black man in forever to get nominated for a major award. As my mother and Sheila told me over and over and over again, it was our duty to turn out for the brother. When he got out of his limo, we would be there for him. So we were. Believe it or not, we got a good look at him. Sheila and my mom kicked their shoes off for better jumping leverage. "Go 'head, Lou. We here for you! You know you deserve it! Go on, Lou." That kind of thing, at the top of their lungs. So loud and determined in fact, that he turned and offered them a broad, perfect smile. Though I was mortified by their screaming, I couldn't help but be charmed by that smile. And they were both struck into grinning, girlish silence for a moment. "Good luck, Lou," my mom finally said softly at his retreating form. We left not long after that. What else were we gonna see that was as good? And that evening, when he won his prize for Best Supporting Actor, the first black man ever to win that award, all three of us sat around our ritual bowl of popcorn, them with their ritual glasses of Zinfandel and me with my ritual glass of sparkling cider, and after we all stopped crying, we raised our glasses in a toast. It was the best Oscar night ever.

22

THERE WAS ALWAYS ONLY THE THREE OF US. NO
one came from anywhere. Not anywhere that they remembered fondly anyway. The only thing I ever heard Sheila say
about her life before Los Angeles was "I was born in Chicago
and my mama died a drunk and Lord help me if I ever go back
there again." My mother was much the same. When I asked her
where Tulsa was, she sucked her teeth and said, "Oklahoma.
Nowhere near here. That's all you need to know, Tam." And
when I was six and she picked me up from a visit to my friend
Ruby's, a whole house in Los Feliz, with two sofas and an orange
tree in the backyard and loud with grandmas and uncles and
brothers and sisters and a mother and a daddy, I asked her,
"Where's the rest of our family? How come I don't have a daddy?"
She didn't answer for a long time. Then, twirling the back of her
hair, she said, "You got a daddy. Everybody does. Can't get born
without one. But he ain't the one raising you. Sheila and I are
doing that." Then she swung into the next lane and she wasn't
going to say one more thing about it. I knew when she was done
talking. But I kept wondering. Where were the rest of us? No
grandmother to cluck over me. No uncle pulling up in a purple lowrider after school for the girls to giggle at. No brother or
sister to roll my eyes at in contempt for his or her stupidity or to

worship from afar. No father to fear or adore or complain about. The three of us might have been born from the desert soil.

On holidays when there was no school, I often went with my mother to Dr. Gillespie's office, where she worked as a receptionist. Dr Gillespie was plastic surgeon to those who wanted to be stars. He adored my mother. I guess that's why he tolerated me hanging around the office as much as I did. His clientele was, by and large, nervous and wildly optimistic, sure that if they got the right look, the life-changing role would come next. My mother was always very at ease and jokingly authoritative with them. Later, I realized she practically had been one of them before I was born, sure that fame was just around the corner. She had to wear a white smock with her name pinned on it, but she always pulled it into a waist-hugging shape with a chain belt across the back and took pains with her hair and shoes so that even in that style-free outfit, she stood out. The prettiest girl in the room. I brought books with me and paper and tried to be quiet and good. It was hard, though. It was so boring.

On the day I'm talking about, I was nine. We had been at the office only about forty-five minutes when the phone rang and, rather than putting it through to the doctor or taking on her usual brisk yet soothing tone, her voice took on the southern softness that it only had when she talked to me or to Sheila. "Hi, Sheila, what is it?" "What? When? And they called you? Yeah, I know you hadn't left for work yet . . . No I never did. OK. OK. I will. We'll talk about it tonight. Right. Right. OK. Bye." She hung up the phone and leaned forward onto the desk, her fingers pressing hard into her eyes.

"Mama, what is it? What's wrong?"

She looked up at me. Her eyes shone with tears. I'd never seen that before. "What is it, Mama?" She wheeled her office chair over toward me, pulled me onto her lap, which frightened me more, even as it comforted me.

"Oh, baby girl . . . my father died. Your grandfather. I didn't
. . . you know we don't see each other much. Not at all." She
reached up and wiped her eyes. "You never even met him, did
you? Well . . . well . . . anyway, he died and . . . that makes me
sad. Sheila was just leaving for work when Jolene called."

"Who's Jolene?"

She laughed shortly. "Listen, Tam. I got a lot to tell you later,
but we can't talk about it now. I'll tell you . . . I'll tell you some
things I should have told you a long time ago when we get
home." She lifted me off her lap, brisk and businesslike again.
"The waiting room's full. I gotta get these people in to see Dr.
Gillespie." I went back to my book, but I kept snatching looks at
her. Who was this Jolene? And Mama had a daddy and she didn't
even go *see* him? I'd have killed for one.

I seethed quietly the rest of the day. I wrote and drew and did
my homework and read *Harriet the Spy* for the eight millionth
time. (My mother didn't understand it with me and books, but
I didn't care. They were my life. Them and the movies.) Mama,
for her part, after her brief show of emotion in the morning, resumed the day with the same gotta-get-it-done attitude that she
always had. There were patients to get in and out of the office, in-
surance forms to be dealt with, nervous breast implant patients to
be calmed. Air Supply played soothingly on the sound system she
controlled. The air conditioner hummed. I thought we'd never
get to go home.

Finally, the day ended. She had just lit her cigarette and
turned the key in the ignition when I asked again. "Who's Jolene,
Mama?"

"She's my sister. Your aunt."

"I have an aunt?"

"Yes. You do. In Tulsa, where I'm from."

"Then what do I need Sheila for?" It just came out. I couldn't
believe it. It just came out.

Mama gazed at me, her eyes narrowed against the smoke. She

reminded me of Claude Rains's mother in *Notorious* (we had just rented it the weekend before), with that same hard, hard look. "Sheila isn't for you. She isn't your aunt. She's . . . she's important to me. She's our family."

"OK," I said in a small voice. "But I got an aunt in Tulsa?"

"Yes, you do. And a grandmother and grandfather and an uncle and a few cousins. You had a grandfather. His name was Johnny Lee Edwards. He was a pharmacist. I . . . well . . ." She took a long, shuddering drag of her cigarette and nosed the car into the next lane.

"Am I gonna get to meet them? Grandma and all, I mean."

"We'll see."

Sheila always got home later than we did, working all the way out at the airport and her hours being 10:00 to 6:00 and usually more like 7:00. When she got home that night, she held Mama tightly for a long time, and said, "Well, Angie, what you gonna do?"

"I don't know. Let's talk about it later." So we watched *Miami Vice,* and they smoked and sipped wine, and I was sent to bed and I could hear their voices late into the night. "You ought to go, Angie."

"I don't know, Sheil. He . . . they didn't ever approve of me living out here. And what would I say about you? I don't want to go back there."

"But he's your father."

"I'll send a note. We can't afford it anyway." Then silence. I drifted to sleep. I never found out what else they said. I never found out how my mother made the decision she did. But the next day my mother made me sign a flowery sympathy card in which she had written this: "I'm sorry I couldn't come. I just couldn't afford it right now. Daddy was a good man and you all have my love." She put in a school picture of me and a snapshot of the two of us together—no Sheila. She let me open the slot of the mailbox to put it in. I did. I always loved doing that. But as I did, I vowed that if I ever found *my* daddy, I wouldn't ever let him go. I would be at his funeral when he died, no matter how much it cost, even if it was $250 or something (I thought that was an insane amount of money at the time). If I ever got hold of the least crumb of information about him, I would never let him go.

23

B Y THE TIME I WAS ELEVEN, THE WAYS I DIFFERED from my mother were set as hard as stone. My mother loved the surfaces of things, how they looked. I wanted to know about the speed of images, how to capture them and make them mine. She'd live with broken switches and blown light bulbs for months rather than attempt even the simplest home repair. She couldn't fathom my longing to be behind the camera, to be the one who makes the picture, not the one in it. But I didn't mind. I liked to keep things at a distance. Machines were more trustworthy. I always knew what was going on inside them, or I could find out if I examined them intently enough. They behaved the same way no matter what I did. Once when I was six, while my mother was in the shower and Sheila was out, I pulled a chair over to our kitchen counter, dragged our toaster oven down by the cord, and, using a screwdriver I found in a drawer, completely disassembled it before she got her mascara on. As she stepped out of our tiny bathroom, resplendent as always, I looked up from a sea of small metal parts, two gears in my hands. I smiled. I had never been so content; at last I could see inside an object and find out what made it work.

From the time I was about seven, Mama's favorite thing to do was to come home from the video store with a box or two under her arm and announce grandly, "Let's watch Mommy tonight!" The three of us ate pizza and popcorn and drank Dr. Pepper, and Sheila and my mother took turns covering my eyes during the really sexy parts and the worst gun battles. They laughed a lot too, remembering. So much sometimes that they forgot to cover my eyes. And they sat right up next to each other, their legs touching, their eyes shining. It wasn't long before I knew all the films by heart, Mama's favorites of the movies she'd appeared in: *Coffy* (third girl from the left who got her dress ripped off in the fight scene). *Cleopatra Jones* (an extra in the airport scene; "I named you after her, baby," Mama invariably shrieked as Tamara Dobson, who played Cleopatra, strode onto the screen). *Street Fighting Man* (dancing in a G-string and no top on the bar in the bar scene). *No Way Back* (she was onscreen for almost ten minutes and had a couple of lines). The movies were loud, confusing, and violent. I got used to them, but I never really liked them much. So much screaming and shooting, and the women were always naked. My own mother was always naked. It was embarrassing. I never asked her about that. What was I gonna say? How weird it was to see my mother rolling and screaming, naked, in a movie? Or ask her how it felt to have Pam Grier rip off her dress? I couldn't ask that. I let her think it didn't bother me.

One time as she was putting me to bed after a movie, she sat on the edge of my bed for a minute and briefly ran her hand over my forehead. It made me feel bold enough to ask a question. "Mama?"

"Yeah, Tam?"

"Was my daddy in the movies?"

Her eyes got big and tearful. I was terrified. "As much as I was, I suppose," she said after a long time. "Not that much." The tears never fell. "He didn't want to be a daddy. And I . . ." She trailed off. I could have asked a million more questions. They were all in my throat, choking me. She gazed past me, absently twirling the hair at the back of her neck. When she started doing that, I knew better than to keep asking. Here was another thing we'd never talk about. "Well, we do all right without him," she said eventually.

"Yes, Mama."

"You go on to sleep now." She got up and left but paused to look at me again before she went out. "I love you, Tam."

"I love you too, Mama."

I probably didn't fall asleep for an hour after that, holding the words in my mouth, hearing them hum in my ears. I could count on one hand the number of times she'd ever said them.

Not long after this, Mama took me to see *She's Gotta Have It*. Typical. The movie is filled with absolutely explicit sex, adult jokes, adult concerns, a rape scene — why wouldn't you take an eleven-year-old? I never questioned her decisions about movies, and after *Raging Bull* when I was five I stopped being frightened by them. Movies were what we did, so I learned to enjoy whatever we saw. I'm grateful now. If I'd been afraid during *She's Gotta Have It*, I never would have learned what I did. If I'd been trying to understand what all the grownups were laughing at, I never would have been able to study the speed of the editing during the men-are-dogs montage. If I'd allowed myself to have any feelings at all when Jamie attacks Nola near the film's ending, I might not have been struck by the beauty of the lighting when Nola sits in her bed surrounded by candles. If I'd given in to my embarrassment as all the lovers in the movie took their clothes off and licked each other in slow (or fast) motion, I wouldn't have been able to admire the full-color ballet in the middle (yeah, it looks ridiculous now, but oh, I thought it was so beautiful then). I was young, but I knew something was going on. I could not have articulated it, but the energy, all the heart that went into making that movie, leapt off the screen, unassailable. All those black people the point of the movie, not the sidekicks or the dupes or just plain absent. I'd never seen that before. Well, that's not true. I'd seen it in my mother's old movies, but they were so . . . I didn't know the word. They weren't alive the way this film was. I couldn't articulate it then, but now I know what the difference was. In my mother's movies, no one paid the slightest attention to craft. Everything was just thrown at the lens as fast as possible. Beauty had no place there. Neither did reality. Speed was the only virtue. But there was something in *She's Gotta Have It* that was just plain true. I could tell by all the excited, recognizing laughter of the grownups. And it was beautiful. I could hear it in my mother's laughter. And as Nola sashayed down what I later learned was the Fulton Mall in Brooklyn, hips swinging, Jamie following right behind her, my mother squeezed my hand. Yeah, I knew something was going on. I asked for a video camera, but I didn't get it until a year later, for my twelfth birthday. It must have taken her that long either to get the money together or decide I wasn't getting over this.

I started out filming everything. I tried to create images like those I saw. As you can imagine, this didn't work out right away. But I kept trying. And my moviegoing got a little crazed. Before, I mostly went with Mama to see whatever she wanted. But now I was reading books of film history the way the girls at my school read *Seventeen*. I started making requests—well, more like demands. It wasn't a problem, though. My mother would take me to anything. We went to any old revival that I asked her to go to. I saw *Mean Streets, Badlands, Days of Heaven, The Godfather*—everything good from the 1970s—by the time I was sixteen. I made my mother take me to the library every week for more and more complex books about filmmaking. I started wearing a baseball cap my every waking hour. I railed at the limitations of natural light. My mother rolled her eyes, convinced I was a changeling.

When I was twelve, most days I came home after school not to our apartment but to Miss Tillie's house. Miss Tillie was an elderly neighbor who watched me and four other children after school for a few dollars an hour. Boring was not the word for it. It was a desert of tedium that I traversed each afternoon without complaint only because I knew that my mother and Sheila needed me not to mind, and though I never would have admitted it I was a little frightened to stay home by myself. Miss Tillie's smelled like a thousand cats and all the various sweet potions and sprays and failed deodorizers that she had used over the years to make it seem as though there weren't a thousand cats. I spent as much time as possible in the backyard, as did the other children she watched, Tracey, Shakira, LaTasha, and Darnell (the only boy). They were all younger than me, eight and nine years old. They always had runny noses and never wanted to do anything out back except fill their lungs with life-giving, cat-free oxygen so that they could go back inside to watch television. Once I got my video camera, they blossomed, in my mind, into the perfect cast for my first feature. Miss Tillie didn't care what we did as long as we didn't draw blood or break anything. And her backyard, overgrown and full of fruit trees run rampant, was ideal for my script, *The Jungle Chase*. So with Angela and Miss Tillie's permission (and the amused permission of the other children's parents), shooting began on March 15, 1988.

Tracey and LaTasha had to hide behind a hydrangea bush for the first scene. Darnell and Shakira were supposed to chase them. I was forced to referee my first actor's dispute when they fought over who would wear the pith helmet I had picked up at a yard sale. There was only one, which I had thought might be a problem, but I also thought that it gave a nice touch of authenticity to the scene. In the end, I made like a director and decreed that Darnell could wear the hat in the first scene and Shakira would wear it in the second. This led to some pouting from Shakira, but I bought her off with the promise of an extra close-up and two Milky Ways, to be paid the next day. Tracey and LaTasha were inhabitants of a tribe of people who were unaware of the existence of humans beyond their jungle (I had seen a PBS special about a tribe like this, and I was dazzled by the idea).

Darnell spoke first. "Look there, I think I see some of the elusive members of the Hantomami tribe" was what he was supposed to say. What he said was, "I want to wear the hat for both scenes." I turned off the camera, furious. "Look, Darnell, we've gotta share the hat. It's the only one we have. You getting to wear it now, right?"

"Yeah, but I like it. I want to be like Indiana Jones, where it never comes off."

"Well, this isn't Indiana Jones," I said. I felt tears, sharp and vital, at the back of my eyes, but I'd be damned before anyone got to see them.

"Well, I'm not going to be in your stupid movie, then. I'm gonna go watch cartoons. Come on, y'all. *Teenage Mutant Ninja Turtles* is on anyway." They all followed Darnell into the house, LaTasha throwing a quick apologetic look my way.

I stood clutching my bulky camera at my side, staring at the space where my cast had stood. Being a director was going to be considerably harder than I had imagined. But there had been that crystalline moment when I was looking through the camera, and LaTasha and Tracey were still, clutching each other's hands. The light filtered through LaTasha's hair and it looked as though it was lit from within. The image was under my control. I could make them look as beautiful or as ugly as I wanted to. My heart hammered behind my breastbone, and then they dropped hands and the moment was gone. But I'd held them in my hands for that minute. And they were perfect. I sighed and followed everyone into the house, my heart slowing as I walked. I felt a little better when I remembered that I had my copy of *Spike Lee's Gotta Have It* with me. I thought maybe I'd read that.

This story makes me sound like a real film geek. Here's a secret: most filmmakers are kind of geeky, even if well dressed. I include myself in that, of course. For all the cultural currency of the job, most of it is an incredible obsession with ridiculous amounts of detail, an ability to watch the same thing over and over and over and over without the slightest lessening of interest, very neat handwriting, and a love of machinery. Look under Steven Spielberg's cap, and behind the dollar signs, and what do you see? A lonely suburban kid with thick glasses and a bad haircut who sat in the back of the classroom, doodling in a notebook. And Spike? My man Spike? Do you think anyone that short, wearing those glasses, with those skinny, skinny legs, ever — I mean *ever* — had a date at Morehouse? You do the math. But we see things. Other things. The elongated, odd angle of Anthony Perkins's neck in that scene in *Psycho* as he leans over the desk to talk to the private detective played by Martin Balsam. Or the glow of the boxing ring in *Raging Bull*, that the soft gray against the knife-edge black against the pure white of the floor in the foreground. Or those hayfields of light in *Days of Heaven*. I wanted to be one of the company who saw things, even if they were a bunch of nerdy guys.

But I was only twelve. And black. And a girl. A girl not much like the other girls in my middle school. And you know that's never good. West Hollywood Middle School in 1988 was in the grip of what was left of *Flashdance* fever. All the girls had enormous hair and sweatshirts falling off of one shoulder and leg warmers covering tight Gloria Vanderbilt jeans. They chewed a lot of gum and thought Scott Baio was the cutest. We weren't separated by money. Most of the other kids' parents had jobs like my mama's and Sheila's; they were the valet parkers, the hospital workers, the waiters and waitresses, the hotel clerks. Like my mama, they were gonna be something else once, a long time ago maybe. But not anymore. Part of the problem was that I was one of very few black kids in the school; it was mostly white and Hispanic. Whether it was race or just my stubborn difference, I don't know. But they wouldn't leave me alone.

I talked to my mother about it only once. It hadn't been a particularly bad day—it was just the day I couldn't take any more. It was just the day I couldn't keep my mouth shut and my head up. Mama picked me up from Miss Tillie's in the little orange Volkswagen that she and Sheila had owned since before I was born. My chest was tight from the sobs squeezed beneath my ribs. They leapt out of me as soon as I got into the car. I didn't even push aside the gum wrappers and pot seeds and rolling papers that always littered the front seat. I sat on them. My head was on fire.

"Baby, what is it? Somebody do something to you at Miss Tillie's today?" My mother got out a cigarette quickly. She always did that when I needed something. I grew up with the smell of smoke in my hair. I still kind of like it. I hitched and sobbed and snuffled a few times and finally choked out the story of how Toni Evans and Diana Perez had knocked over my lunch tray not once but twice and said my mama was a dyke and I must be too until it became apparent that I simply wasn't going to be allowed to eat lunch and so I was starving and if I cried in front of them they'd be even meaner and the teacher wouldn't do anything and I was so hungry and why were they so mean. Why were they so mean? I couldn't stop crying.

My mother took a long pull on her cigarette and stared out the window. "Baby, I don't know. I don't half know why people act the way they do." She touched the back of my neck tentatively. "But I know you can't let them get you down. You can't let them stop you. I kept going toward what I wanted 'til I just had to stop. Just had to. You hardheaded, just like me. I never did fit into Tulsa, not for one minute. But I just stood it until I could leave. You gonna have to stand it too." She took another long drag. I was silent. "Sheila and me. I don't know. We . . . She's always been there for me, since before you were born. If that makes me a dyke, then maybe I am, even though I see these people on TV sometimes and I can't hardly say I'm like them. I'm not. We've just got each other and we do what we can. That's the best we can do." She blew some smoke rings and smiled a little. "You used to love when I did that. But you're growing up. I wish I could make it easier for you. But I can't. Can't always get what you want in this life. But you gotta live it the best way you know how anyways. You know?" I nodded. "Just flip them girl's trays first next time you see them. They'll leave you alone after that. Listen," she said suddenly, "this is kind of perfect, but Sheila's gotta work late, and they're showing *The Breakfast Club* down at the dollar show at the Pavilion. Wanna go? Just you and me. Girls night out."

I took a deep breath. *The Breakfast Club*, which we'd seen three times when it first came out, was one of our favorites. We even agreed about its virtues, which was rare. She hadn't helped me figure out what to do. She never did. It'd be nice to sit next to her in the dark with a big old bucket of popcorn, though. I always loved the feel of her leg next to mine. "Sure, Mama. That'd be great."

"Great. I'll get you a hot dog too. You must be starving. Those little bitches."

I looked out the window. "Yeah, Mama. I am pretty hungry." The lights outside were just beginning to pierce the dusk all around us. I wondered if I had the nerve to flip over Toni Evans's lunch tray. I thought about Ally Sheedy. "That'd be good." Beside me, my mother smoked and drove. Just the two of us, going to the movies.

24

EVER SINCE TAM WAS LITTLE, SHE HAD POSSESSED the ability to get under Angela's skin like nobody's business. She was the kind of a kid who wanted to know everything, for one thing. Everything that Angela didn't know how to answer. How things worked, where her daddy was, what was going on with Sheila, why Angela wasn't in movies anymore. "Hell, I don't know" was Angela's answer to most of these questions. And she felt the weight of each word. Hell. It was hell. It was hell not knowing. It was hell never understanding why she didn't get what she wanted when so many women who were not as pretty, not as willing, not as keen, got to make it in the pictures. It was hell once she decided to have the baby and came back to Sheila and they stood over the crib at night, together, looking at the wailing bundle inside and trying to figure out what in God's name was going on. "Look, Angie. I gotta be at the club at eight. I gotta get some sleep. You figure out what to do," said Sheila. Then she walked out of the room and went to bed. And Angela didn't know. Couldn't Sheila see that she didn't know? She rocked, she walked, she gave bottles and burped, and sometimes it worked and sometimes it didn't and there was no logic to it. Tamara, her beautiful, maddening little Tamara, was impervious to logic. She was just a baby.

Things got better after Sheila quit the club. She came home late one morning, saw Angela on the sofa with the baby, sat down heavily next to them, and said, "You know those old bags at the club that you see still squeezing into that goddamn costume, and we used to say, 'Oh man, that's pathetic, don't let that happen to me.' Well, I'm just about there. Time to move on. Ain't no movie stars around here." Angela, still in her bathrobe at 10:00 A.M., unshowered and covered with spit-up, had to agree.

They never said what they were doing. They never *decided* what they were doing. They just did it. That was how they'd always lived. They got in bed together every night, sleeping spoon-style, got up together every day. Sheila paid rent and managed things until Tam was old enough for daycare, and then Angela got a job too, but they never said, *This is a family. We are each other's loves. We belong with these other women we've been hearing about, these lesbians.* They both kept going out on dates with men at first—guys at the advertising agency where Angela first worked and then later at the doctor's office, and guys at the rental car office where Sheila landed. But then those same guys would meet the other woman and hear about the daughter and gradually put one and one and one together and hit the road. Neither Sheila nor Angela really minded. They had each other. And Tam kept getting bigger. Eventually, they stopped giving their numbers out.

Rafe called one night when Tam was about ten. She was already asleep, thank God. Angela was laid out on the sofa half watching *The Trouble with Angels,* which she'd rented out of sentiment. Sheila was out with a friend. She nearly dropped the phone at the sound of his voice. "Rafe? Rafe? What the hell?"

"It's me, Angie. I know it's been a long time. How you been?"

"I been all right. Well . . . yeah. I'm OK. How'd you get this number?"

"You're still listed, sweetheart. I just . . . I just haven't had the nerve to call before now. Are you still in the business?"

Angela laughed shortly. "Me? No, no I'm not still in the business. The business got sick of us. Didn't you notice?"

Rafe laughed too. "I surely did. I own a little store down on Crenshaw now. Health food, vitamins, stuff like that. Trying to help people get healthy."

"Really?" Her hand spun in the hair at the back of her head.

"Yeah. It's good. It's a good life." He paused. "Listen, Angie. I know things didn't end . . . well. They didn't end well. But I think about that baby every day. What . . . what happened?"

"Well, she ain't a baby anymore." Angela couldn't breathe properly, but she got the words out. "She's asleep in the other room. She's ten now. Her name's Tamara."

"Tamara," he breathed. "That's beautiful. Tamara."

They were both silent for a few long moments. Finally Rafe spoke. "And what about you? Are you . . . is Sheila still around?"

"Yes. She's still around. We're . . . we're still friends."

"Friends like you were before?"

"Yes," she whispered. Why did she feel so funny?

"Well . . . that's all right. I . . . I thought you would be. You two were always kind of special together. The prettiest girls in show biz." He laughed thinly. "Really, girl, I wish you all the best. I don't . . . Could I meet her some time?"

Angela's hand froze in her hair. "Who?"

"Tamara."

"You want to meet her?"

"Yeah."

"Ten years go by, and then you want to meet her?"

"Yeah."

"Uh, no, my brother. Not this way. I don't think that's a good idea. Not at all."

Rafe backed down immediately. "Well . . . I guess I ain't been there. Can't expect you to be happy about having me trying to jump in at this point. But I'm gonna give you my phone number and address and all. You keep it. And when she wants to know. You tell her that she can come to me if she wants to." He stopped. When he spoke again, his voice was ragged with tears. "I'd like to meet my daughter." He gave her the information. She wrote it down. She put it away in the box where she kept special things. She went to bed with Sheila that night without a word. But she didn't forget the way his voice broke when he said "my daughter," either. So she kept the number. Every time Tamara asked about him, she said something like, "I met him through the business, but he's gone now." Then she'd stop talking. Sometimes she thought about the way he used to look at her, the way he used to touch her. He was the only man she'd ever really loved, but it turned out that a man's love wasn't what she needed. Sometimes she thought she ought to tell Tamara that. Or at least tell her that she knew where he was. She might want to know. So she thought about it. Sometimes.

25

W HEN RODNEY KING GOT BEAT DOWN LIVE AND in color, I was seventeen. That's when I started to truly know the power of an image. The tape was everywhere. Everywhere. Mama and Sheila and I didn't pay too much attention to the news, but you didn't have to watch the news to see that tape. It was the air we breathed that spring.

The night of the verdict, Mama got home after I did. I was sitting in front of the TV. I couldn't look away, and I was too scared to move until she came in. As she walked through the door, I jumped up and hugged her like I hadn't since I was little. "Mama, none of those cops got found guilty and people are burning up South Central." I was crying.

"What?"

"Come see." She sat next to me and we watched for a while, the words stricken out of us. "Damn," she finally said. "Damn. I guess them old folks back home were right."

"Right about what?"

"Oh, nothing you need to worry about. Something that happened in Tulsa a million years ago. Damn." She turned back to the TV. The video played silently again. Again. "Mama, didn't the jury see this?"

"Sure they did, Tam."

"Well, then how could they decide what they did?"

"I don't know, Tam. White people . . ." She trailed off. "White people always funny about this stuff. They always stick together. Can't trust 'em, even when you think times have changed. That's . . . that's what my daddy always said." I knew she was truly rattled then. She hadn't mentioned her father since that long-ago time when we didn't go to his funeral.

She didn't make me go to bed that night. There'd be no school in the morning. When Sheila came home she sat right down without a word next to us in front of the television. We watched the city burn until night eased toward day. Then we fell asleep like puppies, curled up uncomfortably on the sofa, the television's colored lights playing restlessly across our faces.

I was the first to wake up. There was a slight smell of smoke in the room, not just Mama and Sheila's old cigs but the smell of buildings burning. My first thought, unbidden, was, *I should go down there with my camera.* I know, I know, I was only seventeen—but that's the kind of seventeen-year-old I was. Mama woke up, rubbing her eyes and pushing at her hair, just a minute after I did. "Tam? Tam, baby, you all right?"

"Yeah, Mama. I'm all right. We all musta fell asleep right here."

She smiled ruefully. "Yeah, I guess we did. Well, I'm glad we were all together."

"Yeah." I paused. "Listen, Mama. I want to go down there. Down to South Central and film some of it. I think somebody ought to. Can I take the car?"

Her eyes got huge. "What?"

"Can I take the car? It's good practice to film something like this, Mama. I'll be careful."

"Little girl, you have truly lost your mind if you think I'm gonna let my seventeen-year-old daughter go get shot at by a bunch of crazy niggers while she carries around her little camera.

You have truly lost your mind." She paused, and then her indignation reared up again. "You see they ain't too discriminating
who they beating up. No, honey, your little narrow butt is staying
right here today. Out your goddamn mind." She started digging
around in her bag for a cigarette.

"Mama—"

"Not another word. Look. I know . . . people get killed in shit
like this. They told me about it. My mama and daddy . . . well,
not them . . . but in town, everybody knew. I used to go to the
movies in a theater that was built up from where one got burnt to
the ground in some shit like this. No. That's the end of it." When
Sheila woke up a few minutes later, we weren't speaking.

I was furious. But I knew she had me beat. I could have tried
to take the car keys or something, but really, I was scared. There
was one little corner of me that was relieved. Finally she was acting like she cared what I did. But after that long day of watching
the city burn, I brought my camera out from under my bed where
I kept it and I held it and I thought. I thought about what pictures
could do. What they could do if you weren't afraid.

When I told my mother how film school worked, I thought she'd
have a stroke. "You pay?" she screamed. "You pay all that money
to go there and then you have to pay for everything on top of that?
You are out your goddamn mind." I never did tell her that thesis
films can run upwards of $50,000. I never did tell her that if you
ain't got the money, you have to get your friends to crew for you
and actors to work for free and eat nasty fried chicken and just
save money any goddamn way you can.

And on so many days, I wondered if she wasn't right, if I wasn't
out my goddamn mind. I had gotten through college (nothing
fancy, just a community college in LA) on a scholarship and
worked shitty jobs for years and years saving up and borrowed a
ridiculous amount of money for NYU and there I was.

My third year began after September 11. Even with the city going insane, I could think only of what it would take to finish. I had to finish. The women were dropping off the directing track of the program like flies. Film school was kicking their asses. They were fleeing to producing, screenwriting, anything but directing. There were hardly any black people left either. Just white-boy filmmakers. They were so sure, so unbelievably sure that the way they understood the world was the way the world was. They were very loud. I had to be small and still and solid just to bear it.

When Colin came in to film production class the first day, we hardly could have missed each other—we were two flies in a sugar bowl, as my mother might have said. He was the last student to come in, and he stood at the door as though he were looking for something special, some particular seat. Then he saw me and came and sat right down. He had dreadlocks the color of wet sand and a scattering of freckles across his nose. "Anybody sitting here?" he asked.

"No." I was smiling and thinking that his eyebrows were oddly light against his medium-brown skin.

"Then I guess I am." He swung his book onto the desk next to mine and made himself at home, smiling back at me. I thought about what it might feel like to kiss him and have my tongue tease the little gap between his front teeth. I wondered how we'd managed not to meet each other before. He spoke: "I'm Colin Walsh. Which *Imitation of Life* do you like better? The Stahl or the Sirk?"

I laughed and said, "I'm Tamara Edwards and I love the Sirk. But I've only read about the other. I'm from LA. I've haven't had a chance to go to Yale and check out the Stahl."

A slight smile crossed his lips. I'd passed the test. "Well, the Sirk's better anyway. My dad teaches at Yale. He got me into the library so I've seen the other one. Fredi Washington's all right, but . . . you gotta give it up for Doug. That boy was all that and a bag of chips."

"Sho' you right," I said. We grinned at each other foolishly. I didn't think he was arrogant. I don't know why.

Then as the professor came in, Colin turned suddenly stern. His eyes were the color of rocks underwater. "Have coffee with me after class." It wasn't a question. So I did.

That coffee was the first of a thousand others we had in a thousand coffee shops. All we did for weeks was talk movies, though I never did stop looking at that little gap in his teeth. We talked about Spike Lee and Oscar Micheaux and Dorothy Dandridge and Charlie Kaufman and Martin Scorsese and Jane Campion and Robert Altman and Todd Haynes and Douglas Sirk and what was playing on Fourteenth Street. We talked about the merits of documentary versus narrative. When we weren't talking we were at the movies and then talking about the movies we went to. One night, we had just come out of *Citizen Kane* at the Film Forum and we were sitting at the bar at Brothers, nursing beers and arguing good-naturedly about the similarities of the opening shots in *Rebecca* and *Citizen Kane*. Our thighs touched under the bar and neither of us moved away. I decided not to acknowledge it. Not to move away, but not to acknowledge it. He was talking and I was watching him talk, his voice velvet in my ear, his leg warm against mine, when all of a sudden he was kissing me and I was free to inch my tongue into that little space I'd been eyeing for so long. My hand slid to the back of his neck, his hand slid gently up my back under my shirt—not too far, but enough so that I could feel him touching my skin. After a while, we stopped and looked at each other, our legs entangled. "I was kind of hoping you'd do that first," he said. "I mean it's not the traditional way, but I don't know . . . I thought you might."

"I don't start stuff like that," I said. "Too risky."

"Do you finish things like that?"

"I try to." I traced his lower lip with my finger. *I want to finish this*, I thought. But I couldn't say it.

"Come home with me." I leaned into him again, feeling dizzy

that someone so beautiful wanted me. We kissed for a long time. Colin finally said, "Let's get out of here." And we blew a ridiculous amount of money on a cab back to Brooklyn and made out the whole way, his hand finally, finally sliding under my bra so that I thought I might cry, and when we got in the house it was almost like a movie. He backed me up against the big *Super Fly* poster on his door and undid my pants and kissed me and did things with his hands until I couldn't stand it anymore and was grabbing at him and saying his name over and over and that's when I knew. This was someone I might love, someone who might let me love him. I was petrified.

After a while, we eased up from the floor, laughing, and he took my hand and led me into his room. His bed was made with a beautiful mud print quilt. The room was hung with framed movie posters (one of them from *Coffy*, which made me think of my mother) and smelled faintly of incense. On the bookcase were a clutter of photographs of him with his smiling brown-skinned family. He had sepia and faded black-and-white photos of relatives from way back too. "Who're all these people?" I said, walking over to the bookcase and picking up a picture of him with a prosperous-looking couple, who must have been his parents. Melted-down candles sat in front of the photos.

"The clan." He smiled and reached to turn down the sheets. "Going all the way back. I like to keep them around."

I was silent. The only photo in my room was a still from *Sweet Smell of Success*. No clan. No history. And I never made my bed. Colin came over and embraced me from behind. My stomach hit my shoes. This wasn't a moment to talk about our families. He kissed me, hard and longingly. I had never been so happy. Isn't that corny? It was the happiest moment of my life.

26

TAMARA KEPT HER HAIR IN A SHORT, BUSINESSLIKE natural. She got it cut at a barbershop. She didn't talk much. And she hated, hated, hated it, when Colin asked her questions. Especially about her family. She had this way of just disappearing. He saw it whenever he asked her a question she didn't want to answer or asked her to do something she didn't want to do, like meet his mother or father. She'd close her mouth, that pretty full mouth, and her eyes would grow black and distant and she'd stuff her hands in the front pockets of her jeans and she'd turn into a wall. Colin never understood what she was running from. But he ran after her. He'd never met a woman who knew more about film. After he was with her for a while, though, he didn't care about that so much. He loved her mind; she was always making connections that startled and pleased him. He loved to stand behind her in movie lines and breathe her in, the softly sweaty odor of her. He loved to make her laugh. He always felt as though he'd won a prize when he succeeded. He loved her. But he didn't tell her for the longest time. He thought she might run away for good after that.

She didn't have the money to do what she was doing. She was getting most of her degree on sheer will and extensive loans. He loved that about her too—she was so damn stubborn. They were in bed at his apartment, talking about their movies, which was all they ever talked about anymore. At least they were talking. When he found out about her mother a week ago, he thought she was going to dump him. It wasn't even something to be ashamed of. But she was so mad. He found out when he came home one night with the DVD of *Coffy*. He knew it was crappy filmmaking, but he loved its energy—and he didn't mind Pam Grier too much either. Tam came over and they made dinner. Afterward he held the DVD up to her, grinning. "I ain't seen this in years," he said. "Let's check it out tonight." He thought he saw her stiffen, saw her eyes go briefly black, but she didn't say anything, just sat down on the couch, ready. The silence roared from her side of the couch until it was halfway over. He thought maybe she was offended because it was so sexist, but then the fight scene came on and she said, "That's my mother."

Colin laughed and turned toward Tamara. He didn't understand what she was saying for a minute. "Right. Pam Grier's your mother and you never told me."

"No, not her. The third girl from the left. That's my mother." Tam's face was coated with tears. He'd never ever seen her cry before. He wanted to reach out and rest his hand on the back of her neck, but something told him not to.

"What?" he said.

"That's my mother. She was in a lot of these movies."

Colin pressed a button and froze Pam's image in midspeech. "Are you kidding?"

"No."

He wanted to comfort her, to tell her she didn't have to be afraid of him. But she also looked so angry that he didn't want to move closer unexpectedly. And he had the undeniable impulse to go back a few frames and see the naked image of his girlfriend's mother in a movie. The impulse to ask a million questions. He couldn't help it. So what he said came out all wrong. "Really. Really? That is cool. Very cool."

"You think so, huh?"

"Yeah. I mean, think of what she saw. Think of what she *did*. Did she ever talk to you about it? About working in the movies back then?"

"No, not much."

"She doesn't like to talk about it, huh?" The image on the DVD was frozen and silent. It was very loud. "You should ask her. You might want to know sometime."

"Maybe."

He was silent a moment. Then he took her hand reflectively, looked down at it for a moment. "What other movies was she in?" he said.

He could have bitten his tongue off as soon as the words left his mouth. The look on her face hit him like a kick in the chest. She yanked her hand back and stood up. "You know, that's why I never told you. Because I knew you'd just want to know all about her. And it would be like she was practically living with us. I came to New York so I wouldn't be living with her. I . . ." She ran out of the room. Colin followed her. They talked for a while that night. She cried a lot but didn't say anything he understood. He didn't see what she had to be ashamed of, or angry about. He loved her. He wanted to know where she came from. And she wouldn't tell him.

They made up. They didn't have time to keep fighting anyway. That was the other thing between them; the money and the time. They never talked about it. He was able to get enough money from his parents to hire a professional cinematographer. And she couldn't. She didn't have anyone to shoot for her. She had grubbed every grant possible, begged for every loan imaginable. Nothing had come through. She could not afford a crew. They were talking about it again on this night. Colin knew she was upset, even though her eyes were resolutely dry. He sometimes had the feeling that she had decided not to cry in front of him anymore since that awful evening with *Coffy*.

They were silent for a long time. But finally, he thought of how he could reach her, how he could love her. "I'll do it," he said.

"What?"

"I'll shoot your movie. Mine's just about wrapped. I can edit at night. I want to help you."

"You do?"

"Yeah, I do."

"But you know how people fight when they do this together. Even friends."

"We'll work it out."

"You sure?"

"I'm sure." He stopped. "I love you."

She lifted her head and looked at him. "Thanks," she said. They kissed. He hoped she would say something more. She didn't. They started shooting two days later.

Colin was surprised by how Tam acted on the set. She was so stubborn in class and in life, he'd thought she'd be the same way on her film. But she was petrified—you could smell it on her. He imagined that if he placed his hand on her heart while she was directing, he'd feel it beating like a hummingbird's. Sometimes he saw her making mistakes, doing things that were too expensive or weren't going to come out or mishandling the actors. But he didn't dare say anything. After the *Coffy* thing and a few days of shooting, he knew his safest course was to keep his head down and his camera up. She didn't even ask him to come over anymore at night. And while he still loved to watch her hands move as she worked, he found himself reluctant to push. She was so scared, and he couldn't help her. One time, when she left her backpack open at his feet as she went to go talk to the actors he spied an old battered copy of *Spike Lee's Gotta Have It* in there.

He had to swallow hard and wipe quickly at his eyes with the backs of his hands. But there was no time for crying, or making love, or talking about anything. They were losing the light and he wasn't even done setting up. He ran through his check of the lenses very quickly. The magic hour was almost over.

27

THE LAST DAY OF SHOOTING MY THESIS, EVERYBODY was late, and Evan, a second-year who'd been doing the lights for me, had trouble setting up, and Colin ran through his lens check really fast, and my actors Sherry and Raymond had an argument over some dumb-ass thing, and we were losing the light. I thought my head would explode. Evan desperately screwed the base into the heavy light once more. He swore nonstop. I struggled to hold it for him as he tried again to mount it properly. My arms shook. Sherry and Raymond sat anxiously on the curb, trying not to look panicked and not succeeding. Finally, Evan let go and the light was steady on the stand. "OK, OK, places, everybody." I lowered my screaming arms, hoping I could stop shaking. "OK, let's do this. You ready, Sherry, Ray? Give it all you got." Sherry did an actressy head roll and up-and-down of her shoulders. Raymond just looked at me coolly. I looked through the viewfinder. It looked all right. "Action!" I yelled. Colin started the film. Sherry and Ray started. Sherry messed up halfway through. I reassured them and started again. The sun continued its gradual descent. "Once more. We can do it once more." They made it through the scene this time. They were not brilliant. They weren't even good. But the light was gone and I was at the end. We were done. After we stowed the equipment, we all went out for a beer and I tried not to act as glum as I felt. I got very drunk. I wouldn't let Colin come home with me. He didn't try very hard to get me to change my mind.

I got home at 3:00 A.M. I picked up the phone and called Mama. I got the machine: her and Sheila in chorus. "You know what to do. So do it." So goddamn cutesy. They were so goddamn old. Why did they have that cutesy message? "It's me, Mama. Everything's all fucked up. This movie sucks. Why'd I do this, anyway? Mama? Mama?" I hung up. I couldn't stand how pathetic I sounded. I knew she wouldn't call me, back anyway. She never did. Whenever we spoke, it was on my dime. She always said she was happy to hear from me, but it was on my dime. And don't let me call when I was sad. That never worked. She'd just say to go see a goddamn movie. I wanted to call Colin, but I didn't dare. I got in bed with *Spike Lee's Gotta Have It*. I pressed it close to my face. The paper smelled old. Some of the pages were about to come out. Did Spike ever feel this way? I moved the book away from my face a little so I wouldn't ruin it with my tears.

I woke up to a hangover and the unbelievable knowledge that it wasn't over yet. Now I had to look at my footage (no dailies for us broke-ass film students). I groaned and put my head under the pillow. Could Spike ever have felt this crappy? Ever? I passed out again and didn't get up until noon.

I dragged myself to campus that afternoon feeling slightly better. I mean, I was done after all. I had something in the can. It was a beautiful, crisp clear winter day. There were cinnamon scones, my favorite, at Starbucks. Life might be worth living after all. I took my film into the screening room, set it up, and started it.

At first I thought it was some kind of mistake. I squinted. I fiddled with the projector. I stopped it and started it again. I put on another reel. But there it was. Every single goddamn shot. The entire movie. Colin, my lover, my fucking rich-boy boyfriend who could hire a *real* director of photography because he was so motherfucking rich, had shot the entire film out of focus. I watched to the end. All the footage. Not only were the silences between the actors long and stupid and awkward and the magic-hour shot completely unusable, but the whole thing was out of focus. Not a lot. But enough that this thing would never, ever, ever be accepted into a festival. There was nothing I could do. I was helpless. I started crying like I never have before. Like my life was ending. I howled and cried until I couldn't anymore. And then I called him. You can imagine what I said. I don't even want to repeat it. I called him every name in the book. I was out of my mind. When he could finally speak, his voice was shattered. He said, "I am really, really sorry about the film. You'll never know how much. But you know what? I just can't deal with you any-more. I'm not gonna be sorry I have money. I'm not gonna be sorry my parents love me. For Christ's sake, I'm sorry I messed up your film, but you don't have to take out your whole goddamn life on me." Then he hung up. And I stood in the hallway alone, holding a crushed coffee cup. I was finished crying.

28

IT'S NOT EVEN WORTH GOING INTO THE REST OF THE gory details. I recut the thing so I could graduate; I can't bear to watch it. But they did give me a degree. I started writing a new script and I kept thinking about how frightened I'd been the whole time I'd been shooting. I couldn't finish. Colin's film looked magnificent, and he got this very big deal American Film Institute grant and moved to Harlem and e-mailed me his phone number and we were done. I kept his number. And I missed the way we knew things about each other.

I tried for a while. I applied for grants. I worked PA on raggedy straight-to-video crap. I watched white boy after white boy get the grants, the deals; I watched them not be scared. And when I went to the alumni career office and saw the ad for a second camera assistant on *Law and Order* I went for it. I was tired of eating ramen noodles and thinking about how I couldn't write and applying for grants I didn't get and working for free and sleeping alone and thinking about the out-of-focus piece of shit that was my only film.

Smash cut. Eight months later. I'm twenty-nine. I'm standing next to the Central Park Reservoir, holding a cup of coffee. I'm bored. The show is shot in an intensely boring style and we were doing the open in which the people who have nothing to do with the rest of the episode are talking about something that has nothing to do with the rest of the episode and they're about to find the body that sets the plot in motion and even the director is bored, clutching his coffee as if it would save him. I carried stuff. Heavy stuff. Wires and batteries and reels of film. That's what I did. That was my function. The day crawled by. Just like every other interminable day.

When I got home from work, my roommate, Lakshmi, was sitting on the couch, watching cartoons. She has a weakness for Bugs Bunny that I had indulged last Christmas with a Looney Tunes boxed set. She said it was the best gift anyone had ever gotten her. She barely looked up when I came in. She was already wearing her expensive black pants and white shirt for work; she's working on a novel and waiting tables at a fancy Midtown restaurant to earn money. She often didn't go to work until after I came home.

"Your mother called," she said.

"My mother?"

"Yeah, your mother. She said it was important and that you should call back."

I sighed. "She probably can't find her lighter."

Lakshmi laughed. She'd heard me rant and rave enough about my mother. "You should still call her back, though. She sounded upset."

I went to my bedroom, feeling wronged, and called. I was afraid really; Mama didn't call unless something was happening. Her voice when she answered was harsh and bristly, like she'd been smoking more than usual. Guess she hadn't lost her lighter after all.

"Hi, Tam."

"Hi, Mama. You called? Lakshmi said it was important."

"Lakshmi. What kind of name is that again?"

"It's Indian, Mama. Her parents are from New Delhi."

"Oh yeah. I forgot."

We had this same conversation every time Lakshmi's name came up. "What's going on, Mama?"

A pause while she inhaled. "Listen, Tam, I . . . do you remember when your grandfather died?"

"I remember you telling me about it. I remember we didn't go to the funeral or anything." I knew I sounded petulant, but I couldn't help it.

She exhaled sharply. "Well, my mama . . . your grandmother, fell and broke her hip in Tulsa and my sister, Jolene, called, and I want to go this time. I . . . she's the last parent I got. They think she's gonna be OK, but I need to go out and see to her." Pause. Another deep drag. "And I want you to come with me. It's time you met your grandmother."

"What?"

"You heard me, Tam."

"Mama, why you want me to go with you now?"

She was quiet for a long moment. "I don't know, baby. It don't . . . I'm not sure I was right not to go before. You got a right . . . you ought to meet your people. My mama ought to meet you."

"Jesus, all right. Jesus. How . . . I . . . I've gotta get a plane ticket to Tulsa. And I can't get away until Friday. Is that soon enough?"

"Soon's you can do it, baby. Sheila can't get off work—"

"You weren't really gonna bring her anyway, were you?"

Mama acted as if I simply hadn't spoken. "I'm going out to Tulsa tomorrow. You get there when you can and let me know when you're getting there. I'll pick you up. You got my cell number, right, Tam?"

"Right."

I stared across the room at the still from *Sweet Smell of Success* that I had pinned on the wall. I'd had it for years. Mama never understood it: "That's such an old movie, Tam. Wouldn't think somebody your age would like it. It's not even in color." In the photograph, Burt Lancaster is holding Tony Curtis's tie, threateningly. They are looking straight at each other. Burt is in charge. Tony's along for the ride, no choice about what to do, just hoping to curry favor. I sighed. I shoved the heels of my hands into my eyes for a moment. Then I walked over to my computer and started looking up plane fares.

I went to my boss the next day and told him what had happened. He just stared at me. Then he said, "Listen, you're a second AC on a network show. Do you know how many people would kill for this job?"

"Yes."

"And you know we're in the middle of the season here."

"Yes, I do."

"So what do you think my answer's gonna be?"

I looked at him. He was such a cliché. He even had this giant unlit cigar in his mouth and was wearing a stupid flannel shirt. "I think your answer is going to be no. But I'm going anyway." And I turned around and left. Goodbye, *Law and Order.* Just like that.

I hadn't seen my mother in a year. Even though once I started working on the show, I could afford it, I kept telling her I couldn't. I couldn't get it together to see her, even when I missed LA's smooth, sunny openness. We talked on the phone when I remembered to call. I listened to my friends' tales of interfering mothers with amazement and, I'll admit, a little envy. What would it be like to have something to push against? Mama met me at the Tulsa airport. As usual, she glowed. She was wearing a tight white miniskirt that most women past twenty-two couldn't have pulled off, a low-cut red satin blouse and big Audrey Hepburn in *Breakfast at Tiffany's* sunglasses. Her hair was in a blond-streaked chignon; she'd had a weave since I saw her last. I felt as wide as a barn door and about as attractive as I struggled up to her, hefting my army green backpack and my camera bag. "Hi, Mama." I kissed her on the cheek.

"Hi, baby. Good Lord, is that backpack all you could find to pack your things in?"

"Yes, Mama. It's cheap, and all I needed was some jeans and shorts and stuff."

"And that camera."

"Yeah, Mama."

She sucked her teeth briefly. "Well, you still could have had some kind of suitcase. You don't have to look like you just fell off a truck," she said.

"Mama, is there any way we could skip this? Or at least wait until I'm in the car to start? Jesus Christ."

"Don't take the name of the Lord in vain."

"*Jesus Christ*, Mama, where's your car?"

"No need to yell, baby. It's just this way. This airport's way smaller than LAX." She paused and I imagined the drag she'd take right then if she'd been allowed to smoke in the terminal. The smooth Bette Davisness of it. The calculated closing of her eyes against the smoke. "Whole damn town's way smaller than LAX." She sighed. "Come on, Tam. Let's go on to the house."

I looked out the window as she drove, still too mad to talk. Smoke wafted out her side window the way it always did when she was at the wheel. I hadn't been in a car with her in a very long time. I remembered the way the sun spilled through the haze onto the wide streets of LA and how small and constricted New York seemed to me when I first moved there. Well, not small. Big yet cramped, like a Great Dane in a ten-pound potato sack. In LA, the room outside seems to spill on forever; the road never ends. In New York, I'd just as soon walk.

Tulsa wasn't like either place. After we got off the highways and into the downtown, it was small and there were more buildings, but it still felt like the country. There were aging, dusty pickups parked in the diagonal spaces in front of a strip of stores. Some of them had gun racks. I spotted more than one old man wearing overalls. Most of the people were white. The sunlight was brighter, unfiltered by smog; the buildings were tall but not assertive and almost noisy like the ones in New York that insisted you think about them when you looked up. "Was it like this when you were a kid, Mama?"

"Like what?" she said, eyeing the light as though willing it to change.

"You know . . . It's real different from LA."

Mama laughed, that special short bark that she reserved for only my most ridiculous comments. "Yeah. It's different all right. You gonna be learning a lot I never taught you, baby. An awful lot. I hoped I'd never come back here," she said. "Or if I did, I'd be wearing furs and folks'd be wanting my autograph. Something like that." I looked out the window again. We were driving past a worn-looking black marble memorial. It was sort of like the Vietnam Vets one, but not quite. I looked back at my mother. She gazed steadily ahead.

29

W E DROVE MAYBE ANOTHER TWENTY-FIVE MINUTES, until we'd left the city well behind and were out in an area of densely packed tract houses, each one uglier than the last. Finally we pulled up at one with two pink flamingos in the yard. My mother turned off the engine, lit another cigarette, and said, "We're staying with my sister, Jolene. She . . . she's been wanting to meet you for a long time. My brother, Otis, will be by later."

"What?" I could think of no other words.

"I know all this is a lot to take in, but I had my reasons, baby. And they all real eager to meet you." *We're staying with my aunt and uncle? What?* I said it again. "What?"

"Come on in and meet them. You'll see." Then suddenly she said, "Bring your camera on in." She'd never suggested I take my camera anywhere. *What* was still the only word in my mind as I walked around to the trunk she popped and got my camera out of its bag. It didn't use film, like the cameras in school, but was a little digital video camera that I had bought with my first *Law and Order* paycheck. I looked at the lens, made sure I had a cassette in, and said, "OK, let's go." And so we walked up to the door. My mother rang the bell. The weight in my hand was comforting.

The woman who opened the door was my mother without the

gleam. Her hair was pulled back into a nondescript ponytail, split-endy and too often relaxed. It's a look you see on the subways, when women have done too much to their hair and it's just given up. She outweighed my mother by about thirty pounds and was wearing a shirt and pants that screamed Kmart, but they were clearly sisters. Same mannerisms, almost the same face, one round, one angular. My mother came from somewhere. Imagine that. I stood a half step behind her the way I used to as a child, afraid to be introduced. "Tam, come on out here. You grown now," Mama said impatiently. "Jolene, this is Tamara. I think the last time you saw her, she was just a lump in my belly."

Jolene smiled broadly, revealing the same strong white teeth as my mother and me (dentists always ask if I've had braces). "Well. Well. I'd never have thought it. Come on in here, girl. Come on in." She extended her arms to embrace me.

I was taller than she was. Over her shoulder as her wide, soft arms encircled me, I could see that the living room was a pink and purple wonder, nearly every flat surface festooned with those little African-American angel dolls that I'd always seen advertised in *Essence* and thought no one bought. There must have been fifty of them. It smelled faintly of cigarette smoke and rose-scented Airwick. She stood back and regarded me, as Mama, out of the spotlight, fidgeted. "Well, your grandma's gonna be glad to see you. Never got to see Angie's baby before." She threw Mama a dirty look. "She's gonna be right pleased." Her voice hummed in my ears like honey. She looked down. "What's that you got there?"

"A camera," I said. "I like to make videos." Not *I'm a filmmaker*, what we all said in school, what I used to always say.

"Well, why don't you take a little video of me and your mama. This is a historic occasion." She reached out and took my mother's arm, pulling her in, and we all walked into the living room, where every piece of furniture had plastic covers. My mother and her sister sat down next to each other. "This girl ain't set foot back here in close to thirty years. We don't even know what all you all do out there in LA."

I looked down into the monitor. My mother and aunt shrunk to the size of the small screen. "I live in New York now"—I paused—"Aunt Jolene." The words felt fractured in my mouth. I'd never called anyone "aunt" before. Sheila was always just Sheila. "I am not nobody's auntie," she would say. "Least of all yours. Me and your mama look like sisters?"

"Do you? All the way up there? Now ain't that something? What you do up there?" Aunt Jolene's voice sung in my ears. The camera made its small metallic breathings. No point getting all into *that* now. I said what was easiest. "I work on a TV show."

"You do? Which one?"

"Law and Order."

"Now, Otis likes that one. Me, I like the stories during the day. *All My Children's* my favorite. You ain't never met Susan Lucci, have you?"

I smiled as I gazed at the monitor. "No. I haven't." Through this whole chat, I'd been shooting, not trying to compose a shot or anything, just recording our talk. My mother and her sister sat with their arms around each other. My mother looked as though she wanted a cigarette, some air, to be anywhere else. She said nothing, muted by the force of her sister's voice. The camera took them both in, my mother's bright flutter and her sister's rootedness.

"I love her," said my aunt cheerfully. "She been that Erica Kane for how long now? Long time. Don't never stop schemin'"

"No, I guess she doesn't."

"Well, I guess I better let you take your bag up. You'll be wanting to meet your grandmother. It's a blessing on her that you come," she said suddenly, her face serious. "She didn't never stop missin' Angie." She looked at my mother. "You know you were al-

ways her favorite. When you didn't come home after Daddy died
. . . it liked to kill her."

My mother's expression didn't change. "I couldn't get away,"
she said levelly. "I was right in the middle of a lot of things. And
Tam was real little still."

"Still. 'Bout broke Mama's heart. I'm just telling the truth."

My mother stood up abruptly. I was still filming. They were
no longer aware of me. "Can I take Tam up to her room?" my
mother said. "She's had a long flight and she wants to get settled."

Aunt Jolene rose heavily to her feet. "Sure can." She looked
evenly at my mother. "Sometimes it sure is hard to sit and hear
the truth, ain't it?"

My mother turned away from her and walked up the stairs. I
swung to keep shooting, not really even thinking, the camera giving me space to hide. "Whyn't you turn that thing off, honey. Let
me show you where you're gonna stay," my aunt said from behind
me. I lowered the camera wordlessly. I could feel her breathing
behind me with all the angels.

30

'D NEVER BEEN IN A CITY LIKE TULSA BEFORE. There was not much to see or think about; not the way I was used to after five years in New York. Not a lot of people walking around. It was mostly strip mall after strip mall, bright signs offering KFC and Wal-Mart and McDonald's. When you got farther out is when things changed. Then you knew you were really somewhere else. There were big industrial farms and two-lane roads with nothing on them but you for miles. It was hard to imagine that there had once been little farms, like in *The Grapes of Wrath*, because now everything was just flat and big and empty. "It was like this when I was a kid too," said Mama, easing smoke out the windows of the car. "That's why I couldn't wait to leave."

I got there late on a Sunday, and Mama said that my grandmother was more lucid and easier to talk to during the afternoon visiting hours. So we spent the morning driving around. I asked her to stop if I saw something interesting. We drove for a long while, neither of us saying much. We were heading back into town and to the hospital when we drove past the black granite memorial I had noticed when I arrived. I said to her, "What's that?"

"What's what?"

"What's that big black thing?

"What thing?"

"Mama, didn't you see it? That big black thing over there. That sculpture, wall, whatever it is."

"Oh, that. That's a memorial."

"I figured. To what?"

A drag on the cigarette. "To some old-time stuff that happened here. Lotta people got killed."

"How?"

"Look, Tam, do you want me to stop so you can see it?" she asked impatiently. "Just ask."

"Stop, so I can see it, please."

By this time, we'd wheeled a few blocks past the slab, so my mother made an elaborate show of turning back and pulling into a side street so we could walk up to the sculpture. Engraved on it were the words 1921 BLACK WALL STREET MEMORIAL, followed by a long description of the "most devastating single incident of racial violence in the 20th century." I read, my mouth gradually dropping open. "Mama, did you *know* about this?"

"'Course I did. When I was a kid, we had this old guy at the ice cream store, was all he'd talk about."

"Mama, this is incredible. I can't believe you never told me about this."

"I don't see why. Ain't exactly news that white folks hate black folks."

"Mama, this goes a little beyond the standard."

"Not really. It all happened a hundred years ago anyway. Not much to say about it now."

"Mama, did your parents grow up around here?"

"Mama did. Daddy didn't come until after that mess. He knew about it, though. Made him plenty nervous. Everybody knew about it around here. Just didn't talk about it too much."

I thought for a minute. "How old is your mother?"

"Ninety-one. That's why this surgery was a big deal. Jolene said she was doin' all right 'til this happened."

"You wouldn't know, though, of course. Not having been to see her in twenty years or so. "

"Listen, girlfriend," she said, suddenly furious. "It ain't like you been burnin' up the phone wires calling me. Sometimes it just ain't right between a mama and her girl. We didn't have too much to say to each other once I got out to LA and then had you and everything with Sheila and all."

"You mean like being a lesbian and all."

"I'm not a goddamn lesbian."

"Right." I wasn't even going to get into that one. I busied myself getting out my camera. "You know, of course, that your own mother must have lived through this if she's ninety-one and has lived here all her life."

Time for another cig. "I know that."

"She never said anything to you about it?"

"No . . . no, not really." Her voice sounded funny. She took a long drag. I grunted, having lost interest in the conversation. I was shooting the words on the memorial now. I don't like to talk when I'm shooting. My mother stood beside me, silent.

After lunch, we went to see my grandmother. My grandmother. It felt so odd even to think those words. After we didn't come to my grandfather's funeral, my mother still got a Christmas card every year with this kind of cheesy-looking photograph of an overweight black woman, her overweight husband, and three chubby-cheeked kids. It was just part of the holidays at our house. Until one year I turned it over and read, "Hope you're still doing A-OK in the big city. We're doing fine, Love, Louann." "Who's Louann, Mama?" I asked.

"Oh, somebody from back when I was little. You don't know her."

"Where's she live?"

"Back in Tulsa, where I'm from."

I could tell by the look on her face not to ask any more questions. After another year or so, the cards stopped coming.

I felt a little ill as we rode up in the elevator to my grandmother's room. I'd even tried to fix up a little; I was wearing a skirt and shoes borrowed from Mama. I felt as if I were wearing a costume. "You look real nice, Tam" was my mother's pleased response to my outfit.

We found the correct room and went in. Aunt Jolene was there already. And there, tucked into her hospital bed, was my grandmother. She was medium-sized and medium-colored; the same tawny brown as my mother, but heavily wrinkled and with wild, curly gray hair. She had beautiful eyes and a mouth just like Mama's. Despite her age, it was lush and inviting. Her head was small against the mass of pillows behind her. I entered the room first, Mama following. When we came in, her eyes widened, and she made a sound half between a gasp and a moan. "Angie? Angie?"

"Yeah, Mama, it's me" came my mama's voice from behind me.

"Angie, you really came back?"

"Yeah, Mama, it's me." My mother's voice was very small. Without really thinking about it, I took her hand and pulled her around in front of me, as I might have with a shy child. "Yeah, Mama, it's me." She stepped forward tentatively. Then my grandmother extended her arms and my mother tiptoed forward to receive her benediction. They embraced for a long time, making little cluckings and murmurings, both crying. Jolene and I looked away. My chest hurt, and I scuffed my sandaled feet against the floor.

After a long time, they let go of each other, and my mother perched on the side of my grandmother's bed. Jolene's face twisted briefly with sorrow, and in that moment I felt a kinship with her: to be the one who is always a little out of focus, off center. I know what that's like. I took a step toward the bed. "Mama, this is my daughter, Tamara." My mother introduced me, wiping tears off her face. I looked straight at my grandmother.

"Well. If it ain't Angie's baby." Her voice was high and quavery but sure. "Come here, you. Let me see you."

I stepped over to the bed. She took hold of my upper arm with strong fingers. "Yeah. Look at you. Ain't you something? Last time I seen you, child, you wasn't even born. To think I've lived to see Angie's baby. What a beautiful young woman you are. You something else."

Beautiful. Colin was the only other person who'd ever said that about me. I didn't move, just looked at the woman in the bed. "Nice to meet you . . . , Grandma," I said hesitantly.

She smiled radiantly. "Nice to meet you too . . . Tamara, right?"

"Right." No one moved. I wished I had my camera.

My grandmother came home late in the afternoon three days later. I shot her homecoming. For the first time in a long time, holding the camera felt right again. So I kept doing it. She seemed smaller in the wheelchair and in the house than she had in the hospital. She looked around uneasily as Jolene wheeled her into the living room. My mother walked behind them, carefully carrying my grandmother's small overnight bag. "Wish I could go on home, Jo," my grandmother said. "I don't want to put you out. And I miss having my own things. I want to be around my own things," she said like a child. Then she looked straight at me, at the camera. "What you doing, child?"

"Filming your homecoming," I said.

"Hmm. Don't know what you think you getting filming an old lady like me. Nothing special about me."

"Oh, Grandma, I bet there is." I'd called her Grandma again. The word felt strange in my mouth.

"Hmf," she said.

My mother put the bag down. I turned the camera to her. "Tam, when you gonna make a real movie? Starring me!" She laughed and struck a pose from her glory days, her hands on her hips, a sweet come-hither smile. A sudden bitter vision of my thesis film passed before me. But I pushed it aside.

Aunt Jolene stood behind Grandma's chair, matronly and quiet. "Girl, you still always got to be cuttin' up, don't you," she said.

My mother dropped her hands from her hips and said, "Well, at least I ain't dried up and half-dead and more interested in other people's business than my own, like some folks I could name."

Aunt Jolene started to say something else, but Grandma said quietly, "Don't y'all start now. I'd like to go to my room." Aunt Jolene gave my mother an evil look and wheeled Grandma to the back bedroom that had been made ready for her.

I turned to my mother, still shooting. The funny thing about these little digital video cameras is how quickly people relax around them. "You and Jolene don't get along too well, do you?"

"Never did. Blood she may be, but she's just the kind of person I left this town to get away from. Have you seen my cigarettes, Tam?"

"They're over there."

"Thanks." She lit up and sat down on the plastic-covered sofa, making a crinkling noise. "I can't believe I'm back here." She looked out at the quiet street. "I can't believe it." A shaft of sunlight made a glowing corona of smoke around her head. It was a great shot.

"When was the last time you were here, Mama?"

She continued to look out the window. "Mmmm. Must be . . . like Jo says, little less than thirty years. You twenty-nine now, right?"

"Right."

"Damn. I can't believe I got a nearly thirty-year-old child."
She took another drag. "Yeah, it's toward thirty years. I wanted
you to have something different. And once you were born, every
spare nickel went toward keepin' your little butt in diapers. I
know Mama would have liked to see you, but back then . . ." She
shifted uncomfortably. "Back then we had a hard time getting
along anyway. I couldn't see no way to bring you back here.
Didn't have no money. Didn't feel like fighting with my mama
and daddy. What was the point?"

"What was your daddy like?"

"My daddy?"

"Yeah. What was he like?"

"Well . . . , I guess he was a good man. He loved us. That's for
sure. He was the only black pharmacist in town—that was a big
deal. He had to go to school for a long time. We had some money
compared to a lot of people. He really liked people. He liked to
tell us funny stories about people who came in the store. And he
knew everything about everybody in town. You know, the man
who sells you your drugs is gonna know you pretty well." She
laughed. "He loved my mama too. But . . ."

"But what?"

"But nothing. Turn that thing off, Tam. We oughta go help Jolene." She stood up, done in that way I knew so well. It was the
same way she was done when I'd ask about my father, who he was
or where he was. The same way she was done when Hilda Díaz
said that I was living with a couple of dykes, and I came home
and asked, What's that mean? The same way she was done when
I was sixteen and we had a fight over me staying out too late and
I screamed that she had never really been an actress anyway, just
a glorified extra who couldn't even hold down a job in the business. Her eyes shut like doors, her body a stone. She was done.

31

I DIDN'T KNOW ANY OLD PEOPLE. IN LA, SIGNS OF aging are greeted with the same enthusiasm as signs of cancer. My mother and Sheila were true LA girls on that front. They coveted plastic surgery but couldn't afford it. Instead every kind of anti-aging cream, potion, or capsule available lined the edge of the bathtub, filled the medicine cabinet, sat out on the kitchen counter. In New York, especially as a recent film student, you were utterly in the country of the young and strong and able. You had to be able to run, to hoist, to manage without much food or money, to scramble. Your willingness had to be enormous, your will titanic. You had to be sturdy and self-involved. So I found my grandmother a little frightening at first.

She was quiet and slept a lot in those first few days. She didn't seem to be in much pain. She was on a lot of medication, I suppose. My mother and Aunt Jolene took turns caring for her, my mother leaving most of the dirty jobs for her sister. My stolid, quiet uncle, Otis, who I don't believe I had heard say more than ten words, appeared periodically with a dish his wife had made and helped with the heavy lifting, moving furniture as needed, that kind of thing. I hung around, relatively useless. I shot a lot of stuff, kind of randomly. Something was forming in my mind.

After the third day, Aunt Jolene came out of my grandmother's room as I lay on the sofa, my shorts-clad legs sticking to it. I was reading an article about lighting techniques in a back issue of *Filmmaker* when Aunt Jolene said, "She asked to talk to you. Go sit with her while she has her lunch."

"She wants to talk to me?"

"Yes. Asked for you particular. Go on now." She looked at me severely. "It ain't like you've been so doggone busy around here."

Sheepishly, I closed my magazine. "Well, I came because Mama asked me to. I haven't . . . I don't have a place here."

Aunt Jolene's face softened. "Sure you do. Go on in there and talk to your grandma."

So I went. She was propped up on a lot of pillows with frilly pillowcases. She balanced a plate with a lot of softish foods on a tray on her lap. There was a chair near the head of the bed and a television, muted now, at the foot. I sat in the chair. "Hi . . . , Grandma."

"Hello, child. Tamara, right?"

"Yes, ma'am." Where'd that come from? Was I channeling old viewings of *Steel Magnolias*?

"I swear, it's getting harder and harder to remember things. Tamara. I'ma try real hard to remember that, but if I forget, you go right ahead and remind me, all right? I've had to keep a lot of names in my head over the years. A lot of names." She trailed off, then seemed to focus again. "I'm mighty glad you come to see me, Tamara. I never did think I'd get to meet you, and I always wondered what you was like. Your mama . . ." She paused, swallowed hard. "Your mama was always hardheaded. Grew up into a hardheaded woman. I couldn't tell her nothing."

"She's still kind of like that, Grandma."

She laughed loudly. So loudly that I couldn't help but laugh too. "Well, I guess folks don't change all that much, do they? You strike me as being a little bit hardheaded yourself."

"You think?"

"I think."

We fell into an awkward silence, until I spoke. "What was she like when she was little?"

"Who, child?"

"Mama?"

"Your mama?"

"Yes, ma'am."

"Well, she was about the prettiest thing you ever did see. Everybody thought so. Couldn't keep her hair together for nothing, when she was little. Knees always dirty. But she was so pretty. That was her downfall, you know."

"What do you mean?"

"Well, she was so pretty, the boys started coming around. She started getting all fast. I couldn't have that. I . . . I was sorry about it later. Always sorry about it. But . . ." She took a deep breath. "What's done is done."

Ain't been no boys coming around for a while now, I thought. But I didn't want to completely freak out an old woman I'd just met. So I remained silent. Then I surprised myself. "Grandma, would you mind if I came in again with my camera? If we talked and I filmed our talks?"

"I seen you with that thing when I came home. You like to use that thing? Take pictures of folks?"

"Yes, ma'am, I do."

"Well, I guess that'd be all right. Though I don't know why you'd want to take pictures of me."

"It's not regular pictures, Grandma. It's movies. It's a movie camera. I saved up and went to graduate school to learn how to make movies." I didn't say "films" as we always did at NYU. Somehow, I knew that to her they were ever and always movies.

"You know how to make movies?" she said. Her voice rose with real excitement.

"Yes, ma'am. I really like doing it."

"Well, I never. A black girl making movies. I never thought I'd see such a thing. I love the pictures. Your mama ever tell you that? We used to go every Saturday, rain or shine, no matter what. We saw everything. You ask her." She stopped again briefly. "Whenever we wasn't fighting, we was at the pictures. We saw everything. Ask her about that *Carmen Jones*." A shadow crossed her face and she leaned back against the pillow. "I don't know why you'd want to make a movie about an old woman like me. But you sure can. Can I ask you one thing, though?"

"Sure, Grandma, anything."

"Show me how the camera works before you start. That's something I always did wonder about."

"Sure, Grandma. I can go get it right now."

"You do that, baby."

I was back in a minute. I helped her sit up a little straighter in the bed and took the camera carefully out of its case. I went over all the parts, showed her the DV cassette ("You mean you can put a whole movie on that little tiny thing? Well, I'll be"), let her look at the monitor and frame up some shots of the room. She laughed girlishly throughout the demonstration. Then she carefully gave the camera back to me. I turned it on without comment. "Tamara, I really appreciate you taking the time to show me all that. I always loved learning stuff like that, but I never got much chance. It was only one person showed me that kind of thing."

"Who was that?"

She closed her eyes. Her hands worked the edge of the bedspread. "Man named William Henderson." She sighed and her face changed utterly as her eyes opened. "He was the projectionist down to the Dreamland Theatre when your mama was a girl. He . . . he was something else. Showed me all about movie projectors, how to do. And about Jacob Lawrence. You know who he is?

"No, ma'am."

"He was just about the finest colored artist you'd ever want to see. Painter. You look him up. And I got a book, a book about him. I'll show it to you sometime."

"So this William, he was a friend?"

She was quiet a long time before she answered. "Yes. He was about the best friend I ever had. You know, in this life, it's some people you meet, and some you recognize. With him and me, it was like that. Seem like we always knew each other."

My chest was getting tight, but I didn't stop shooting. She turned her head to the side. "That's enough for now, baby, I need to rest. You go on. I'll see you later."

"Yes, ma'am." I leaned over to kiss her forehead. She looked out the window, not acknowledging me.

I left the room, glad to get out of there. I felt like crying, and it had been a mighty long time since I'd done that. I thought of the pictures of Colin's family all over the bureau, the candles he kept before them, the look on my grandmother's face as she held my camera, as she told me about William. I went to go ask my mother if I could take the car into town and get some more DV cassettes.

She said she wanted to come with me. "I'm 'bout to lose my mind sitting up in this house. I don't know how much more of this I can take. Ain't nothing happening around here," she said. So much of our life together has been in the car. She drove, like always.

"You gonna have to get back to work soon, Mama?"

"To tell the truth, yeah. I had some vacation time saved up, and I've been there a long time so I can get another couple of weeks unpaid, but it's kind of hard to swing it without a paycheck for long. You know."

"I know."

"How about you, baby girl? You need to get back soon?"

Well. No time like the present. "No. I . . . Mama, I quit my job so I could come down here. I'm just gonna have to look when I get back."

"What?"

"I wanted to meet Grandma. And I wanted . . . I wanted to see you. So I came. I can get another job. It's all right."

Mama just looked at me. "You are crazy." Then she smiled. "Just like me. Christ. I can't believe you quit a good job to come to Tulsa."

"I'm glad I did. This is interesting."

Mama snorted. "You think so?"

"Grandma says I should ask you about *Carmen Jones*. That you two used to always go to the movies together."

Mama's eyes narrowed against her cigarette smoke. "She told you that, huh?"

"Yeah."

"We used to go to the Dreamland every week. This big old theater downtown. I drove by the spot where it was when I first got here. Wanted to see if it was still there. But it's gone. They put a Payless there. I got me some shoes instead." She laughed a little, but her eyes were sad.

"You never told me anything about *Carmen Jones*, either," I said.

"Nothing to tell. Mama had already seen it a million times by the time she took me. It came back through town, you know. I loved it, that's all. Same as I love some movies now. Same as you do." She laughed again. "I did want to wear a flower behind my ear for a while. But Mama wouldn't let me. Just as well. I'd have looked pretty silly."

"Oh, I don't know," I said. "You were just a kid."

"Still." We were turning into the mall parking lot now. "Mama always was worried about how things would look. That's why she couldn't stand when I went off and got into pictures. Her baby taking off her clothes in a movie . . . she never understood that I had to. That was what was out there."

"Must have been hard for her to understand."

"Yeah. I guess it was."

"Kind of like you understanding why I quit to come down here."

She grinned suddenly. "Yeah. Kind of like that."

That night, I couldn't stop thinking about what my grandmother had said: "Some people you meet, and some you recognize." I thought about the way Colin sat down next to me the day we met and asked me about *Imitation of Life* before he even asked my name. He knew I'd know. He knew I'd care. He knew me. And I knew him too. I recognized him. I lay on my too narrow bed, tears running into my ears. Colin would understand how I felt now that I had found all these people, my family. I leaned over and rooted around in my backpack and got out my cell phone. His number was still in there. I felt stupid every time I scrolled by it. But I couldn't get myself to delete it. I sat up and called him, my mouth as dry as sand. He answered on the third ring. "Colin?"

"Tam? Tam, is that you?"

"Yeah." Why wouldn't my voice stop shaking? "Yeah, it's me."

"Jesus. Where . . . how are you?"

"I'm good. I . . . I work on *Law and Order* now. Well, I did."

"I heard that." He paused. "Why'd you say you 'did'?"

"I quit."

"Why?"

"I had to." I stopped, switched the phone to my other, unsweaty hand. "I miss you." Just came out. Didn't even know I was gonna say it.

"Really?" He sighed. "You said some evil-ass things to me. But I miss you too." He sounded a little surprised. "I can't even kind of find a girl who's as much of a film geek as me."

"Well, I can find plenty of film geeks . . . , but they're not you."

We fell into a brief silence. Then he spoke. "Yeah." Big sigh. "Yeah. Why'd you call, Tam?"

"I'm in Tulsa, with my mother and my grandmother. Who I've never even met before. And she's so amazing. The whole thing is . . . I want to tell you about it. You're the only person I know who'd understand. I'm so sorry, Col. But I want to talk to you. You're the one I want to talk to. Will you?"

I could picture him shifting the phone up closer to his ear, moving his dreads out of the way. I could picture him scowling a little, thinking. "I will. I probably shouldn't. But I will. Tell me," he said. So I did. I sat on the edge of the pink-and-white bedspread, talking, my heart breaking open, unwilling to think of something beginning.

32

OW THAT TAM WAS GROWN AND GONE AND
barely talking to them, Sheila had to admit that she
missed her, though she'd never thought of herself as that
child's mother. More like her much older sister or something.
That goofy way she had of going around filming everything, that
stupid baseball cap, her unwillingness to be a silly, overgrown
girl. God only knew where she got that. And she and Angie had
ridden her about it plenty. But secretly, Sheila kind of admired it.
Tamara would never end up stuffed into a skimpy costume, dodg-
ing hands. She was sure she was meant to make the pictures, not
be in them. God only knew where she got that either.

As Tam grew up and she and Angie got older, Sheila couldn't
help but notice that Tam was right about one thing: men did
decide everything in Hollywood and lots of other places too. And
there were an awful lot of half-naked women used to sell everything, and the half-naked women (she should know, she'd been
one of them) never did get paid as much as the men at the top in
the suits. It was funny she'd learned all this from Tam because
she'd never even meant to have a child. Angie either. And yet
there they were. They'd raised this girl. The two of them. Dancing around the living room together, getting whatever jobs they
could, raising a baby girl. Who'd have thought that possible?

Just like what she'd decided to do since Angie went off to see to her mama seemed impossible. This girl, Heather, down at the office, kept telling her and telling her about this program at Los Angeles City College for people who hadn't gone to college at the usual time. Heather reminded Sheila of Tamara: she gave that same impression that she could have what she wanted if she worked hard enough, like she deserved something good. Sheila wasn't used to seeing a black girl who really felt like that. She sure hadn't felt like that when she was their age. But she liked it. That's why she went along with Heather's coaxing and signed up for a class. They had this special program for people over fifty. She had to admit that she was over fifty to get in, but she figured she didn't have to go telling everybody that. She just admitted it to get in to the program. She couldn't wait to tell Angie about it, called her the morning after the first class. It was an English class; they were reading *The Bluest Eye*, that book Oprah had recommended awhile ago. Sheila, who hadn't read a book since the Bunny training manual, found she absolutely could not stop reading. She finished at 4:00 in the morning, her eyes grainy with fatigue and red from crying, holding the book to her chest. Then she turned it over to look at the author photo. Then she held it to her chest again. She waited until it was late enough in the morning to call. Angie answered on the first ring. Sheila pictured her eyes half-closed against the smoke of her cigarette, the way she was probably sitting, one leg folded up underneath her, as she held the phone. She missed her.

"Angie, girl, how you doing? How's your mama?"

"Sheila! I'm so glad you called. I . . . it's been weird. You know how long it's been since I've seen her."

"I know. How is it?"

"It's kind of all right. She's too old to be picking with me so much anymore, you know?" She stopped. "And I guess I'm past needing to pick with her all the time too. It feels different. I'm glad I came, to tell the truth. I think I'da been sorry if I hadn't. You know what happened the other day?"

"What?"

"I was in her room, just sitting with her, and I got bored and so I started changing the channels around, and guess what was on?"

"Just tell the story, girl, all right?"

"*Splendor in the Grass*! I ain't seen that in years. In years. Mama sits up and I leaned right in and we were watching it, and she said, 'You know, I never did see what you saw in that Warren Beatty,' and I said, 'Mama, look at him. Come on, he's perfect,' and she said, '*You* say.' But then she said, 'You always did know your own mind, girl. You something else. Like to kill me. But you something else.' And then guess what I said."

"What?" Sheila cradled the phone as though she were cradling Angela.

"'I love you, Mama.'" She paused, her voice soft. "Been more than thirty years since I said that. And she told me she loved me too. Didn't look at me or nothing. Just staring at the screen. But she said it. That's something, huh?"

"Yeah, Angie. That's something." A silence. Then Sheila spoke again.

"Y'all talking OK? You and Tam. How's she taking it?"

"Well, she's mad at me, you know. 'Why didn't you bring me to meet her sooner? Why didn't we come to Grandpa's funeral?' That kind of stuff. I guess I should of. You know. I should of. Just too hard. Well. They getting along good, though. Tam's in there almost every day filming her. You know her and that damn camera. But Mama don't mind. It's funny. I think she kind of like it. She ain't perking up like we hoped, though. They thought she'd be doing better by now."

Sheila heard the anxiety in her lover's voice. She said what she knew would help. "Well, you know, you don't need to rush back. We all right for money. I got a little bit saved. If old Doc Gillespie get funny with you about not coming back right away, we'll get by. You'd always be sorry if you didn't do the right thing now. You know that, right?"

"You know, Sheil, I finally do. Thank you, baby. I do need to stay. I don't know. I still can't talk to her, you know. But I need her to know I'm here. I need to be here."

"Right." Sheila paused. "Listen. I got some news too."

"Aw, girl, you ain't pregnant is you?" They both howled with laughter. "Seriously, Sheil, what's up?"

"I'm . . . I'm going to college." She rushed on. "I told you about this girl Heather at my job, right? She told me about this program at LACC for people . . . well, people our age. And you get to go real cheap, and then it's free when you're sixty, and I just read this book, the first book I read . . . well, you know I don't read, and it was called *The Bluest Eye,* and I just cried and cried. Girl, you've got to read it. You've got to read it. This might be all right. College. I never thought I'd go to college."

Angela was quiet for a long time. When she spoke she said, "You ain't gonna get so smart you won't be interested in me, will you?"

"That could never happen. You my girl for good."

More silence. "You don't think I could do that program, do you?"

"I don't know why not. We both been lying about our ages for the last thirty years, but I know how old you is, heifer. You old enough."

"I'ma think about it. Really, Sheil. Don't want you passing me up."

"Never happen, Angie Bangie."

"Right."

"Right."

Sheila held the phone to her ear, not speaking. Angela did the same. They sat that way for a long time.

33

FROM THE DAY I HAD THEM, I LOVED THEM. DIDN'T always like them. But I loved them. Angie most of all. She was the easiest one, the aching and the sweating and the pushing and then the tearing rush. She was born with a caul. Special, the old ladies always said. Gonna have second sight. I don't know. She always saw me, right from the first. Only one of the three of them who always saw me. She saw me better than J.L. too. And I saw her. She didn't know it. I couldn't tell her. But I did. Only other person it was like that with was William and I couldn't keep either of them for nothing in this world. Anybody sees you like that, anybody you see like that, it's just too clear. It's so clear, it's like before the burning when my mama took me down home with her one summer and I went in a lake down there, a green one, so deep that it was up over my head. I felt the water go all up between my legs and in me and in my ears and when I opened my eyes, I was part of the water, part of the little silver fish going by part of the bitter green cold, and I felt myself going all out into the water until I wasn't there anymore. When you see somebody like that and they see you, it almost hurts, same as swimming in that cold, cold water did. Like you disappeared.

This new girl, my daughter's daughter. I recognize her. We

could be like that. But I ain't strong enough for it anymore. Got to give her what I can before I go. William taught me that. J.L. did too. Always gave what they could, both of them. Her mama ain't learned it yet. Always running. I did what I could for her. All those Saturdays in the dark together. Wish it had been enough. I surely do. I wish they knew how much I loved them. I don't know if I ever did tell them that so they could hear it. Some folks just can't hear it no matter how you say it. I don't know. Wish I could tell them about the color of the sky. The silver fish. The bitter green water. What it takes to truly see it. I wish they knew. I surely wish I could tell them.

34

I COULDN'T STOP SHOOTING GRANDMA. I FELT — NO, I knew—I was getting a story that I would have looked right past if it wasn't for that time we spent breathing together, looking over my camera, enjoying a well-made machine. I had never met another woman who loved my camera as much as I did. I couldn't believe that that woman was my grandmother.

We talked and talked. I shot and shot. Jolene and Mama looked at us both skeptically but didn't stop us. After that first day, she told me more about William, shy at first but then softly admitting how much she loved him, even though it had caused great pain. Even though she loved my grandfather too. She didn't tell me whether or not they'd "had an affair." But that part didn't seem to matter: "Not everyone gets to love somebody like that," she said. "I was lucky. Wish I could have held on to him somehow. I miss him still." Then she pressed her lips together and stopped talking for a little while. She told me about Jacob Lawrence too. She showed me the old catalogue she had and told me how much she would have loved to see one of his pictures for real. "I did a little painting myself. Just tried to teach myself," she said, her hands moving over and over the cover of the book unconsciously. "It's hard. I don't know . . . I did some things I liked. But it's hard."

"It's hard getting it right," I said.

"It surely is." Her hands stopped. "Here." She shoved the book toward me. "I want you to have this."

"What?" I didn't pick up the book. Still shooting.

"I want you to have this. Take it. Put that camera down and take it."

I did, shaking. "You take care of that now," she said.

"I will." Then she lay back on her pillows and closed her eyes, her signal that we were finished for the day.

A couple of days later, I asked her about the riot. I'd been going down to the library, looking through old archives, getting more and more freaked out. I knew I was going to have to ask her, on camera, but I was afraid of what she'd say. Finally, as we sat alone one sunny day in the backyard, she in her wheelchair, I at Aunt Jolene's picnic table, I asked her.

"Grandma, you were in the riot, weren't you." It wasn't a question.

Her eyes widened. She bit her lip, and her eyes filled with tears. But then she turned her gaze to me, immutable, and her voice was firmer than I'd ever heard it. "You get your mama. You get your mama and then you ask me again."

I was startled, but the steel in her voice left no alternative. Still holding my camera, I went in the house and called Mama. She came out, blinking in the sunlight, a copy of *Entertainment Weekly* in her hand. "What? Is everything all right?" she said. Without us ever discussing it, she had stayed out of the time I spent with Grandma.

"Yeah, everything's fine. Grandma wants you out here now." I still didn't quite know what was going on. We both walked back to my grandmother. She gazed at the lawn, lost in memory.

"You got your mama?"

"Yes'm, I do. She's sitting right there."

"Got that camera on?"

"Yes'm"

"Ask me that question again."

So I did. Were you in the riot?

She turned her head and looked directly at Mama, her eyes unwavering and clear. "Yes, I was. They killed my mama, Anna Mae Stableford. Liked to kill my daddy and me. But they shot her dead in front of me. I was eight years old." Mama gasped. The only other sound was the flutter of the magazine falling to the ground and the caw of a faraway crow.

My hands were shaking, but I didn't stop. I knew she didn't want me to. "Tell me about it."

She told us her story. Five minutes or five hours, I had no idea how long she talked. I didn't think how I'd use it. I only listened. Mama only listened too; occasionally I heard a low moan from her, but that was all. My grandmother told the whole thing, barely pausing for breath, tears running freely down her face. When she finished, she said, "Your mama has the picture. The picture of my mama. The only one we had left. My daddy kept it for me, and I gave it to her." She took a deep breath. I looked at mama, whispered, "On your bureau?" She nodded. Grandma went on. "I ain't never had the strength to talk about it. Neither did her daddy. We was young. Everybody knew. But nobody talked about it. We didn't know what to say. I'm sorry about that now. But now you know. You got it right in that thing, that camera. And one more thing. There's a work shed out back of my house. Jolene can tell you where. It's got a lock on it. You go on and cut that lock off. If Jolene or Otis give you a hard time, tell them I asked you to. You do that for me, all right, Tamara?"

"I will, Grandma."

She sat back in her chair, relieved. "You do that for me. We all done now?"

"Yes, ma'am. We're done."

"Take me back inside then, I need to lay down."

My mother just sat there, ankles crossed, sun gleaming her smoothly weaved hair, magazine at her feet. She didn't even look up as I wheeled Grandma past her. Once I got her settled, I came back out, camera in hand. Never drop the camera. I pointed it toward my mother. "Well?" I said.

"Well, what? What am I supposed to say? Jesus Christ, Tam, what do you want me to say?"

"Whatever's on your mind. What do you think, hearing that story?"

"I . . . my God . . . I can't believe." Here her voice went soft. "I can't believe she lived through that and never told us all of it."

"Why do you think she never told?"

For the first time, she looked at me, at the camera. Her voice wavered. I lifted my head to gaze at her. "Sometimes it hurts too much to tell the truth."

"Do you wish she had?"

A sigh older than the world. "Maybe. Maybe. But what would that change?" She stood up. "I gotta go have a cigarette, Tam. Turn that thing off. Wouldn't hurt you to do something without it for five minutes." She stalked off. I stood shooting the sharp green grass, the rusting chair where she had been seated, for a minute more. Then I turned off my camera, sat down on the wooden bench of the picnic table, lowered my head, and cried.

35

AFTER THAT DAY, MAMA WAS GETTING ITCHIER and itchier to run. I could see it. The cigarettes, the nervous tapping of her left foot, her hand straying to the back of her head and twirling, twirling. Staying in one place, feeling stuff she doesn't want to feel, hearing stuff she doesn't want to hear—that's just not something she does. Before I started filming Grandma, I got in Mama's face about why we hadn't ever been here before, but like always, I didn't get anywhere. So we retreated to our separate corners. She went to a lot of movies. She didn't ask me to go with her, which hurt my feelings, but I didn't want to let her know that. So I didn't say anything. She talked to Sheila sometimes until late into the evening, laughing their private laugh into her cell phone. She helped Aunt Jolene with a tight-lipped show of effort that I had never seen in her. She was trying to stay, to focus, not to fight with her sister, not to fight with me. But she wasn't gonna be able to do it much longer.

In the days after Grandma told us about the riot, we were very, very careful with each other, circling, circling, not saying much more than was necessary to take care of her. Grandma slept a lot, most days and often into the evenings. Some nights she was horribly agitated, crying out names from long ago, my mother and Jolene and I taking turns holding her hand in the bed as she sobbed and tossed. During the days, I felt a little lost, but I kept filming

Grandma when she was lucid and I read and talked to Aunt Jolene about living in Tulsa. I filmed her too and went to the library
and learned more about the riot.

One night, I came home from the library after dark. I went
straight to Grandma's room when I got home and looked in, the
way you might look in on a child. Her face was relaxed, her hair
wiry on the pillow. When I came out, my mother had appeared
on the sofa, staring out into the blue night, her legs curled beneath her. Her hand worked in her hair. She looked up when I
came in. I could hear Jolene laughing at something on television
distantly from her bedroom. There were crickets outside, a sound
I could not get used to. Sometimes they kept me up at night, all
that chirping. Mama looked away from the window, picked up
her cigarette, took a drag, put it out, and said, "You know, I have
your father's phone number."

Sometimes, when people say things, it really is like in a movie.
I turned to her, my ears ringing. I could hear my voice going up,
up, up. "What?"

"I have your father's phone number. His name was Rafe Madigan. I think . . . I think I should give it to you."

"How long have you been in touch with him?"

She looked away. "I'm not in touch with him. But I know how
you can reach him."

"And you didn't tell me."

"No."

"Did you tell Sheila?"

"No. No. I didn't tell anyone. I didn't see him. I talked to him
a couple of times. He'd always call and make sure I had his right
number. But I didn't know what to do. He . . . I loved him, but
he was gone, and I love Sheila, all right? And he wasn't never
there for you. Called out of the goddamn blue. What was I supposed to do? He didn't come around. I didn't want to let him
around you . . . I . . . ."

"Why are you telling me this now?" I was crying, standing up, walking frantically around the room. It suddenly seemed very small. I went to the door. I don't know why.

"Because . . . because we're here and I see . . . I see." Her voice got very small. "I see what it might have meant to you. You're grown now. You ought to know."

"Jesus Christ, Mama. Jesus Christ." I opened the door and went out.

The stars were very clear overhead, almost comically so, and the air was cold. I just stood there. I didn't know what to do. I stood there a long time before I felt a hand on my arm. My mother stood beside me. "I'm sorry, baby. I just didn't know what to do."

"You never do."

"But I did my best. I hope you know that."

"Right."

"Well, I got his number for you when you want it. I love you. I do."

"Right." I knew it was cruel, but it was all I could manage. "Mama, I'm gonna go for a drive."

She nodded. I got into the car wordlessly. I looked out the back window at her as I drove off. She looked sadder than I'd ever seen her.

When we lived in LA, she never let me drive. Whenever we went anywhere together, even after I learned, she was at the wheel. We went where she wanted to go. I opened the window and let the cool air blow on my damp face. There were very few streetlights out here where Aunt Jolene lived. I pressed the pedal to the floor, and the car sped forward. I shouted, screamed. "Dammit, why didn't you tell me? Dammit, why didn't you tell me?" I eased off the gas pedal, my throat raw. Now what? Now where was I going? I turned the wheel. I wasn't thinking. I was just going.

I drove all the way downtown. It was late. No one was out. I thought how busy it would be back home right now, the lights pounding, everyone on cell phones, walking and talking. I wondered what Colin was doing, what my father looked like. I thought about my mother saying, "Sometimes it hurts too much to tell the truth," and the look on my grandmother's face as she heard the gunshots again, the gunshots that tore her mother open, left her bloody in the street. I pulled up in front of the memorial. The car stopped and I got out. I stood there. I just stood there. Words formed in my mouth, soft. I could almost taste them. For once, I couldn't think of a movie scene that this was like. "I can do it," I said to the smooth black stone in front of me. I touched it with my bare hands. First one, then the other, then I leaned forward as if I were going to push it over. "I can do it. I can do it. I will." I stood like that for a long, long time. My hands were very cold. The air was still. The breath of my ancestors was all around me.

36

WHEN MILDRED DIED, ANGELA WAS SHOCKED right to her shoes. Even Angela could see that her mother wasn't recovering the way she should have. Even though she could see the intensity with which her mother talked to Tamara, like she was trying to say everything at once. Even though she carried the trays of food back to Jolene's kitchen nearly untouched, looking much the way they had when she brought them into Mildred's room. Even then, she wasn't ready. She didn't think she'd mourn the way she did.

Tam found her, of course. Going in there with that camera, the way she had been almost every day, getting quieter and quieter, only saying, "I can't tell you yet," whenever she or Jolene asked about what she was gonna do with all this film. She went in first thing in the morning. And then just a couple of minutes later, she came right back out. Angela was sitting on the sofa, reading *People*. "She's gone, Mama," she said.

"What you mean gone, Tam? Where's she gonna go? She can't walk."

"I mean she's dead, Mama. Grandma's dead. Come in here with me, I'll show you."

Angela's knees started shaking. She took her daughter's hand. They went in together, two little girls in the woods. Mildred lay in bed, eyes open, face relaxed, curiously beautiful, her hair spread about her on the frilly, frilly pillow. They stood there for a long time, holding hands, before they left the room to go tell Jolene and begin the long work of making it real.

So then she had no mother, and Tam had no grandmother, and they were both crying all the time. Once Angela heard Tam talking tearfully on the phone to that boy Colin, that boy she used to date, and she thought, Well, that's one thing that's different, when you break up with somebody now, you don't stay broken up. And she called and asked Sheila to come to her because she couldn't hide it anymore and Sheila came on the first thing smoking and was there holding her up and she couldn't even make a pretense of not needing her, a pretense that they weren't lovers. Angela could no more have slept alone at this moment than she could have flown to the moon. She didn't even think about how it would look. She just did it. And no one said a mumblin' word. Tam asked everybody if she could film everything and no one said no. The camera just seemed like part of her, and she was careful to respect them, careful to turn it off when it might have been embarrassing. But it was part of her, that camera. Tam was who she was. Angela was beginning to feel all right about that. She'd done all she could; maybe not so much, but all she could.

A couple of days after the funeral, Tamara asked Angela to spend some time with her, alone at Mildred's house. Jolene's had been such a swirl of old people, people who went to church with Mama or knew Jolene or Otis, people who were rooted in this place, that they hadn't had a moment together in days. Just as well. They hadn't been speaking to each other much before Mildred died, what with Angela finally deciding she had to tell about Rafe and all. "I want you with me there," Tamara said. Her voice was even, her reddened eyes steely.

So Tamara and Angela went to Mildred's house and watched a movie together one more time. They watched some of Tamara's footage of Mildred. They sobbed like children together as she talked about William, about Angela's father, about the riot and her mother's murder. They sobbed and sobbed and sobbed. Every now and then they had to stop the video. But they watched it to the end. And after it was over, Angela looked at her daughter and said, "Let's go see what's in that shed, all right?"

Tam was dressed for it in jeans and a T-shirt; Angela was not, in high heels and a bright red dress. They found an old crowbar lying in front of the door ("like God put it there," said Angela), and Tamara pried open the door.

At first they didn't see what they were supposed to be looking for. It was just an old shed. Here a broken old baby carriage—probably the one she herself rode in, Angela thought—there a toolbox, everywhere dust and dirt. Tamara stepped in cautiously, spoke to Angela cautiously. "What do you think?"

"I'm not sure," Angela said. She stepped in too. "Let's look on the worktable."

So they did. And that's when they found them. Not many. Ten or fifteen. A few careful paintings, mostly done on large pieces of plywood. So careful. Some clumsy and not much good, the colors rough and untutored, the images cartoonish. But then there were more. But some, two or three that took their breath away, had photographs collaged into them and showed an assurance that was almost frightening. Vivid collages—one with a singed old postcard of *The Last Supper* in the middle of it, then covered with shellac and painted gloriously a rainbow of colors, with bottle caps and rocks and shells and beads heavily layered all around it. Here was one with an old family photo. And here was one with Johnny Lee. And here . . . here was one of Angela. Her headshot from around the time of *Coffy*, right before she got that speaking part, before she found out she was going to be a mother herself.

She barely remembered sending it; she'd sent it to prove to them that she was really trying to get work as an actress. It was before that movie where she danced on the bar and Mama called her, her heart torn out of her chest. She and Tamara stared, transfixed.

She was the most beautiful woman in the world. Her eyes wide-set and long and falsely lashed, her Afro proud and new, her skin like poured honey, her throat like a song. "That's me," said Angela. "That's me."

"Yeah," breathed Tamara. "You're beautiful, Mama."

They stood there together for a long time, Angela clutching the collage, unable to speak. Tamara spoke first. They both kept gazing at the photo. "Mama, I'm gonna come out to LA to see you when this is over, and I get things settled at home. And I'm gonna call Daddy. I want that number."

"I want you to have it. I should have given it to you a long time ago."

For once, Tam didn't bite her head off. "Yeah. Well. I'm glad you're gonna give it to me now. You're so beautiful, Mama."

"Thanks, munchkin. So are you." And they looked at the picture again and then at each other with surprise and delight and broken hearts. Angela spoke first this time: "Let's take this stuff out of here, OK?"

"OK," said her daughter. And together, they gently began to remove Mildred's art.

Dreamland

2005

Here is the opening scene of *Dreamland:* The screen is black. You hear my voice: "My mother was an actress. In some ways, she doesn't look very different from the way she did back then. She still has honey-colored skin and eyelashes that make you think of fur or feathers. Her movies were all made in the early 1970s, before I was born. You know the titles of some of the big ones: *Shaft* and *Super Fly* and *Blacula.* She wasn't in those. Then there were the little ones that blew in and out of the dollar theaters in Cleveland and Detroit and Gary inside of a week, until the last brother who was willing to part with $1 had done so: *TNT Jackson* and *Abby* and *Savage Sisters.* She's in some of those. You wouldn't know her, though. She was no Pam Grier. These are her credits: Girl in Diner, Murder Victim #1, Screaming Girl, Junkie in Park. She was the third girl from the left in the fight scene in *Coffy.* When I was little, sometimes she woke me late at night and we sat down in front of the television to watch a bleached-out print of a movie with a lot of guys with big guns and bigger Afros. They ran and jumped and shot. They all wore leather and bright-colored, wide-legged pants made of unnatural fibers. They said, 'That's baaaad' as percussive, synthesized music perked behind them. The movies made their nonsensical way along, and then suddenly my mother said, 'See, see, there I am, behind that guy, laying on the ground. That's me.' Or she said, 'That's me in that booth.' Then Richard Roundtree or Gloria Hendry or Fred Williamson sprayed the room with gunfire, and my mother slumped over the table, her mouth open, her eyes closed. Blood seeped slowly out from under her enormous Afro. I looked away from the television at the mother I knew. She smiled watching the gory death of her younger self. Her pleasure in her work was so pure, even though all she was doing was holding still as dyed Karo syrup drained from a Baggie under her wig onto a cheap Formica table."

Then you see my mother's face. First in an old headshot, so beautiful, and then her voice comes over it, cigarette-hoarsened and wised-up: "I was gonna be a movie star. The biggest there ever was." Then there's a sudden cut to the aged face of her mother, Mildred Edwards, saying, "They killed my mama, Anna Mae Stableford. Liked to kill my daddy and me. But they shot her dead in front of me. I was eight years old." Then you see the photograph of Anna Mae. It is weathered with age and cracked and wrinkled with sweat. Then a cut to some old footage of Angela, dancing on a bar in a scene from *Street Fighting Man* with Fred Williamson. Then an old picture of Angela as a girl, hair in neat braids, photograph turned sepia. And then Angela in the fight scene in *Coffy*, getting her dress ripped off and smiling, just a moment. She's gone almost before you can see her. And then Mildred's collage with her *Last Supper* postcard and then a picture of me and Sheila and my mother all together at Venice Beach, laughing. And then I speak again. "My mother raised me in Los Angeles with her lover, who was an actress too. My mother has never called herself a lesbian, even though she's made a life with this woman for nearly thirty years, and they love each other very much. My mother raised me the best she could, but she gave me so little history. She had such a hard time with the truth. Me, I want to tell the truth. So here's my version." And then you hear Sly and the Family Stone singing "Thank You Falettinme Be Mice Elf Again" (full speed ahead, I'll come up with the money for the music rights somehow), and there's a whirling collage of every picture of every family member I could get, and then my grandmother starts to speak. And then my mother and then me. And there we are. My mother is beautiful and my grandmother is beautiful and I'm beautiful. You see that beauty as it finally is even though no one wants to see it as it is in a black woman in America, not a hoochie, not a ho, not a mammy, not a dyke, not a cliché, just a woman. A lot of women. Real women doing what they can, making art where they can, making their lives mean something where they can. And there's so much music in it too, and beauty and love, and as you go from image to image and hear our voices and know our story you know that there's a power here, a power that can't be denied. As you look at our beautiful, beautiful faces, there's no getting around it. There is something there that can't be denied.

Acknowledgments

I have so many people to thank. Anne Rumsey, Sharon Guskin, Stacey D'Erasmo, Bridgett Davis, Jacqueline Woodson, and David Petersen all read drafts of this book at various stages and provided thorough comments that were both thoughtful and helpful. Anne, bless her heart, read it twice. And David never let me forget that art is what's important. He also showed me how a digital video camera works, which was crucial to my understanding of Tamara.

Mo Ogrodnik generously filled me in on the workings of film school. Carmen Fields talked with me about the black community of Tulsa, Oklahoma, in the 1960s. Richard Wesley was very helpful in reading a portion of the manuscript and talking with me about the film industry in the 1970s. He also helped me make the link that brought the Tulsa riot into the story. James Hannaham and Rosie Sultan provided language that I was only too grateful to include in the book.

The MacDowell Colony provided vital time and space for me to work on this novel, not once but twice. Thanks also to the New York Foundation for the Arts for its generous fellowship. And the Writer's Room in Manhattan has been my home away from home for two novels now.

And thanks to Video Edge on Flatbush Avenue in Brooklyn for keeping that "Players Club Pix" section up to date.

271

ACKNOWLEDGMENTS

To my editor, Jane Rosenman: Words fail me. You're the best.

To my agent, Geri Thoma: You've stood by me through thin and thicker. Thanks so much.

To my husband, Jeff Phillips, and my children, Nathaniel and Ruby Phillips: Your love and support mean everything to me. I truly am much blessed.